DARK ANGEL

MARI JUNGSTEDT

Translated from the Swedish by Tiina Nunnally

CORGI BOOKS

TRANSWORLD PUBLISHERS
61–63 Uxbridge Road, London W5 5SA
A Random House Group Company
www.transworldbooks.co.uk

DARK ANGEL
A CORGI BOOK: 9780552159968

First published in Great Britain
in 2012 by Doubleday
an imprint of Transworld Publishers
Corgi edition published 2013

A CIP catalogue record for this book
is available from the British Library.

Addresses for Random House Group Ltd companies outside the UK
can be found at: www.randomhouse.co.uk
The Random House Group Ltd Reg. No. 954009

The Random House Group Limited supports The Forest Stewardship Council (FSC®), the leading international forest-certification organization. Our books carrying the FSC label are printed on FSC®-certified paper. FSC is the only forest-certification scheme endorsed by the leading environmental organizations, including Greenpeace. Our paper-procurement policy can be found at www.randomhouse.co.uk/environment.

Typeset in 11/14½pt Giovanni by
Kestrel Data, Exeter, Devon.
Printed and bound by
CPI Group (UK) Ltd, Croydon, CR0 4YY.

2 4 6 8 10 9 7 5 3 1

For Bosse Jungstedt, beloved brother – always
in my heart

She looked so beautiful standing there. Wearing a white dress with a wide belt around her slender waist. Her blond hair pinned up high in a knot. Very stylish. She was smiling at the photographer with her head tilted to one side. Flirting with the camera, as usual. Always well dressed. Sometimes she wore her hair tied back with a ribbon. And that dazzling smile of hers. Standing in front of the stove as she fried Falun sausages, picking apples out in the country, walking out to the car with the children. A façade. As fragile as the glass in the frame of the photograph. He picked up the portrait and hurled it against the wall.

The shattered glass flew all over the room. That was his life.

The blinds drawn, shutting out the springtime sun. Silence in the room. From far off the sound of car doors slamming, dogs barking. Sirens. The muted conversation of passersby, an occasional laugh. Street sounds, the sounds of life. It has nothing to do with us. My story is etched into the face of the person sitting across from me. As if the lines had deepened, the eyes filled with compassion. Neither of us says a word.

Once again I have described a memory from my childhood. In truth, nothing out of the ordinary, not at all. Just a fragment from daily life. Yet the image is still razor-sharp in my mind, although twenty-five years have passed.

I was seven when I decided to surprise my mother by serving her breakfast in bed. The idea came to me the minute I woke up and realized that everyone else was still asleep. I was ecstatic at the thought. I would make Mamma happy again. She'd been so sad on the previous day, sitting on the sofa and crying for such a long time. She never seemed to stop. I didn't know why she was so sad. Mamma was often like that. She would cry and smoke, and smoke and cry. Then she would talk on the phone all evening, and afterwards we had to go to bed. There was nothing I could do. Or my siblings either. It made all of us sad. But now I'd come up with a good plan. I would serve her breakfast in bed.

Eagerly I climbed out of bed and padded down the hall to the bathroom. I tried not to wake anyone. I wanted to do this on my own, without any help from my siblings. I wanted to be the one she would thank, the one she would hug. Her face would be beaming with joy when I came into her bedroom carrying the tray. And then everything would be fine again.

Cautiously I crept down the stairs. I remember how I cringed at every creak of the steps, scared that the sound might wake her. In the kitchen I got out a cereal bowl and a spoon. But the box of cornflakes was high up on a shelf in the pantry. I couldn't reach it. I went to get a chair from the table. It was so heavy. With great effort I lugged the chair into the narrow work area and then into the pantry. I climbed up on it and stretched out my hand for the box. Pleased that I'd managed to grab it, I filled the bowl and then poured just the right amount of milk over the cereal. Mamma was very particular about things like that. It had to be done just so. Not too much and not too little. What about sugar? She usually wanted sugar on her cereal. But where was it? There, behind the porridge oats. Good. I used the spoon to scoop out what I thought was the proper amount of sugar, but not too big a spoonful. Mamma always complained if her cereal was too sweet; I'd heard her say that so many times.

What was I missing? Oh, yes, an open sandwich. I looked inside the bread box. There was a loaf of bread. Skogholm Bakery, it said on the wrapper. I knew how to read. My older siblings had taught me. I found the bread knife in a drawer, but now came the hard part: cutting two slices. I thought I could manage it, but if the pieces ended up being too big, Mamma didn't have to eat all the bread. She was a grown-up, and grown-ups didn't have to obey the same rules as children. The problem was that she hated slices of bread that were too thick. They had to be thin. I sawed at the loaf with the knife, but it went in crooked. Thick on top and thin at the bottom. I studied the first slice with a frown. It didn't look good. I didn't dare throw it in the trash, because then Mamma would get mad. I knew she would. She often complained about how much everything cost. Cheese was so expensive that my siblings and I were each allowed only one slice on our sandwiches. Mamma always had two. And if I occasionally asked for a second glass of milk, she would always look so displeased that I didn't ask again. I held the piece of bread in my hand. What should I do with it? This slice would never do. All of my efforts to make her breakfast would be ruined because she'd be so annoyed by the size of that piece of bread. If only the slice were the proper thickness, everything would have been fine. Now I was not going to see the look of total joy on her face that I longed for. Instead a deep furrow would appear between her eyes, or lines of disapproval would form around her mouth. All because of that darn slice of bread.

I cast a glance out in the hall, listening for any sounds. It was OK; everyone was still asleep. Quickly I stuffed the piece of bread in my mouth in order to get rid of it. Then I tried again, and this time I made a better job of it. The butter was hard and I couldn't get the lumps to spread out evenly. I covered up the lumps with cheese. Then I had an idea. What if I put on three pieces of cheese instead of the two she usually ate? Wouldn't that make her even happier? But when I saw the three pieces piled on top of each other on the bread, doubt seized hold of me again. It looked like a lot. What if she got angry because I was being wasteful? I didn't dare take that risk, so I ate the extra piece of cheese too. Then I studied my handiwork. I was almost done.

In a cupboard I found a tray and a small plate. Mamma hated to set sandwiches directly on the bare tabletop. After I'd arranged everything on the tray, I could see that something was still missing.

Of course – how could I be so stupid? Coffee. I mustn't forget the coffee. That was the most important part of all. Mamma always drank coffee first thing in the morning, otherwise she didn't feel human, she said.

And a paper napkin! She needed something to wipe her mouth with. She was always annoyed if the kitchen roll wasn't on the table. I rushed over to the breakfast nook and tore off a piece. It looked a bit ragged. I tried again and managed to tear off a whole sheet. The first one I crumpled up and tossed in the bin. Now for the coffee. Again I was in doubt. How exactly was it made? I'd watched my mother cooking it on the stove. After that she would pour it into a thermos. Ours was made of red plastic with a black spout and lid. I needed water and coffee grounds, which were kept in a metal tin in the pantry. I got out the tin but then wondered how to get the powder inside the thermos. And it had to be cooked too. I turned around to look at the stove. I'd seen how my mother turned those knobs to make the burners hot. That much I knew. I paused to think. This was the only thing left to do, and I had to work it out for myself. Then my mother could have her breakfast. And be happy again. I chose one of the knobs and turned it to the number six, thinking that the biggest number must be the hottest. I waited for a moment, and then I held my hand over the burners. The one closest to me was getting warm. Hurray! I was excited, now that I was so close to achieving my goal. I picked up the thermos and turned on the tap. I had to climb up on the chair again to reach it. Then I filled the thermos half full of water. That seemed like enough. I picked up the coffee scoop and put a lot of grounds into the water. Now all

I had to do was put it on the burner to cook. Proud of my ingenuity, I set the thermos on top of the hot burner. Just then I heard someone go into the bathroom upstairs. Darn. I hoped it wasn't my mother.

At that moment smoke began pouring from the stove. The smoke smelled terrible. Something must be wrong. The next second I heard Mamma come pounding down the stairs. My heart froze.

'What the hell are you doing?' she roared, yanking the thermos off the stove. 'You must be bloody well out of your mind! Are you trying to burn down the whole house?'

Thick smoke was now swirling around in the cramped kitchen. Mamma was furious. Through the billowing haze I saw the scathing look on her face. She was shouting and screaming. Behind her I heard my siblings come into the kitchen. My sister started wailing.

'I was just trying to . . .' I ventured, feeling my lower lip begin to quiver. I was paralysed with fear.

'Out!' she bellowed. 'Get out of here this minute, you stupid child!' She was shaking one hand at me. In the other she held the thermos. 'You've wrecked the sodding thermos. Do you have any idea how expensive they are? Now I'm going to have to buy a new one. And I can't afford it!'

Her voice rose to a shriek, and then she started sobbing. Scared out of my wits, I raced upstairs to my room, closing the door behind me. I wished that

I could have locked it. Wished that I could have run away and never come back. I crept under the covers like a frightened animal, shaking all over.

I lay there for hours. But she never came.

And the hole inside me grew.

The dedication of the new conference centre in Visby was decidedly one of the high points of the year. The centre would put Gotland on the map in terms of hosting conferences and help to bring people to the island all year round – not just sun-seeking tourists in the summertime. Their shoulders hunched against the capricious April wind, the invited guests hurried towards the main entrance. The Visby brass band was bravely playing their horns in the gusts, which ruffled their hair and fluttered their ties like banners.

The wind also hampered the efforts of the photographers jostling for space near the red carpet.

Everyone from the local press corps had turned up. Even a couple of paparazzi from the Stockholm tabloids had been sent over from the mainland to cover the event.

The building gleamed in the evening sunlight. Magnificently modern, it was constructed from glass and concrete and centrally located just outside the ring wall near the verdant park called Almedalen, only a stone's throw from the sea. An unnecessary showpiece of a building, according to some people. A visionary project that would benefit all of Gotland, others claimed.

Most of the faces in the crowd of people were well known to the island residents. Local politicians, the top business people, the county governor and the bishop, the cultural élite as well as famous summer guests who had flown over from the mainland to take part in the festivities. The number of celebrities and bigwigs who bought summer houses on Gotland seemed to increase every year.

In the lobby of the conference centre stood the evening's host, the event planner Viktor Algård. Along with the governor and the chair of the county administrative board he had formed a receiving line to greet the guests. There was the steady sound of people kissing each other on the cheek as polite words were exchanged.

The foyer quickly filled, accompanied by the cheerful buzz of voices. It was at least 10 metres to the ceiling, and the décor was done in an authentic Gotland style, with pastel colours. Young waitresses moved deftly among the assembled guests, offering hors d'oeuvres and chilled Moët et Chandon. White lilies had been meticulously arranged in slender crystal vases, and candles were burning in lanterns placed on cocktail tables scattered about the lobby. The view from the enormous picture windows was magnificent: Visby seen at its very best. Almedalen, with its green lawns, the pond with the ducks and the rippling fountain. The ring wall, partially covered with ivy, surrounding a hotchpotch of medieval buildings. The thirteenth-century ruins of St Drotten and St Lars churches, and crowning everything the cathedral's three black spires reaching up to the heavens. Beyond it, the endless sea. The site chosen for the conference centre was perfect.

When all the guests had arrived, the county governor ascended a podium that had been positioned in a corner of the lobby. She was an elegant woman in late middle age, wearing a black floor-length skirt and silk blouse. Her blond hair had been stylishly cut.

'I would like to welcome all of you,' she began, letting her gaze sweep over the festively clad audience. 'It's a great honour for me to dedicate, at last, our new conference centre here in Visby. The project has taken five years and so many of us have been longing to see the final result. And what a result it is.'

She made a grand gesture to indicate the setting. Then she paused for dramatic effect, as if wanting to give everyone time to truly take in the atmosphere and savour the tasteful furnishings. The light grey floor was made of Gotland limestone from Slite, the walls were adorned with guild banners, and the long reception counter was decorated with knotted wool from Gotland sheep. A wide, illuminated staircase made from American cherrywood led up to the next floor, which was to be the setting for the banquet and after-dinner dancing.

'Of course there have been sceptics,' the governor went on. 'Anyone who wants to change things will always face opposition. But I think that most people realize what an asset the conference centre is going to be for Gotland.'

She cleared her throat. What she had just said was a vast understatement. The protests against construction had been both numerous and loud. She had been surprised at the force of the opposition. A never-ending flow of complaints had been lodged with the municipality and the county administrative board ever since the plans had been made public. The debate had raged in the local newspapers. Many feared that the scanty tax revenues from Gotland residents would be eaten up by an unnecessary luxury building at the expense of childcare and services for the elderly. Islanders still had fresh memories of other ventures that had ended in disaster. They were apprehensive of another Snäck, the plan to build a hotel and condos just north of the city. The project had gone to pot and cost the district millions. When the construction project went bankrupt, the municipality was forced to sell the whole kit and caboodle to a local entrepreneur for a paltry sum. No one wanted to see that sort of fiasco repeated.

And that didn't even take into account the opposition

that arose because of the location of the conference centre. The monstrosity stood smack in the line of sight from the Gotlanders' beloved park, Almedalen. To top it all off, the structure blocked the view of the sea.

Environmental activists had staged demonstrations during the entire construction process, chaining themselves to fences surrounding the site. Their protests had caused delays, which in turn had led to cost overruns. Yet in spite of everything, the building was now complete. The governor was relieved that the project had finally been brought to a successful conclusion.

'At the moment it may be hard to see what the significance of the conference centre will be, but one thing is certain: this is a step in the right direction so that Gotland will be able to grow. And it's totally in keeping with the favourable development that has taken place on the island over the past few years.'

A delighted murmur and nods of approval from members of the audience.

'The community college has been growing year by year, and we're managing to entice more and more students to attend,' she went on. 'Our young people no longer need to leave the island to study on the mainland. Many respected teachers have moved here and, in my view, the future looks bright for Gotlanders. Businesses have put their faith in our future and the tourist industry is enjoying an upswing. Last year there were forty thousand more nights spent at our tourist facilities, compared to the previous year. Let's all rejoice at this development and celebrate our important new asset, which will help to promote Gotland. Let's all drink a toast! Cheers for the conference centre!'

The governor's voice wavered and her eyes were shining. There was no mistaking her emotion.

All of the assembled guests raised their glasses.

Viktor Algård opened a bottle of Ramlösa mineral water and looked around. So far the dedication celebration had proceeded largely as planned. There really hadn't been any reason for him to be nervous. He'd organized so many events over the years that by now it was mostly routine. He was Gotland's very own Bindefeld, the party king. Slightly older, a bit thicker around the middle and without the same network of contacts, but still a local celebrity. Viktor Algård was elegantly attired in a black suit tailored in a fashionably modern style. His lavender silk shirt was handsomely cut, giving him a touch of the dandy. He was past fifty but clearly in excellent shape. Hardly any wrinkles were evident on his open, friendly face except when he laughed, which he did frequently. His hair was still dark and thick. In honour of the occasion, he had combed his long hair back so it reached almost to his shoulders. He had an olive complexion, which he'd inherited from his Tunisian-born father, along with his dark eyes and full lips. In general, he was quite satisfied both with himself and with his appearance.

Now he gazed with pleasure at the building's hypermodern banquet hall, which could hold up to a thousand guests.

He took a certain pride in being allowed to arrange a dedication, in being the very first on the scene. He'd spent the past few months meticulously planning this event, fine-tuning all the details down to the very last minute.

He raised his hand to give a wave to the governor, who smiled at him. He could understand why she was so happy. The only disappointment was the blustery wind, which had forced them to hold the welcome ceremony indoors. But what did that matter when the champagne was expensive and the glasses gleaming?

He went upstairs to the kitchen to make sure everything was going as it should. He found the place in a frenzy, with eight chefs working to create the perfect meal. The appetizer was being plated. On the menu were: salmon and lemon parfait with feta and arugula creme, followed by mustard-marinated roast lamb with root-vegetable gratin. And dessert was a nougat panna cotta with raspberries marinated in elderberry juice. All typical Gotland fare, elevated to a sophisticated level. He shouted encouragement to the chefs, who were sweating over the stoves, before he returned to the bar. He noted with satisfaction that the glasses were being rapidly refilled. It was important not to be stingy with the booze; the guests needed to be warmed up as quickly as possible. Linen tablecloths had been placed on the tables and the waitresses, all dressed in white, were lighting the candles in the silver candelabras. It looked as though it was going to be a perfect evening.

The lobby was crowded with guests and, judging by the laughter and chatter, they were already in a festive mood.

A short distance away stood his lover, carrying on an intense conversation with two of the island's foremost artists. Her fiery red dress and platinum-blond hair made her stand out among the other guests. Almost queenlike, if it weren't for her exuberant spirit. She laughed loudly and waved her arms about to underscore her words as she apparently regaled the artists with one of her countless anecdotes. Both men stood very close to her, their expressions rapturous.

Algård chuckled and gave her an amorous glance as he hurried past.

Their relationship had begun two months ago. It happened at a gallery opening that he had arranged in town. She was strolling about, looking at the paintings, and they had struck up a conversation. They got on so well that they left the event together. They took a walk along the seafront and ended the evening by having dinner. By the time they parted, late that night, he was in love.

So far no one knew of their relationship. They had chosen to wait to make their love public. Visby was such a small town that gossip was rampant, and his divorce from Elisabeth was not yet final. He didn't want to hurt her any more than necessary. Elisabeth was so weak. Fragile, both physically and psychologically.

Nothing like his lover.

Detective Superintendent Knutas didn't particularly care for this type of event. The small talk and overblown friendliness felt horribly insincere and rarely involved a single sensible conversation at any point in the evening. His wife Lina had persuaded him to attend. Knutas had been head of the Gotland criminal police for close to twenty years and his position carried certain obligations. There were some events that he simply couldn't avoid, and the dedication of the new conference centre was an important occasion for the island. Besides, Lina thought it was fun to mix with the crowds. In Knutas's eyes, his wife was a social genius. She knew how to chat easily with anyone she happened to meet, always giving them her full attention. She could start up a meaningful conversation with everyone, from the lowly civil servant who worked in the municipal administration offices to the country's most famous pop singer. Knutas had no idea how she did it.

This evening Lina wore a loose-fitting grass-green dress with embroidered silk flowers. Her red, waist-length tresses hung loose over her shoulders, giving her the look of a wood nymph. She was energetically gesticulating, waving her pale, freckled arms about as she sat across from him at the long banquet table. He couldn't help smiling.

For once he'd been lucky with the seating arrangements. On his right sat Erika Smittenberg, the charming wife of the chief prosecutor. She was a ballad singer from Ljugarn who wrote her own songs, which she often performed at rural community centres and small pubs all over the island. Knutas had always been intrigued by the Smittenbergs; they were so different from each other that it was almost comical. Prosecutor Birger Smittenberg was tall, lanky and pleasant in an unobtrusive way, but bone-dry and proper in all situations. His wife was petite and plump with a boisterous laugh that made the glasses on the table vibrate and caused people to turn their heads in surprise to stare in her direction. Knutas thoroughly enjoyed her company and they talked about all sorts of subjects – but not about his job. He appreciated her discretion. One topic to which they devoted a good deal of attention was golf, since it was one of Knutas's chief interests. Gotland, with its wide-open spaces and mild climate, was perfectly suited to the game. Erika told him hilarious stories about her struggles when she first took up the sport the previous year.

Spring had arrived and the lawns had turned green. The sun was putting in an appearance more and more often, warming both the ground and their frozen winter souls. He really should go out to Kronholmen, his favourite golf course, one of these days. It had been a long time since he last played. Maybe I'll go there tomorrow, he thought. If only the wind would stop blowing. He was hoping to take the kids along. As they got older, he felt that he was losing contact with them. The twins would soon be seventeen and they were in secondary school. It was alarming how time was rushing past. He couldn't keep up.

Suddenly he felt Erika give him a playful poke in the side.

'What kind of dinner companion are you, anyway?' she pouted, feigning indignation, but the next second she broke into a smile. 'What are you daydreaming about?'

'Sorry,' he said. He gave her a smile and then raised his glass. 'All that talk about golf made me yearn for Kronholmen. *Skål!*'

The dance floor quickly filled as the band began playing a 'slow' tune. Everyone had finished their coffee and the bar was open. The party was going well, Viktor Algård decided, now that they'd made it through the most difficult part of the evening. Serving dinner for over five hundred people was always a juggling act, but it had gone off without a hitch. Now the guests were leaving their assigned seats at the tables to seek out other company. Some headed for the dance floor; others settled themselves on the sectional sofas arranged along the walls.

Algård exchanged a few words with the waiters, making sure that everything would continue to run smoothly. After that, it was time for him to take a well-deserved break. He tried to catch a glimpse of his lover in the crowd, but he couldn't see her anywhere. He would have liked to share a private moment with her. Provided they could do so without drawing attention, that is. But she'd probably been invited to dance by the man seated next to her at the table. Viktor glanced at his watch. Eleven forty-five. The dinner had lasted longer than expected, which was actually a good sign. Everyone at the banquet tables had seemed in high spirits right from the beginning, with plenty to talk about. The surprise event of the evening was scheduled for midnight, so he might as well wait until the show began. He took a sip of his mineral water, allowing his thoughts to drift. His wife's face popped up in his mind. She wore an accusatory expression, as if she knew. Not that it would really be a surprise. Their marriage had lost its spark long ago. They continued to live side by side, but their paths seldom crossed any more. They lived in a large, isolated manor house out in the country near Hamra in Sudret, the southern part of the island. Elisabeth spent all her time at her loom out in the barn, which had been turned into a weaving studio. It was as if she didn't really need him any more. He in turn devoted himself to his job and his extensive social network. He'd acquired many friends over the years, but Elisabeth didn't like most of them. She was a loner who detested events such as this. The migraine that she'd developed in the afternoon was probably just a pretext to get out of attending the dedication celebration. It was an effective way of avoiding anything she didn't want to deal with, although no one could question her motives when she lay in bed in a darkened room with a towel over her face. To be honest, he was actually grateful for her absence. It meant that he could slip away with his mistress after the event and stay overnight at his flat in town.

When he'd fallen in love with such shattering effect, the deficiencies of his marriage had been brought into even sharper focus. This dream woman had come whirling into his life and turned his whole world upside down. He was completely infatuated with her. Only now did he realize the full extent of what he'd been missing. Passion. Lust. Interest. The sheer pleasure of being in another person's company. Companionship. Togetherness.

The children had left home long ago to settle on the mainland. They had their own lives now. He was longing to be free. And not have to sneak around any more.

His thoughts kept getting interrupted by people who wanted to talk to him, thank him for such a splendid party, or simply shake his hand. He smiled at everyone, happy to see that they were having a good time.

Then the music stopped, to be replaced by a drum roll. The lights were dimmed and a spotlight lit up the stage. Everyone turned their attention in that direction. It was time for the evening's surprise.

Wild applause broke out when Afro-Dite, the popular vocal group, appeared on stage. The three beautiful and glamorous women, Kayo Shekoni, Gladys del Pilar and Blossom Tainton, sang like soul goddesses, but they were also full of warmth, humour and charm that enchanted their fans. There aren't many artists in Sweden with such star quality, thought Viktor, pleased that he'd managed to book them for the evening. He'd made the choice based on the fact that five years earlier the group had captured the hearts of the Swedish people when they won the Eurovision Song Contest. Suddenly he felt someone taking him by the arm.

'Hi. How's it going?'

She looked happy and glowing, her face a bit shiny. Her eyes were sparkling.

'Good. I was hoping you'd turn up. I was thinking of taking a break, but wanted to wait until the show started. Want to come with me?'

'I'm sorry to bother you, but—' The bartender abruptly appeared at their side, holding out a drink. 'For the lady – with greetings from an admirer.'

Viktor felt his face cloud over.

'What on earth . . .' She laughed, gazing around in confusion. 'Well, this is certainly flattering.' She looked at the colourful drink. 'Who's it from?'

The bartender pointed towards the other side of the bar.

'Oh, looks like he's left.'

She turned back to Viktor.

'Honey, I need to go to the loo. Where should we meet?'

He pointed to the stairs beyond the bar.

'Go downstairs to the lounge. That section is closed for the evening, so we can sit there in peace.'

'I'll make it fast. Could you take my glass?'

'Sure.'

Viktor Algård told the bartender that he was taking a short break and then slipped away before yet another talkative guest claimed his attention. Most likely no one would notice his absence, since everyone was watching what was taking place on stage.

Downstairs was a lounge area with a small bar and several groups of sofas. A door led to a paved terrace and a deserted side street. He opened the door and stepped out, lighting a cigarette as he gazed at the sea. He savoured the quiet. Standing there in the dark, all he could hear were the waves rolling on to the shore.

He took several deep drags on his cigarette.

The temperature had dropped significantly and he shivered. The chill air forced him to put out his smoke and go back inside. He sat down on a sofa, shoved a couple of pillows behind him, and then leaned back, closing his eyes. All at once he could feel how tired he was.

A sudden sound very close made him sit up with a start. A faint rattling over by the employee lift. He couldn't see the lift from where he was sitting on the sofa, but he knew that it was over there in the corner, near the exit to the terrace. He froze. It was too soon for his mistress to be returning from the ladies' room.

He listened tensely. The last thing he wanted at the moment was someone's uninvited company.

The music and noise from the floor above were clearly audible, although somewhat muted at this distance. He glanced at the bar, but it was closed and deserted. He looked out at the street, but it was just as dark and empty as before. Had someone slipped inside while he was having a smoke? He had, in fact, stepped away from the door with his back turned to the room. His thoughts vacillated nervously. But now it was quiet again. Nothing moved.

He shook his head; he must have imagined it. Or maybe a couple had come down here from the party, looking for an out-of-the-way corner. That sort of thing happened at every festive gathering. But then they must have noticed him sitting on the sofa. He glanced at his watch. Ten minutes had passed. She should be here any moment.

The drink she'd handed him looked enticing, and he was thirsty. He reached for the glass.

He had barely taken a gulp before a burning flame shot up his throat. Surprised, he held up the glass to look at the contents. The drink had a bitter taste that reminded him of something, but he couldn't think what it might be. Now he also noticed a pungent odour.

At that instant he was overcome by dizziness. He could barely breathe, and powerful convulsions surged through his body. With an effort, he stood up and staggered forward a few steps, his lips trying to shape the words to call for help. Not a sound came out. The room blurred.

Viktor Algård lost his balance and collapsed.

The Kronholmen golf course was beautifully situated on a promontory surrounded on three sides by the sea. Unfortunately, the idyllic setting was not having a positive effect on the prevailing mood. Anders Knutas shook his head at his son Nils, who for the third time in an hour was throwing a fit because he'd failed to sink a putt. Inspired by the conversation with his dinner companion on the previous evening, and by the advent of such glorious weather, Knutas had brought the twins out to Kronholmen for a few hours of pleasant camaraderie. He'd quickly realized that he should have known better. Both of his children were in the midst of an explosive puberty and the slightest thing could set them off. The past six months had been almost unbearable. A simple question, such as whether Petra might like to have some juice at breakfast, could prompt her to sputter: God, why do you have to keep nagging at me, Pappa! Nils thought Knutas was interfering too much if he dared to ask his son how football practice had gone. Two sixteen-year-olds undergoing the same hormonal chaos was nothing to joke about.

When Knutas had gone out to fetch the Sunday paper from the letterbox that morning and looked up at the cloudless spring sky, a round of golf with his kids had seemed a splendid idea. The wind had died down. The day was fair and calm. The sun was shining and felt wonderfully warm on his back.

But none of that had made any difference. He was already regretting his decision.

'Bloody sodding piss! I hate this fucking game!'

His face bright red, Nils raised his club and shoved it with all his might into the golf bag next to him. The club went right through the leather, making a huge slit in the bag and also breaking a bottle of Coca-Cola. The Coke sprayed out like a fountain, drenching Nils's new jeans.

Knutas felt his fury rise. He'd put up with the kids' sullen expressions all morning; now his patience had finally run out.

'That's enough!' he shouted. 'What do you mean by wrecking that bag? It was a present and it was really expensive! I'm cancelling your allowance until you pay me back enough to buy a new one!'

Angrily he gathered up his things as he continued to rant.

'Here I am trying to arrange something fun and have a good time with the two of you, and all I get are surly looks. That includes you, Petra. This is just not acceptable. You're both behaving like spoiled brats!'

'I don't give a shit,' yelled Nils. 'And I don't want a new golf bag, because I'm never going to play golf again! I hate it!'

'Don't yell at me,' Petra sulked. 'I didn't do anything.'

Knutas stomped off, heading for the car.

He was angry, hurt and disappointed. He just didn't understand his children any more. Sometimes he really felt inadequate as a parent.

A heavy silence descended over the car as they drove back to town. Nearly 30 kilometres without a single word spoken. Knutas felt he no longer knew how to talk to the twins. No matter what he said, it was always wrong. So he thought it better not to say anything at all.

He'd had such ambitious plans when the children were born. He'd thrown himself into the role of father with the greatest spirit and gusto, determined not to spend too much time at work. He played with the kids whenever he had time, took them fishing and hung hammocks for them out in the country when they went on holiday. He also made an effort to attend at least a few football matches every season. Whenever the children's friends came over to the house, he was always friendly and polite. One year he was even the parent representative for their school. He'd been naive enough to think that the good relationship he'd established with the twins would last a lifetime, and that the foundations he and Lina had worked to build would remain stable. The past six months had disillusioned him. Chastened, he'd gradually come to the painful realization that his relationship with his children was terribly fragile and brittle, liable to shatter at any moment. Yet deep in his heart he wanted to believe that everything was fine and fundamentally solid.

He parked the car outside the house, relieved to see that the lights were on in the kitchen. Lina was home, which meant he'd at least be able to share his misery with someone else. His offspring swiftly strode up the gravel path, several metres ahead of him. The rigid set of their backs signalled their disdain.

'Hi. Did you have fun?' called Lina from the kitchen as they entered the front hall.

'Yeah, sure. It was great,' muttered Nils sourly as he kicked off his shoes and disappeared upstairs.

Knutas heard him slam the door to his room. He sat down at the kitchen table and sighed with resignation.

'Good Lord, what am I going to do?'

'What do you mean?'

'I keep doing everything wrong. I can't understand why they're always so grumpy. Especially Nils. Do you know what he did? He got so angry that he wrecked his new golf bag. I told him he'd have to pay for a new one, and then he said he didn't give a shit because he wasn't going to play any more!'

'It's called finding their independence,' said Lina dryly as she set two coffee cups on the table. 'All you can do is try to remain calm and on an even keel.'

Knutas shook his head.

'I don't remember behaving like this when I was a teenager. God, talk about a generation gap. In my day, you were expected to treat your parents with respect. You didn't just say and do anything you liked. Am I right?'

Lina pushed back her thick red plait so it hung down her back before she poured the coffee. Then she sat down across the table from her husband, giving him a sardonic look.

'Can't you hear what an old curmudgeon you're being? Have you totally forgotten what it was like to be young? You told me that when you weren't allowed to go to Copenhagen on a camping trip with your girlfriend, the two of you hitchhiked to Paris instead, without saying a word to your parents. All they got was a postcard of the Arc de Triomphe. Your mother even showed it to me. How old were you back then? Seventeen?'

'OK, OK,' said Knutas. 'I take your point. It's just so strange not to have any control any more. Or contact. I can't reach Nils at all. He always has his guard up.'

'I know. But just think of it as a phase he's going through. Right now it's probably worse for you than me. He needs to free himself from you in order to become his own person. They're both growing up, you know, Anders.'

'But it makes me feel so helpless.'

She placed her hand on top of his.

'Of course. But don't you remember how it was

last autumn when Petra barely said a word to me for months on end? Things are much better now. I think Nils is going through the same thing. Just relax. It'll pass. It's painful for them to free themselves from us. The only way they can do it is to belittle us for a while. It's completely normal.'

Knutas looked at his wife doubtfully. He wished he could be as calm about it as she was. He opened his mouth to say something more but was interrupted by the phone ringing.

The sergeant on duty told him that a dead body had been found in the conference centre.

All indications pointed to murder.

Dawn has arrived again, painfully confirming that life goes on. I'm sitting, or rather reclining, on the sofa, as usual. A sense of unreality has settled over me, as it always does.

I've been lying awake for several hours, having moved from the bed to the sofa in a desperate attempt to fall asleep. Memories from my childhood keep intruding. It's as if time has caught up with me. I can't escape it.

One summer, we were staying – as we often did – with my grandmother in Stockholm. On the day in question we were supposed to go to the amusement park and zoo called Skansen. Mamma had been promising us this excursion for a long time. I'd been looking forward to it for weeks and couldn't think about anything else. When Sunday morning arrived, I was so excited that I could hardly eat my breakfast. I loved animals and kept talking about getting a dog. Or a cat. Or at the very least a guinea pig. I was eight years old, and this was going to be my first visit to the zoo.

The sun was shining outside the windows and Mamma was in a cheerful mood.

At the breakfast table she wolfed down her food and coffee. She was eager to get everything packed up so we could leave.

'It's going to be really fun to see all the animals, isn't it, kids? And Skansen is so beautiful!'

She bustled about the kitchen, getting ready as she hummed along with Lill-Babs, who was singing her Swedish version of 'It's My Party' on the radio. She made open sandwiches with lettuce, cheese and ham; she made fruit punch from syrup and water; and she took cinnamon buns out of Grandma's freezer to thaw.

'We'll take along our own lunch so we can sit in that wonderful park over near Solliden. From there you have a view of the whole city, let me tell you. Oh, it's going to be marvellous!'

She dashed into the bathroom to put mascara on her beautiful long lashes, making them even longer. I sat on the lid of the toilet and watched with admiration as she got ready.

'You have such beautiful eyes, Mamma.'

'You think so?' she replied, giggling with pleasure. 'Thank you, my sweet little boy!'

Grandma was too frail to go with us. Instead, we were going to meet Aunt Ruth and my cousin Stefan at the zoo. He was a few years older than me. Aunt Ruth was on her own, just like Mamma. Her husband had left her because he'd fallen in love with his secretary. The family used to live in Saltsjöbaden and were 'well to do', as my mother put it. Now Aunt Ruth and Stefan had moved to a small flat in Östermalm.

We took the train, since Grandma lived some distance outside the city. I grew more and more excited with every station we passed. I could hardly sit still. My siblings chattered away with Mamma, commenting on the view from the window and discussing the people who walked past on the platform whenever the train stopped at a station. *Look at the strange hat that old woman is wearing! Where are we now? Did you see that man – was he drunk? Are we almost there? What a cute puppy!*

I couldn't concentrate. I just wanted to sit in silence until we reached our destination.

After what seemed like an eternity, we finally arrived at Stockholm's central station. From there we took a bus out to Skeppsbron in Gamla Stan. That was where we could catch the ferry to Skansen. Mamma didn't like taking the underground. She said it smelled bad, and it was filled with so many unsavoury characters.

Aunt Ruth and Stefan were waiting at the ferry dock when we arrived. Mamma and Ruth hugged each other, while my siblings and I shook her hand. We didn't see her very often, only a few times a year. Stefan seemed happy to see us, which was a relief to me. It was something I'd been worrying about.

We boarded the ferry and I stayed out on deck with the other kids. The sun shone; the water sparkled. It was May. Soon it would be summer and I would be out of school. Stefan and I stood next to each other, leaning over the railing and looking at the churches and other buildings in the narrow streets of Gamla Stan, which was receding more and more into the distance behind us.

Mamma and Aunt Ruth were sitting inside to stay out of the wind. Both of them had pinned up their hair under a scarf. Ruth's scarf was navy blue, while Mamma's was pink. That was her favourite colour. She was looking stylish in a tight-fitting black dress and a short pink jacket with big buttons. I was proud of my mother because she looked so pretty. In comparison, Ruth looked like an old woman, even though they were almost the same age. Mamma was slender and seemed much younger. She sat inside the ferryboat, laughing and looking lovely. I was glad to see her so happy.

And soon I was going to meet in real life all the animals that I'd seen only in pictures or on TV. I could hardly believe it.

All of a sudden the zoo was right in front of us. Stefan pointed. 'Do you see the amusement park? And the rollercoaster? Over there. I've ridden on it a whole bunch of times. Don't you think it looks scary?'

I shook my head. I'd never been there before, but at that moment it didn't matter. I was going to Skansen.

*

The boat docked and everybody disembarked. There were a lot of people and I lost sight of the others in the crowd in front of the entrance to Gröna Lund. Suddenly I felt somebody give me a hard pinch on the arm.

'Where on earth were you?' snapped Mamma in annoyance. That ugly voice of hers was back, even though she had just been laughing so merrily. 'You need to stay close. Don't you understand that?'

The lump in my stomach came back, settling into its familiar place. I tried to block out its presence from my mind, tried to forget it was there. We had almost reached the zoo. I tossed a remark to Stefan in a half-hearted attempt at a joke, making a great effort to act normal. We were here to have fun. I'd been looking forward to this day for such a long time. The animals were waiting inside.

At the entrance we had to stand in a queue. Mamma started looking tense because there were at least thirty people ahead of us. The nervous feeling in my stomach got worse. 'I'm sure it won't take very long, Mamma. Here, let me carry the bag.'

The sun was shining, it was warm outside, and no one else seemed at all concerned about the wait. They were talking and laughing and joking. I wished that Mamma could be as relaxed as they were.

The queue slowly moved forward. Ruth powdered her

nose. Mamma lit a cigarette. 'God, why is this taking so long? What can they possibly be doing up there?'

When we finally passed through the turnstile, everyone had to use the loo. But I was too excited to pee.

Skansen was located high atop a hill and we began making our way up the slope. Suddenly we found ourselves right next to an ice-cream stand, and Ruth stopped.

'OK, I'm treating everybody to ice cream! Then we'll sit down and get re-energized before we climb any further. Skansen is a big place, kids. It takes a long time to walk all the way around. Right over there are the elephants, but you have to finish your ice cream before we can go and see them. Or else they might swipe the cone right out of your hand! All right. Choose any kind of ice cream you want!'

The strained look on Mamma's face disappeared when she sat down at a café table with a cup of coffee and a vanilla cone.

'This is exactly what we all needed,' she told Ruth, giving her sister a grateful smile.

The mood immediately lifted, and I breathed a sigh of relief.

When we each had to choose the ice cream we'd like to have, I was too timid at first to ask for a soft ice cream in a waffle cone, which is what I wanted most. But Ruth refused to give up until I admitted that was what I wanted. The man in the ice-cream stand gave me a wink and let the soft ice cream come swirling out of the machine until I had the tallest ice-cream cone I'd ever seen. Delighted, I carefully took the cone from him. It was a blend of vanilla and chocolate, and it tasted wonderful. I'd only had a soft-ice cone a few times before, and this was the best one of all. I sat down at the table next to Mamma.

I felt butterflies churning in my stomach as I looked towards the entrance to the elephant house. Soon we'd be going inside. All the kids had ordered the same kind of cone, but when I looked around at everyone else seated at the table, I was happy to see that mine was a little taller than everyone else's.

As if my cousin Stefan could read my thoughts, he suddenly cried: 'Who has the biggest cone?'

He leaned forward, holding out his cone to compare it with mine. I rose halfway out of my chair to do the same. But in my eagerness, I happened to bump into Mamma's coffee cup. It toppled off the table and landed in her lap. I can still hear her angry shout as the hot coffee spilled over her skirt and bare legs. I jumped up so quickly that all the ice cream fell out of my cone.

'What the hell do you think you're doing, you little idiot!' she bellowed. The next second she burst into tears.

Ruth leaped up and nervously began wiping Mamma's skirt with paper napkins from the holder on the table as she tried to console her sister. 'Hush now, it's not so bad. We'll just wipe you off here and then go into the loo to wash off the rest with water. Your skirt will dry in no time in the sun. You'll see.'

The other children and I sat in horrified silence as Mamma sobbed. She kept switching between feeling sorry for herself and yelling at me.

'Why does everything always have to get wrecked? Why can't I ever be happy for just one minute?'

I noticed that the people at the other tables were staring at Mamma with a mixture of surprise and alarm. And then, to my dismay, I suddenly felt something running down my legs. When Mamma saw it too, she got even angrier.

'So now you're peeing your pants like a baby? Haven't you already done enough? Haven't you? You stupid sodding brat! You always ruin everything – absolutely everything!'

Terrified, I sat frozen to my chair, incapable of moving. In one hand I still held the empty cone.

Mamma was silent and withdrawn the whole way back to Grandma's flat. I never got to see the elephants. I would never visit Skansen again.

Sunday started off slowly at the editorial offices of Regional News in Visby. Johan Berg rarely had to work on Sundays; it only happened a few times a year. What annoyed him most was that on this particular day, the editors in Stockholm had decided that they didn't need any stories from Gotland. The news reports would consist entirely of stories compiled at headquarters on the mainland. Having to sit in the office when nothing was going on seemed to Johan like the stupidest waste of resources. But there's no use trying to second-guess the managers of Swedish TV, he thought morosely. He really could have used a few more hours' sleep.

At the moment he was sitting at his desk, having his morning coffee and eating a sandwich. He listlessly rocked his chair, casting a critical eye at the cramped quarters of the editorial office. He let his gaze wander over the bookshelves, the computers, the bulletin boards and the windows overlooking a park. He also glanced at the stacks of jumbled documents and the map of Gotland, which always gave him a guilty conscience because there were so many small parishes that they almost never visited.

Although Gotland was Sweden's largest island, the distance between the northern tip of Fårö and the southernmost district, Hoburgen, was no more than 180 kilometres. And the island was barely 50 kilometres at its widest. That's why we ought to be doing more, thought Johan. We should be covering more of the island.

As a reporter for Regional News in Stockholm, with Gotland as his beat, he'd become a bit jaded after so many years of meeting deadlines and working with inadequate resources. Although things had definitely improved: they'd moved from a musty cubbyhole of an office into the new and modern building that housed Swedish TV and Radio, only a ten-minute walk from the centre of Visby. The premises were admirably suited to their jobs, but they'd been forced to change their routines. They'd had to become much more organized. Now they set themselves goals, and pursued a specific strategy in their work. Usually he or his cameraperson, Pia Lilja, decided which stories to investigate, yet, since they were the only two employees in the local editorial office, it was difficult to find time to do the necessary research. Their boss in Stockholm, Max Grenfors, wanted them to deliver a story every day in a steady stream so that he had no problem filling the TV news programmes. He preferred their reports to be no more than two minutes long, which was considered just right in terms of newsworthiness and relevance, since the further away from Stockholm the programme ventured, the less important the news was deemed. At least that was how Grenfors viewed things. Johan couldn't even count the number of times he'd beaten his head bloody against the brick wall that was Max Grenfors, trying to stir up interest for some issue on Gotland. The issue might be a regional problem, but it could still be placed in a larger national context.

Johan switched on his computer. They were working on an urgent topic that was even relevant to Stockholm – and the rest of the country, for that matter. It was the increasing incidence of violence among young people. He pulled up a photo of a sixteen-year-old boy that filled the entire screen: Alexander Almlöv, brutally assaulted late one night outside a popular club for teenagers in Visby. He had been beaten so badly that he had been taken into intensive care at the Karolinska Hospital in Stockholm. Now, two weeks after that fateful night, the boy was still in a coma, hovering between life and death. He'd got into a fight with a classmate outside the Solo Club down near Skeppsbron. The club had advertised a special evening for students. Hundreds of young people from all over the island had turned up, and even though no alcohol was served to anyone under eighteen, the kids had brought their own booze from home and consumed great quantities of it out on the street. The fight had started with a row inside the club and escalated when those involved were thrown out by the bouncers. Then several others jumped into the brawl. It ended with Alexander getting chased down to the harbour, where he was beaten unconscious behind a shipping container. He was kicked and punched, receiving blows both to the head and to the body. After he passed out, he was left on the ground to his fate. Some of his friends went out looking for him and found him only a few minutes later, which undoubtedly saved his life. If he survived. The outcome was still uncertain.

The number of assaults among young people had increased dramatically over the past few years, and they were getting more severe. Weapons were being used to a greater extent – knives, clubs and even guns. Johan wanted to do a story on the growing violence and its possible causes. Fights among teenagers usually occurred in the summertime when the island was invaded by tourists. Visby was popular because of its sunny weather, long sandy beaches and the lively bar scene.

'Hi.'

Startled out of his reverie, Johan looked up from his editing. He hadn't noticed that Pia Lilja had come in.

With a big yawn, she sat down at her desk across from Johan and switched on her computer.

'How boring that we have to work on a Sunday. Is there really anything we should be doing?'

'Not a thing, apparently. Are you tired?'

She gave him a sly look. As usual, she had put on a good deal of eye make-up.

'Yeah. I didn't get much sleep last night.'

'A new boyfriend?'

'You might say that.'

Pia seemed to have a steady stream of new boyfriends. Her appetite for men was apparently insatiable, and the men seemed equally infatuated with her. Pia was twenty-six, tall and slender, with black hair sticking out in all directions. She'd had both her nose and her navel pierced and adorned with gemstones in various colours. And it was no exaggeration to say that her choice of eye shadow was vibrant. Right now her lids were painted a bright turquoise.

Johan was glad that she'd never tried to put the moves on him; he wouldn't have been interested anyway. Just after they started working together, he had met Emma Winarve, who became the great love of his life. And they were now married.

'Anyone I know?' he asked.

'I doubt it. He's a sheep farmer from Sudret. A real hermit. But cute and sexy. Big muscles and tons of energy.' A dreamy look came into her eyes.

'How'd you meet him?'

'I drove past his farm early one morning, and in the haze I saw hundreds of lambs in one of the pastures. It was an irresistible scene. I just had to stop and take a picture. And there he was, appearing out of the mist like some character in a fucking fairy tale. But what about you? Are you hungover from the party last night? Was it fun hobnobbing with all the society bigwigs?'

Pia hadn't stopped mocking him ever since he'd agreed to go to the dedication festivities at the new conference centre.

'Sure. It was actually OK. Free champagne and great food. Those of us who are parents to little kids don't get out very often, so we have to accept any invitation we can get.'

'Oh, right. You're a journalist, for God's sake. You need to preserve your impartial status,' said Pia, throwing out her long arms in exasperation. 'What happens if the owners of that bloody consortium, or whoever is behind that building, have been embezzling taxpayers' money? What if some of the construction work was done by illegal workers? Or if the guy who organized the celebration, that mafia type – Algård – starts selling booze under the table to teenagers at his club or turns out to be pushing drugs?'

'I would hope I know how to keep my work and my social life separate,' said Johan with a faint smile.

Of course he'd had his doubts. A handful of reporters had been invited to the celebration, and he was one of them. He'd felt flattered, but at the same time he was ashamed that he'd allowed himself to be so easily taken in by the very people he was supposed to scrutinize. Yet he couldn't very well turn down all invitations just because he was a reporter. That had been Emma's argument when he discussed the invitation with her. Was his attendance at one party really going to influence how he did his job? If it came out next week that the chairman of the municipal board had fiddled the bill for the booze, wouldn't he report the story as usual, even though he had attended the party? Of course he would. And besides, Emma had said, wasn't it a good idea for a journalist to get out in society by going to this sort of event? Gather impressions of people in the community and make contacts? Just because he occasionally socialized with certain people, that didn't mean they had to be his best friends.

Johan had decided to go, although it went against his gut feeling. Was it really possible to keep his distance? Once a reporter started socializing with people privately, sooner or later sympathetic feelings were liable to arise and muddy his judgement. To minimize the risk, he probably ought to refrain from that sort of fraternizing. Pia was undoubtedly right, but since she'd spoken to him in such an annoying tone of voice, he wasn't about to admit that he actually agreed with her. Instead he changed the subject.

'Speaking of our work, I think we should plan on doing more segments about violence among young people. And if, contrary to all expectations, we need to put together a report for the late news broadcast, we could always do something on the Alexander case. His condition hasn't changed, but we could talk to kids about what happened. According to the desk sergeant, things have been relatively calm in town, apparently as a result of the assault. And by the way, Alexander is just the latest in a long series of victims, although he ended up suffering worse injuries than most.'

Johan rummaged through the pile of folders on his desk until he found the one he wanted, which he handed to Pia.

'I've found forty-five assault cases involving teenagers during the past year here on Gotland. No one has been seriously hurt before, but it looks like it's just a matter of time before somebody dies – if Alexander manages to pull through, that is.'

'Yeah. What a bloody mess,' sighed Pia. 'Some of my cousins were present when a fight took place last summer and a kid was badly beaten. He's probably included in your statistics. The boy over at the Östercentrum mall, if you remember the case.'

'Remind me.'

'He was attacked with iron pipes and clubs, but I think they mostly aimed at his body, not at his head. My cousins weren't involved in the fight itself, but they saw the whole thing. I just can't believe that anyone would stand around and watch something like that without intervening.'

'It's strange all right. But it's hard to predict how you yourself would react in a similar situation. That's another aspect of the whole thing. And something else that I think people forget, both in general discussions and with regard to youth violence, is the role of the parents. Where are the parents? What are they doing? What do they think? How do they feel? How much responsibility do they have for the fact that things have gone so far? What are they doing to stop the violence? As in the case of Alexander, for instance. No parents have made any sort of statement to the media – neither the parents of the victim nor of the perpetrators. There were five boys involved, according to the police. You'd think that someone would say something.'

'I don't think it's strange at all. They're obviously ashamed about what happened. Just think what it's like here on this little island, where everyone knows everyone else, more or less. Or at least knows someone who knows someone. It's not that easy to make a public statement, saying that your son is a brutal bully. Especially if he might be charged as an accessory to murder, if things go badly. They've been detained, haven't they?'

'Three of them have. The other two were released pending trial because they're so young. Only fifteen.'

They were interrupted by the phone ringing. The editor in Stockholm was calling to say that they could go home. The evening news programmes already had more than enough material.

But they were told to keep their mobile phones switched on, just in case.

Everything was calm outside the conference centre when Knutas arrived. A couple of police vehicles had been parked haphazardly in front of the main entrance; otherwise there was no sign of activity. Inside he found crime-scene technician Erik Sohlman, who had also just arrived. One of the uniformed officers showed them to the area where the body had been discovered. Several members of the cleaning staff, looking upset, stood next to their carts as they talked to police. A woman with Asian features sat on a sofa, sobbing loudly.

Knutas had a strangely surreal feeling as he passed through the foyer. This was the same place where less than twenty-four hours ago he had been drinking champagne toasts and mingling with hundreds of other festively clad guests. Now the scene was completely different. They walked through the deserted and littered salon on the ground floor until they came to a smaller lounge furnished with a few sofas and a bar. This part of the centre had been closed off during the Saturday-night celebration.

Tucked away in a far corner of the room was a small lift used by employees. Inside on the floor lay the body, with the legs partially sticking out of the lift door. The dead man was wearing a silk shirt and black trousers. His hair was dark and combed back. On his feet he wore shiny black shoes with soles that looked almost untouched.

'Do you see who that is?' asked Knutas tensely.

'No, I don't recognize him,' said Sohlman.

'Viktor Algård. The man in charge of organizing the whole celebration yesterday.'

Images of the previous evening flashed through his mind. The event planner had been elegantly dressed, as always. Brimming with enthusiasm, he had greeted all the guests and then dashed about, talking to people right and left, attending to everything. Making sure that everything ran smoothly. Now here he lay, dead as a doornail. It was an alarming sight, and Knutas felt sick to his stomach.

'Look at his complexion. How strange,' murmured Sohlman. He squatted down to inspect the body.

The colour of the dead man's face surprised Knutas too. He couldn't recall ever seeing anything like it. The skin was a bright pink, almost the hue of a newborn piglet. The same was true of the skin on his hands and arms.

The crime tech leaned closer and began sniffing at the victim's face. Cautiously he opened the pale lips, stuck a finger between the man's teeth and prised open his jaws. Then he started back, grimacing.

'What are you doing?' asked Knutas indignantly.

Sohlman gave him a knowing look.

'Come over here and smell it for yourself.'

Knutas leaned forward and noticed an acrid odour.

'What's that smell from?'

'Bitter almonds,' muttered Sohlman. 'It means that he was most likely poisoned with potassium cyanide. It usually has that strong smell of bitter almonds. The body's colouration also points in that direction. Remember that old detective novel by Agatha Christie called *Sparkling Cyanide*? It seems horribly apropos in this situation. You were at the party last night, weren't you? And didn't they serve champagne?'

Knutas was so taken aback he didn't know what to say. He tried to recall the last time he'd seen Algård during the festivities.

'How long do you think he's been dead?'

Sohlman carefully lifted the victim's arm.

'Full rigor mortis has set in, and signs of livor mortis are also present, so we're talking about at least twelve hours, maybe more.'

Knutas glanced at his watch. Four forty-five. He'd run into Algård on the way to the gents. That was after dessert had been served and right before the dancing began. What time would that have been? It must have been at least eleven or eleven thirty. That was the last time Knutas saw him. But with so many guests, there had been a great deal of commotion when everyone got up from the dinner tables and scattered in different directions. Knutas had spent almost all evening dancing with his wife Lina, except for the few occasions when he'd stepped outside to have a smoke. They had stayed until the band stopped playing around two in the morning. He had no memory of seeing Algård when they left. Lina had been so involved in an intense discussion with the county governor that they'd had a hard time getting away. They were probably among the very last guests to leave the conference centre.

Patches of blood and drag marks were visible on the floor outside the lift. Viktor Algård also had a gash on his forehead where the blood had coagulated.

'How'd he get that wound on his forehead?' asked Knutas.

'God only knows,' muttered Sohlman. 'Look at the blood spattered all over the floor.' He got to his feet and pointed. 'The perpetrator obviously dragged the body into the lift. You can see the marks.'

Knutas looked around. A glass door opened on to a stone-paved terrace with several tables next to a narrow side street and a small car park. In the other direction was the sea, the open-air swimming baths and the harbour.

A woman walking her dog passed by outside, casting an inquisitive glance at the big picture windows. Those damned windows, thought Knutas. They were everywhere. The street outside needed to be cordoned off. He called to Detective Inspector Thomas Wittberg, who appeared in the doorway.

'Cordon off the building, the side street and the immediate vicinity! Right now anybody can look inside. It won't be long before we've got journalists swarming all over the place. Call for back-up. I want the police dogs brought in.'

'OK. The cleaning woman who found the body is about to leave. Do you want to have a word with her before she goes?'

'Absolutely.'

Wittberg pointed at the Asian woman who was sitting on the sofa and leaning against an officer's shoulder. She was crying so hard that her thin form shook. Knutas went over to her and introduced himself.

Knutas's colleague, whose name he'd forgotten, got up to make room for him on the sofa. The cleaning woman looked about twenty-five, with long dark hair pulled back into a ponytail. Not until Knutas sat down next to her did he realize how petite she was.

'What's your name?'

'Navarapat, but everyone calls me Ninni.'

'OK, Ninni. Can you tell me what happened when you came here?'

'I was with Anja, one of my co-workers. Everyone else had already arrived. The locker room and cleaning supplies are in the basement. We changed our clothes and started working on the ground floor. She cleaned the cloakroom and this area. I started on the other side.' The young woman stretched out her thin arm to point. 'And when I got over there, I found the body.'

'Tell me exactly what you saw,' Knutas told her. 'Try to remember everything. Even the smallest detail could be important.'

'I was pushing my cart past the bar.' She pointed again. 'And that's when I caught sight of him lying there on the floor, inside the lift. He was on his stomach, so I couldn't see his face.'

'What did you do?'

'I called for Anja, and then we rang the police.'

'What time was it when you arrived?'

'We start at four, and it was probably five to four when we got here.'

'And how much time passed before you found him?'

'Ten minutes, maybe fifteen.'

'You said you were with one of your co-workers. Anja? How did the two of you travel to work?'

'We both live in Gråbo, and we came by bicycle.'

Knutas decided that was enough for the moment. He thanked the woman, telling her that she'd be summoned to a more official interview at the police station later in the day. Along with Anja.

Johan's mobile rang just as he was falling asleep in the double bed with one arm around Emma and the other around Elin. Emma had been happily surprised when he came home from work so early. Since they were both tired after the big party the night before, and Elin was worn out from a bad cough, all three of them had gone to bed even though it was only two in the afternoon. They had settled themselves comfortably among the duvets and pillows, and then he had read a story aloud until both he and Elin began to doze off.

It was Pia Lilja on the line.

'Hi, were you asleep? Well, rise and shine. A man was found murdered at the conference centre, and it's not just anybody.'

'When? Now?'

Johan's voice was groggy. He cleared his throat and gently moved his daughter, who was sleeping soundly with her mouth open.

'From what I understand, they found him just a short time ago. It's Viktor Algård. Can you believe it?'

Pia sounded out of breath. He could hear her going outside as she talked.

'I'm on my way out to the car. I'll meet you at the conference centre.'

'OK. How'd you find out about this?' he asked as he climbed out of bed.

'The body was discovered by someone on the cleaning staff, and I happen to know one of their colleagues. See you there.'

She ended the call. Johan wasn't surprised that she'd heard the news so fast. Pia had an amazing network of contacts that extended all over the island. She had been born and raised on Gotland with six siblings and relatives in every parish. This meant that she had at her disposal countless conveyors of information who kept her up to date on everything going on. Not that it was always newsworthy.

Johan cautiously poked Emma.

Her hair had fallen over her face. Endearingly, she stretched out her long legs, turned over and pulled the covers closer around her. He gave her another poke, a bit harder. This time she reacted by sitting up in bed with a big yawn. She peered at him, not yet fully awake.

'What is it?'

'Viktor Algård was found murdered in the conference centre. I've got to go.'

He kissed his wife on the forehead and left the room before she even had time to respond.

*

Half an hour later Johan parked his car outside the conference centre. Uniformed officers were putting up crime-scene tape.

He said hello to his fellow reporters from the local radio station and newspapers. Word had obviously spread quickly. Pia was already busy with her camera. She had taken up position in a side street and had been filming through one of the big picture windows until she was chased off by a policeman.

'The body's still here,' she told Johan. 'God, how awful. There was blood on the floor. I hope I got something, but I'm afraid it's probably just footage of the detectives' backs.'

'Maybe that's just as well,' said Johan dryly.

Pia was a highly professional cameraperson, but sometimes she lacked a sense of what was ethically acceptable to show on TV.

The minutes were ticking by and they needed to get back to their office soon if they were going to get the story edited before the evening broadcast. The editor in Stockholm had already called to say that the national news programme also wanted to include a report about the murder. So they needed to be quick about it. None of the police officers was willing to say anything, and Knutas had not made himself available to talk to the press.

At that moment the detective superintendent happened to come out of the building. He was immediately showered with questions by the assembled reporters. He briefly answered a few of them before climbing into a police car.

Johan finished the report by doing a stand-up in front of the conference centre, presenting the meagre information that they'd been able to gather so far.

'The dedication of the new conference centre here in Visby was a lavish affair with more than five hundred guests. But the festive celebration had a tragic end. Just after four o'clock this afternoon, a man was found dead inside the centre. He attended the party last night but apparently never left the building. The cleaning staff found his body in the area directly behind me, inside an employee lift on the ground floor of the centre. That part of the building was not used during yesterday's festivities. Evidence found at the scene, including traces of blood on the floor, indicate that a crime was committed. The police have confirmed to Regional News that the case is being treated as a possible homicide. The conference centre and surrounding streets have been cordoned off, and this evening the police are going door-to-door to interview anyone who might have seen anything. The police dogs have also been brought in. As of now, no arrests have been made, and so far there is no known motive for the crime.'

It was late by the time Knutas finally had a moment to himself. He had called Lina to tell her what had happened, and to let her know that the family should go ahead and eat dinner without him. He had no idea when he'd be home.

The body had been transported to the morgue, and from there it would be taken to Stockholm and the Forensics Division in Solna.

Knutas had already had a long conversation with the medical examiner. She told him that it was very possible that the cause of death was cyanide poisoning, but she wouldn't be able to say for sure until she'd done the post-mortem. She was hoping to have time for it on Tuesday. At this point she couldn't say much about the blow to the victim's head. Knutas had known the ME for a long time. She was utterly meticulous and never made any statements until she was absolutely sure of the facts.

Knutas took out his old curved pipe from the top desk drawer. This evening the investigative team had held its first meeting in order to parcel out the necessary tasks.

The top priority was to focus on those friends and family members who were closest to Algård.

Knutas was sorry that Karin Jacobsson wasn't able to attend the meeting. She was both his deputy and best friend at work. She had gone to Stockholm for the weekend to celebrate her fortieth birthday. He'd tried to ring her in the morning to wish her a happy birthday, and again this evening to tell her about the murder, but she hadn't answered either call, which worried him a bit. It wasn't like Karin to switch off her mobile.

Something had been going on with her over the past six months. She was more reserved and taciturn than usual, if that was even possible. She'd always been reticent about her personal life – that was something Knutas had been forced to accept. On the other hand, when it came to her job, she was alert, outgoing and assertive, always ready and willing to participate. But lately he'd noticed a significant change. Karin seemed to be constantly slipping into her own thoughts and daydreaming at their meetings. She also seemed to be having trouble concentrating on her work. It was as if some sort of veil had come down between them. Something was getting in the way, but he had no idea what it was. It was frustrating, because he needed her as much as ever – maybe even more now.

He pushed these worries aside and went back to thinking about the murder case. What about the motive? he thought. What could it be? There was no indication that Viktor Algård had been killed during an attempted robbery. He still had his wallet and Rolex watch.

So far they hadn't been able to interview his wife, Elisabeth. When the police went to the family home in Hamra to deliver the news of Viktor's death, she had been suffering from a severe migraine, which made it impossible for her to answer any questions. She had asked them to come back another time. The police decided to postpone the interview until later. The two Algård children were grown up and lived on the mainland. They had been informed about their father's death and would be flying to Gotland the next day.

Did the wife have any motive for killing her husband? Or could the murder have anything to do with the terrible assault on the teenager outside the Solo Club a few weeks ago? Algård had been very much involved in the case, giving statements both to the police and to the press, because he was the owner of the club. A sixteen-year-old boy had been beaten so badly that he'd had to be transported by helicopter to Stockholm. He ended up in a coma and was still unconscious, a patient in the intensive care ward of the neurosurgery division of Karolinska Hospital.

It had proved nearly impossible to find out exactly what happened that night. There were many witnesses, but they gave conflicting accounts. Most of them were very young and exceedingly drunk. It had been dark and difficult to see what was going on or who was doing what. Three teenage boys had been arrested. Viktor Algård landed in real hot water afterwards. Ever since the club opened, plenty of people had questioned his decision to hold parties for underage kids at the club. He was subjected to harsh criticism because alcohol was sometimes sold to minors in connection with the parties, resulting in frequent drunkenness and brawls. On the night in question, things got seriously out of hand. The bouncers stationed at the club entrance were accused of failing to intervene effectively when the fight broke out. It later turned out that both men also lacked the necessary training. One was an old jailbird; the other was a member of a motorcycle gang which had a dubious reputation on the island. Several demonstrations had been held to protest about the increasingly brutal incidents of youth violence. The newspapers had been filled with outraged letters to the editor ranting about the ineptitude of politicians, the failure of parents to take responsibility and the ever-growing exposure of teenagers to violence via the Internet, computer games and TV.

It seemed plausible that Algård's murder might be somehow connected. The whole episode had certainly made him plenty of enemies.

Knutas couldn't resist lighting his pipe. Then he opened the window and stared out into the darkness. He wasn't in charge of the case dealing with the assault on the teenager. He'd assigned it to another colleague. He'd had to, because he happened to be personally and emotionally involved: he knew the victim quite well. For many years Alexander Almlöv had been in the same class as his own son Nils, and the boy's father used to be one of Knutas's best friends. Both families had spent a good deal of time together. But a few years ago, the friendship had ended abruptly. And then Alexander's father had died.

It was all a very sad story.

Five hours after Knutas left his office, he was back again. His eyes were stinging with fatigue as he opened the door to the police station and said hello to the sergeant on duty.

He had barely settled himself at his desk before someone knocked on the door. Karin Jacobsson poked her head inside. Knutas felt a wave of relief when he saw her. It was almost ridiculous how much he missed her whenever she wasn't at work.

'Hi. What the hell is going on here? I was shocked when the sergeant told me about it. Viktor Algård, of all people! And nobody told me anything!'

She plopped down on the visitors' sofa in front of Knutas's desk and fixed her intense gaze on his face. She flung one jeans-clad leg over the other and straightened her black shirt, which looked like something his daughter Petra would wear. In terms of her appearance, Jacobsson tended to look like a teenager. She was unusually slender for a police officer and only five foot three, a tomboy with dark hair cut short and brown eyes that she rarely accentuated with any make-up other than a trace of mascara.

'Nobody told you anything?' Knutas repeated dryly. 'I can't tell you how many times I've tried to reach you on your mobile.'

She threw out her hands.

'My phone ran out of juice yesterday afternoon and, like a bloody idiot, I'd left the charger at home. On the other hand, I was off duty, you know. I had a good time in town, went out to eat, and then caught the night ferry home. I slept like a rock in my cabin and didn't wake up until we arrived. I just had time to stop by my flat before coming here.'

'And you didn't listen to your voicemail?'

'No. How was I supposed to know that Viktor Algård would get himself murdered and, to cap it all, at the dedication festivities for the conference centre? Thanks for the flowers, by the way. They were left outside my door. That was a nice surprise.'

'You're welcome. As I said, I did try to call you.'

'So tell me all about it.'

'Algård's body was found inside an employee lift on the floor below the banquet hall. That part had been closed off for the evening. Presumably he never left the building after the dedication ceremony and celebration. At four o'clock yesterday afternoon the cleaning staff found his body. He probably died from cyanide poisoning.'

'Cyanide?' said Jacobsson, raising her eyebrows. 'That sounds rather unlikely. Are you sure?'

'We won't be sure until we get the report from the post-mortem, but everything points in that direction. The victim's complexion was bright pink, and he actually smelled of bitter almonds.'

'Bitter almonds?'

'Yes. Apparently cyanide has the same smell.'

'I've heard that bitter almonds can be poisonous if you eat too many of them – but you'd have to scoff fifty or so. As if anyone would ever do such a stupid thing. Who in the world even uses them nowadays?'

'I assume they're used as ingredients in Swedish curd cake and almond buns. Aren't they?'

'I'm always surprised by the range of your knowledge, Anders.' She gave him a wry smile. 'You don't really do much baking, do you?'

'You're forgetting my upbringing.'

Knutas's parents had run a bakery on their farm in Kappelshamn in the north of Gotland. Even though their speciality was unleavened flatbread, Knutas had grown up surrounded by all sorts of baked goods.

'But it wasn't bitter almonds that caused his death. It was cyanide,' he said.

'Is there anything to indicate that the murder is connected to all that uproar about Algård's club – and the latest assault case?'

'Not so far. But it's certainly an interesting theory.'

'Is Alexander's condition still unchanged?'

Knutas nodded gloomily.

'Did you know Algård?' asked Jacobsson.

'I wouldn't say that I knew him exactly. But we'd always exchange a few words whenever we met. I've attended a number of parties that he arranged. He was a nice guy, cheerful and easy-going and very sociable, of course. He had to be, in order to do that kind of job.'

'Was he married?'

'Yes, although we haven't been able to interview his wife yet.'

'Any children?'

'Two. Both grown. They live on the mainland, but they'll be here today.'

'What about the guests?'

'We're going to bring in every one of them to be interviewed. It'll be a big job, since there were five hundred and twenty-three invited guests.'

'Good Lord.'

'We need to get help from the National Criminal Police. I talked to them last night. Kihlgård is apparently out on sick leave. Did you know that?'

Jacobsson's face clouded over.

'What? No, I had no idea.'

Martin Kihlgård was the NCP inspector they'd had the most contact with. He almost always came over to Gotland if they needed help. He loved the island and was very popular with his colleagues in Visby. He and Jacobsson were especially close. Occasionally their fondness for each other had been so blatant that Knutas felt annoyed. Embarrassed, he had reluctantly admitted to himself that this was an entirely selfish reaction because he didn't want to share Karin. For a while he almost thought that a romantic relationship was starting to develop between Martin and Karin. But then at one of the daily morning meetings, Kihlgård just happened to mention that he had a boyfriend.

Now Knutas saw the concern in Jacobsson's eyes and he tried to smooth over what he'd just said.

'I'm sure it's nothing serious. Maybe he's just home with the flu.'

They were interrupted by Thomas Wittberg, who appeared in the doorway.

'Hi. I just heard something interesting.'

He stopped what he was going to say and grinned when he saw Jacobsson sitting on the visitors' sofa.

'Happy birthday, by the way. Or are we not supposed to congratulate you on joining the ranks of middle-aged women? You're already looking more worn out.'

Jacobsson glared at him and frowned. Wittberg was always taunting her about being ten years older than he was.

'Get to the point,' said Knutas impatiently. 'We've got a meeting in five minutes.'

'Viktor Algård was in the middle of divorce proceedings. They filed the documents with the district court a week ago.'

Ever since last night, I've been preparing myself. It started at eight o'clock, after the *Rapport* programme was over. I watch the TV news every evening, even though I don't care a whit about what happens in the world. But it's the only thing I have left that gives me some sort of anchor in reality. Otherwise my life is nothing more than a pseudo-existence. One day follows the next in a steady stream; all of them look very much alike. I sit here in my self-imposed prison, and the furthest I have to walk is from the kitchen to the bathroom.

I see only one other person, and today it's once again time to do that. It means that I have to venture outside. And that requires preparation.

Last night I rummaged about until I found some clothes that were presentable, clean and without any holes. I never think about such things when I'm alone. I placed them on a chair: underwear, socks, a shirt, jeans. Before I went to bed, I set three alarm clocks, each fifteen minutes apart, so that I'd be sure to wake up. Since I take sleeping tablets, I tend to sleep very soundly and I'm out for a long time.

I put one alarm clock on the bedside table, one on the window ledge so I'd be forced to get up, and the third, which rings the loudest, I put in the kitchen so I wouldn't be tempted to go back to bed and pull the covers over my head.

All three were set to give me plenty of time to wake up and carry out the obligatory morning ablutions required of normal people who do normal things. Such as venturing outside.

This morning I took a shower and washed my hair, which was quite a feat, considering my condition. It takes an enormous effort for me to slip out of my sleep-warmed pyjamas and get into the shower. It never gets any easier. Yes, I wear pyjamas to bed, just as I did as a child. They're my armour: against fear, evil spirits, and any malicious, sinister creature that might happen to enter my bedroom. Sometimes I lie there in the dark imagining that someone is inside the flat. There are plenty of nooks and cupboards and wardrobes to hide in. I live in the only occupied flat in the entire building. The rest are all offices. No, that's wrong. There is one other residential flat on the same floor. But it belongs to a family who live abroad, somewhere in Saudi Arabia, I think. I don't know when they're coming back.

That's why the building is so quiet at night. Very quiet. Outside these walls, it's a whole different matter. That's where life in the city goes on.

I've had my coffee and forced myself to eat two open cheese sandwiches on rye bread. Energy is required if I'm to manage the walk I have ahead of me. I always read while I eat. Right now I'm reading *The Red Room* by August Strindberg. It's a book that I spent a brief period reading aloud for Pappa when he wanted to rest on Saturday afternoons. I remember that once my nose started to bleed. It left a red spot in the book that's still visible today.

A few days ago when I got out this book, which had been packed away for so long, a photograph fell from between the pages where it had been lying, forgotten. It was a picture of Pappa, taken in the boat out at the lake. He's wearing shorts and a light blue shirt, smiling slyly at the camera. Wrinkling his nose at the sun the way he always used to do. I don't think I've ever seen a picture of Pappa in which he's really happy. He might make a face or smile, but he never laughed when anyone took his picture.

Mamma and Pappa divorced when I was five, and after that they seldom saw each other. The day before my thirteenth birthday, he died in a car accident. My memories of him are few and fragmentary, but occasionally images appear in my mind's eye. The dark hair on the back of Pappa's neck as he drove; the way he would floor the accelerator on that bumpy hill out in the country so that the three of us kids sitting in the back seat would screech with delight. His inimitable way of chewing on a bun, making it look so heavenly; the way he inhaled through his nose; his dry hands; and the way he tossed back his head when he laughed. He had a big round belly and the indentation of his navel was clearly visible under his shirt. Pappa smelled so nicely of aftershave. The bottle of Paco Rabanne stood on his shelf in the medicine cabinet.

During one summer holiday in Norrland, I remember playing in a deep, dark lake in the woods. Pappa was romping with us, chasing us about in the water. I laughed so hard that I nearly choked when he grabbed me and I landed in his big, soft embrace.

Pappa worked on the mainland and came home only at the weekends. I remember how Mamma would always hum as she cleaned up the flat before he arrived. She would set the table with the good china and candles, take out a bottle of wine, and cook steak with French fries and Béarnaise sauce. When he finally turned up on Friday evening, my siblings and I would stand in the hall, our eyes sparkling, as if the king himself was coming to visit.

I never heard any explanation for why they split up. Only that something had happened that Mamma couldn't forgive. She was the one who wanted the divorce. Even so, she was inconsolable afterwards, and everyone in her circle of friends was fully occupied trying to take care of her. The poor woman, left on her own with three small children. And so young. Without money in the bank or any sort of education.

The grey days became weeks, months, years. No one had time for the feelings of loss that my siblings and I were trying to deal with. We ended up in the shadows. And that's how things were to remain.

Actually, I've been in the shadows ever since I was born. Like someone who really has no right to live. I wonder why I was born at all.

Mamma never wanted me. She told me that herself.

She has always said that she thinks it was a miracle I could be such a happy child when she was in such despair while she was pregnant with me. At first she was utterly beside herself when she found out she was going to have another baby. Then she wept every day as I grew inside of her. Apparently it was hard to tell that she was even carrying a child until close to the end. That was how strongly she tried to deny me.

I must have been about fourteen when I heard the story for the first time. She related the tale as if it were a funny anecdote. I don't remember having any particular reaction; I didn't feel angry or upset. I assume my response was the usual one. Acceptance. I simply accepted the insult – hook, line and sinker. Just as I put up with everything she said about me, no matter how denigrating her words. I can hear her voice echoing inside my head.

'And just imagine – even though I was so upset about having you, you were incredibly happy when you came out! Right from the very beginning!'

Sure, Mamma. Imagine that. And why exactly are you telling me how unwanted I was? I have no bloody idea.

I'm dressed now. I have to go out of the door, take the lift downstairs, and mingle with all the people out on the street. I take a breath. A deep breath.

Lina phoned just as Knutas was heading down the corridor to the investigative team's morning meeting. He'd left home very early, before she was awake. Knutas's Danish wife was on her way to her job as a midwife at Visby Hospital. She'd started taking a walk every morning before breakfast. It was another of her countless attempts to lose weight. Knutas didn't think there was anything wrong with his wife's plump figure, but she was always trying to get rid of a few extra pounds. At the moment she had high hopes for the diet based on the glycaemic index, which was the current fad. Consequently, whenever it was her turn to do the cooking, their meals consisted of meat, fish and salads. Potatoes, pasta and rice had been replaced by lentils and beans, although Knutas and the children weren't happy about the substitution. Because of their protests, she had relented enough to serve whole-grain pasta.

'Good morning,' Lina gasped on the phone, sounding out of breath. 'How's it going?'

'OK, but we're really busy. We've got a meeting in a few minutes.'

'I just had to phone you because Nils is sick.'

Knutas stopped in his tracks.

'What's the matter with him?'

'This morning it was almost impossible to wake him. He said that he'd hardly slept at all and that his stomach hurt.'

'Hurt in what way?'

'He says it aches but he hasn't thrown up, and he doesn't have a fever. At any rate, I let him stay home from school.'

'That's good. I've got a lot on my plate today, but I might be able to drop by to see him later on.'

Lina's work schedule was not as flexible as his since she was assigned specific shifts at the hospital.

'That would be great. I know you have to go, so we'll talk later.'

'I'll phone Nils.'

'No, don't do that. He went back to sleep.'

'OK. Love you.'

'Love you too.'

Worry instantly settled over Knutas. Nils hadn't been himself lately, and maybe it wasn't all due to puberty.

Still thinking about his son, he went into the conference room for the first meeting of the day with the investigative team.

Chief Prosecutor Birger Smittenberg was already in his place at the table, intently leafing through the morning newspaper. He glanced up at Knutas and gave him a distracted greeting. Wittberg and Jacobsson were sitting next to each other, leaning close and conversing in low voices. The police spokesman, Lars Norrby, was missing. He'd taken a two-month leave of absence to sail around the West Indies with his children. While Lars was away, Knutas had to handle the press himself, which he didn't really mind. Things were actually calmer this way. He and Norrby didn't always agree about what information should be made public.

Knutas had just sat down in his customary place at the head of the table when Sohlman came in. The crime-scene tech's face was ashen and he looked as if he hadn't slept all night.

He sank down on a chair next to Jacobsson, who patted him lightly on the shoulder. Sohlman reached for the thermos of coffee on the table.

'Good morning,' Knutas greeted everyone. 'You all know about what happened. Viktor Algård was found dead yesterday afternoon inside the conference centre. According to the ME's preliminary examination, Algård died of cyanide poisoning. But he also had a wound on his forehead, and there were bloodstains both on the cocktail table near the bar and on the floor underneath. Marks on the floor indicate that the perpetrator dragged the body into the lift, presumably to hide it. We don't know yet what caused the wound on the victim's forehead. The body is being taken on the afternoon ferry to Stockholm and the Forensics division in Solna. We're hoping that the post-mortem will be done tomorrow. Sohlman, can you describe what we know so far about the injuries and crime scene?'

Knutas nodded to his colleague, who got up to stand next to the screen at the front of the room.

'First let's take a look at the victim. Certain circumstances make this a particularly interesting case. You can see that the victim's skin is bright pink. Livor mortis, which is a light crimson or rose colour, has fully developed. This points to cyanide poisoning, since cyanide obstructs the airways, making it impossible for oxygen to get out of the bloodstream. The victim also smelled strongly of bitter almonds, which is typical of cyanide poisoning.'

'I don't know anything about cyanide,' said Jacobsson, 'but it must be an extremely unusual method for killing someone. I've only heard of it used as a murder weapon in old detective novels.'

'I know. I've never handled a homicide case in which cyanide was used,' Sohlman agreed. 'But I've actually had a couple of instances of suicide by cyanide. It's extremely toxic. In this instance we're probably dealing with potassium cyanide, which is cyanide in crystal form. It dissolves easily in water.'

'Why did you make that assumption?'

'Because that's the easiest form to handle and carry around. It can be kept in small glass vials. Then all you need to do is empty the contents into a glass of water, or some other liquid.'

'What about alcohol?' asked Jacobsson.

'It doesn't dissolve in alcohol, but the perpetrator could have mixed it in water first, before adding it to a drink. If that's how the poison was administered to Algård, that is. We don't know for sure. But it's not the sort of substance that anyone would drink voluntarily. The perp must be at least somewhat familiar with cyanide. Handling it can be quite risky. For one thing, it's fatal if inhaled. Hydrogen cyanide was the gas that the Germans used to murder the Jews in the concentration camps in the Second World War. As I said, it can knock out your respiratory system in a matter of minutes.'

'How does it work?' asked Knutas.

'The cyanide instantly blocks the airways. You could say that the cells are suffocated, and the victim will have trouble breathing immediately after ingesting the poison. I presume it's sometimes used as a method of committing suicide because it's such a lethal substance. If you take a sufficient amount of cyanide, you will definitely die. And it happens so fast, taking anywhere from thirty seconds to a few minutes, depending on the amount. The Nazi Hermann Goering killed himself by swallowing a cyanide capsule when he was sentenced to death for genocide at the Nuremberg trials.'

'How difficult is it to get hold of cyanide?'

Sohlman shrugged.

'These days you can buy just about anything on the Internet. Or make it yourself if you have an interest in chemistry. It may also be used in certain industries. I don't really know.'

'We'll need to find out about that,' said Knutas. 'Will you look into it, Thomas?'

'Sure. At the same time, I think we have to ask ourselves what type of person would use poison to commit a murder. It indicates a certain amount of calculation. And who would be capable of handling such a dangerous poison?'

'Something that distinguishes a killer who uses poison is the absence of physical contact between the perpetrator and the victim,' Sohlman interjected. 'That type of murderer watches the victim ingest the poison, but usually leaves the scene as quickly as possible. So he doesn't leave any incriminating evidence behind. No fingerprints or strands of hair, no skin scrapings, no blood. In this case, the perp did drag the victim into the lift, but he must have felt a need to hide the body for some reason. There's also a psychological aspect. Death by poison is often extremely painful, even though it happens fast, which indicates that the motive is most likely personal. So the victim and killer knew each other; they had some sort of relationship.'

'If we assume that someone put cyanide in Algård's drink, shouldn't he have noticed from the smell that something was wrong with it?' asked Jacobsson. 'Since it would have smelled so strongly of bitter almonds?'

'Hmmm,' said Sohlman and then paused, rubbing his chin. 'That depends. I've heard that only fifty per cent of human beings are able to smell the scent of bitter almonds. Algård might have belonged to the group that can't. Or else it all happened so fast that he noticed the smell too late. It's also possible that he was forced to drink the poison. We found a chair toppled over at the crime scene. And he'd suffered a blow to the head.'

Silence settled over the room, as if everyone were trying to imagine what might have happened on the night of the dedication festivities. Knutas broke the silence.

'Let's leave the speculations for now and concentrate on what we know about Viktor Algård. I didn't really know him. I only met him a few times in connection with various events that he'd organized. Anyone else know him?'

Everyone shook their heads.

'OK.' Knutas glanced down at his notes. 'Algård was fifty-three years old, born and raised in Hamra. Married, with two grown children who live on the mainland. A son who's twenty-eight and a daughter who's twenty-six. He'd worked as an event planner for years, and I know that he was quite successful. His problems started when he bought a building down by the harbour and turned it into a club for teenagers. We all know what has gone on since then. There has been trouble at that club from the very beginning, and now, to top it all, we have the recent case of assault and battery.'

Knutas got up, picked up a red marker and began writing on the whiteboard at the front of the room.

Assault.

'The incident that took place in front of his club is an important factor, and we need to explore a possible connection, of course. According to several witnesses, Algård was in the process of divorcing his wife.' Knutas wrote the word *Divorce* on the whiteboard. 'Wittberg, can you tell us more?'

'The Algårds filed for divorce in district court a week ago. They've been married more than thirty years. We've just started on the interviews, and unfortunately we haven't been able to talk to any of the family members yet. We'll be meeting with his wife, Elisabeth Algård, later today. Both children will also be interviewed – I hope sometime today. The only people we've talked to so far are employees of his company, which specialized in PR and event planning. Algård had two people on staff and his company is called Go Gotland. The office is located on Hästgatan and the client list includes major players, such as Wisby Strand, Kneippbyn and the municipality of Visby itself. I've talked to the two employees, a young guy named Max and a girl called Isabella. They had only good things to say about Algård as a boss. In addition, both of them are positive that he was having an affair. They hadn't seen him with another woman, but apparently he'd exhibited all the signs of being in love. They said that he'd started having lunch with someone, but he refused to tell them who it was. He was gone from the office for long periods of time, and would return looking flushed and very pleased with himself. He'd started going to a gym – apparently he used to work out, but had let it lapse – and he'd even hired a personal trainer just a few weeks ago. He'd told his employees that he was going to take a trip to Paris in May, and he'd contacted an estate agent to help him find a large flat in the centre of Visby, since he was planning to sell his small pied-à-terre.'

'So now we have another motive,' said Smittenberg, twirling the ends of the moustache he'd recently affected. 'The mysterious mistress.'

Knutas wrote *Mistress* on the whiteboard and then turned again to Thomas Wittberg.

'You might as well write *Wife,* while you're at it,' Smittenberg suggested. 'From what I gather, Elisabeth Algård doesn't have an alibi, does she?'

Knutas did as the prosecutor requested.

'There's one theory that may be a long shot, but we still can't rule it out,' Wittberg interjected. 'The fact is, the conference centre has been a very controversial construction project. It's possible that someone murdered Algård to protest against the dedication of the building.'

'A statement from rabid environmentalists, maybe? That sounds really credible,' Jacobsson teased him.

'We need to keep all avenues open,' Knutas countered, his voice sharp.

He added the words *Conference Centre* to the list and again turned to Wittberg.

'What have you found out so far from talking to the waiters and service personnel?'

'According to a bartender, shortly after midnight Algård told him that he was going to take a break. It was the first time all evening that he left the party. After that no one saw him again.'

'And no one missed him?' asked Jacobsson in surprise.

'The dinner was over by the time he took a break, and then the dancing started up and there was a lot of commotion. We're talking about more than five hundred guests, after all. The people that we've interviewed so far seem to have taken it for granted that Algård was on the scene somewhere, but none of them can pinpoint exactly the last time they saw him.'

'Was he alone when he left?'

'Yes, he headed downstairs to the section of the building that was closed off for the evening.'

'The perp could have been someone he worked with,' said Jacobsson. 'What do we know about any problems on the job? We should look into that.'

Knutas wrote *Work Colleague* on the board.

'As of now, we haven't come up with anything significant other than the trouble at his club,' said Wittberg. 'We need to keep working.'

The group from the National Criminal Police in Stockholm arrived in the afternoon. There was none of the hullabaloo that always ensued whenever Martin Kihlgård was part of the group, and Knutas reluctantly had to admit that he missed his charismatic colleague. Even though Kihlgård frequently drove Knutas crazy, at least he was entertaining. Jacobsson politely greeted their newly arrived associates, but displayed what seemed like a deliberate lack of interest in talking to them. Knutas found that annoying. It wasn't their fault that Kihlgård was ill.

In charge of the group was an inconsequential-looking man by the name of Rylander. Under his direction, they immediately set to work on the most pressing task: scheduling and recording the huge number of interviews. Some had already been conducted, but hundreds of others still needed to be done.

Viktor Algård's two children were coming to the police station to be interviewed, but his wife couldn't muster the strength to do the same. So the police would have to go to the Algård house. Knutas thought that was actually just as well. He wanted to see Algård's home to get a better picture of what the man was like as a person. The police had already searched the house without finding anything of interest. The same could not be said of the victim's flat on Hästgatan. In the bathroom the police had found perfume, a hair dryer and other feminine toiletries. In the bedroom were shoes and clothing belonging to a woman, but of course they might be his wife's. Knutas had decided to wait to ask about these items until he could talk to Elisabeth Algård in person.

As soon as the morning meeting was over, Jacobsson and Knutas headed for Hamra to interview the widow.

First, however, they made a detour to Bokströmsgatan and parked in front of Knutas's house.

'I just need to run in and see Nils for a moment,' he explained. 'He stayed home from school because he had a stomach ache this morning.'

'But isn't he sixteen by now?'

'Children still need their parents. Don't let anyone tell you otherwise. They're never too old for a little parental concern.'

Knutas gave her a wry smile as he opened the car door. Jacobsson made a choking sound, as if something had got lodged in her throat. Then she had a coughing fit.

'Are you coming down with something too?' Knutas asked.

He pounded his colleague on the back as tears

ran down Jacobsson's cheeks. Knutas looked at her in astonishment.

'What's the matter?'

'It's nothing,' she told him. 'I must have swallowed something the wrong way. That's all. I think I'll wait in the car.'

'OK.'

The house was dark and silent. Knutas tiptoed upstairs so as not to wake Nils if he was asleep. Cautiously he opened the door. Nils was sitting at his desk next to the window with his back turned. His computer was on. Knutas saw at once the picture of Alexander Almlöv that had been published in the newspapers.

'Hi, Nils. How are you feeling?'

His son turned around with a start. His eyes were shiny with tears.

'What are you doing at home?'

Knutas went over to Nils and placed his hand on his son's shoulder. The boy was much too thin. That was something he'd been noticing for a while now.

'I just wanted to look in on you. Mamma said you had a stomach ache.'

Knutas's expression turned grim as he looked at the picture on the computer screen. The photo had been taken at Tofta beach in the summertime. Alexander, his face suntanned and his hair wet, was smiling at the camera. Now he lay in a coma.

'What are you doing?' he asked gently.

'Nothing.' Nils turned off the computer and went over to his bed to lie down. 'Just leave me alone.'

'But how are you feeling?'

'Better. Nothing to worry about.'

He turned over to face the wall. Knutas sat down on the edge of the bed.

'Are you thinking about Alexander?'

'Why are you here, anyway? Don't you have a lot to do because of the murder and everything?'

'Yes, I do,' sighed Knutas. 'We're on our way down to Sudret. Karin and I. She's waiting in the car.'

'So go. I'm fine.'

'Shall I get you something? Are you thirsty?'

'No.'

'You sure?'

'Yes. I said I'm fine.'

Knutas made his way back to the car, filled with anxiety. He had to find some way to reconnect with Nils.

They drove south, taking the coast road. It was a beautiful day with the springtime sun shining over the fields and meadows. The hides of the cattle gleamed as they grazed in the pastures. On the right-hand side of the road Knutas and Jacobsson occasionally caught glimpses of the sea, which glinted with promise. After the long and dreary winter, it was as if someone had lifted a hazy grey curtain that had been hovering over the island for months and now nature had come back to life. A few fiery red poppies were visible in places along the road, and suddenly summer didn't seem so far away. The air was already warmer. Knutas rolled down the window.

'Beautiful day,' he said, casting an enquiring glance at Karin.

'It really is.'

'So how are things going?'

'Fine, thanks.'

She looked at him and smiled. She had a relatively large mouth for such a narrow face. The big gap between her front teeth was particularly endearing.

'We haven't had much time to talk lately.'

'No.'

'You've seemed a bit down.'

'You think so?'

Karin's face seemed to close up. It was obvious that she didn't want to discuss the topic. They continued driving south in silence.

Knutas looked out of the window again, wondering what could be weighing on her. He'd worked with Karin Jacobsson for more than fifteen years and she was his closest confidante. At least from his point of view. He told her everything, including any problems he experienced with his family. She was a good listener, always willing to offer encouragement and advice. But when it came to Karin's own personal life, that was a whole different story. As soon as the conversation turned to her, she became guarded and silent.

A year ago Knutas had promoted Jacobsson to Deputy Detective Superintendent and second in command, which had stirred up some bad feelings at the station, even though most people were positive about her new role. Malicious comments were heard from a handful of older male officers who didn't like being passed over for a much younger colleague who also happened to be a woman. Jacobsson's petite stature hadn't made it any easier for her to win their respect. The fact that she didn't live according to the expected norms had also given rise to speculations. Although she was forty years old, she still lived alone with her cockatoo named Vincent. She devoted most of her free time to football, both as a coach and as a player in the women's league.

'Have you heard anything more about Kihlgård?' Knutas asked, mostly just for something to say.

'Yes. He was in Karolinska Hospital for a week, and they did a lot of tests, but he's home now. The doctors don't know what's wrong with him.'

'I didn't even know that he was in hospital. What sort of symptoms does he have?'

'He just generally doesn't feel good. He's suffering from nausea and dizziness.'

'How long will it take to get the results of the tests back?'

'A week or two.'

'We should send him flowers.'

'That's a good idea.'

He glanced at Karin. She looked more tired than usual.

'You know that you can talk to me if there's something bothering you,' he said. 'I'm always willing to listen.'

'Thanks, Anders. I know that. Maybe we could talk some other time. Not now.'

'Are you sure?'

'I'm sure.'

Knutas changed the subject in order to break the oppressive mood that had settled over them.

'What do you think about the case? Any ideas about a motive?'

'It's impossible to say. There are several likely motives, but I don't think it's any coincidence that Algård was murdered just a couple of weeks after Alexander Almlöv was assaulted. Especially considering all the criticisms that have been hurled at Algård lately.'

'Who do you think is a likely candidate?'

'Either someone who is close to Alexander, or someone connected to the bouncers, who both happen to be involved in criminal activities. Or maybe some fanatic who's tired of all the youth violence and wants to take matters into his own hands. There are all sorts of variations to consider. Nine times out of ten the perp is a member of the immediate family. So it could also be someone like that.'

'Maybe it's no coincidence either that Algård was in the process of getting a divorce.'

'Sure. And it's a strange thing about this mistress of his,' said Jacobsson pensively. 'We need to find out who she is. And does Mrs Algård know that her husband was playing around on the side? Maybe not, if the love affair is relatively recent, but somebody in their circle of friends must know something. Do you think the mistress was at the party?'

'Maybe. We'll have to wait and see what the interviews can tell us. She may have been out of town. Maybe she doesn't even know about the murder yet.'

When Jacobsson and Knutas reached the Hamra Inn, they pulled over and stopped in the deserted car park. The inn was incredibly popular in the summertime, but now it looked practically abandoned. Several signs indicated that the Coconut Bar was to the left, while Pepe's Tex-Mex was on the right. The rustic wooden tables were stacked against one wall and the restaurant was glaringly empty. A few messages had been tacked up on a decrepit-looking bulletin board near the car park. 'Flea market in Burgsvik', 'Weaving class in Havdhem', 'Alcoholics Anonymous meets every Tuesday in the Hablingbo community centre', 'Sheep shearing – cheap', and 'Lost cat'.

'We need to go left here and head down towards the sea,' said Jacobsson, turning the car on to a gravel road. The flat landscape was mostly cultivated fields. This was farm country, with one farmstead right next to another. Healthy-looking cattle grazed in the pastures and flocks of sheep stared at the car as they drove past. The sea glittered up ahead. They were almost at the southernmost tip of Gotland, far from their own familiar stomping grounds.

They drove along a narrow road that followed the shoreline. The farm at the end of the road belonged to the Algård family. As they pulled into the gravel-covered yard in front of the house, two greyhounds appeared, barking loudly. Knutas, who was afraid of dogs, hesitantly climbed out of the car, never taking his eyes off the two animals. Jacobsson called out to them and they instantly loped over to her, barking happily. The front door of the house opened and a shrill whistle rang out across the yard. The dogs immediately stopped their romping and raced to join their owner.

Elisabeth Algård showed Knutas and Jacobsson into the house. They sat down in a big country kitchen replete with all the farmhouse charms: blue-and-white-checked cotton curtains, exposed ceiling beams, a big brick fireplace, a scoured wood floor and a gate-legged table, which was the biggest and most rustic Knutas had ever seen. The tall windows offered an expansive view of the fields and, off in the distance, the sea. The widow served them coffee and almond buns without first asking if they'd like any. She shooed the dogs out of the kitchen and closed the door. With a heavy sigh she sat down on a chair across from the two officers. Her thin, sinewy figure was clad in jeans and a short-sleeved cotton blouse. Her wispy, smoky-coloured hair was pulled back and fastened with a clasp at the nape of her neck. She wore no make-up. Her lips were thin, making a narrow streak of her mouth. She couldn't be described as a beauty, but she had pleasing, distinctive features. As she poured the coffee, Elisabeth Algård looked Knutas right in the eye.

'What do you want to know?'

'First of all, we want to offer our condolences. Unfortunately, we do need to ask you quite a few questions. When was the last time you saw Viktor?'

'Saturday afternoon, before he left for the party.'

'How did he seem?'

'He was in a great mood, even though he tried to hide it.'

Knutas looked at her enquiringly.

'Viktor wanted a divorce,' she said tonelessly.

'We know about that. Can you tell us why?' said Jacobsson as she bit into a bun.

'It was a bolt out of the blue. I can't understand it. Good Lord, we've been married for thirty-two years. We have two grown children, this farm with all the animals and my studio. Viktor had his own company. Our life was good. It was calm and pleasant and the days passed enjoyably. All of a sudden he wanted to destroy everything we'd built together.'

'When did he tell you that he wanted a divorce?'

'A couple of weeks ago. Right after that boy was assaulted. At first I thought that was the reason – because

Viktor was so upset by all the uproar and criticism. But he said it had nothing to do with that.'

'So what did he give as his reason?'

'Reason? He didn't have a reason. He just said that he wanted to lead his own life. Have you ever heard anything like it? He said he was longing to focus on himself, on his own happiness. "You only live once," he said, "and I don't want to end up a bitter man."'

The widow shook her head.

'Bitter! How could he even utter such a word, considering everything we've accomplished during all these years together? Two well-brought-up children who have become independent and successful individuals with their own lives. An entire farm that we renovated from the ground up. It's frequently included on lists of the most beautiful farms on all of Gotland. We live here in this marvellous natural setting and close to the sea, which we both love. We have dogs, and we raise chickens that give us the best eggs for breakfast every day. I have my weaving, which actually now provides me with a full-time income. He has his company and the club, both of which were doing amazingly well – at least up until that awful beating incident occurred. We can afford to travel and do all the fun things we want to do. We eat well every day. So how can he talk about being bitter and wanting to finally put himself at the top of his priorities? I'm sorry, but I just don't understand it.'

Elisabeth Algård's voice had risen in volume. She leaned across the table, shifting her gaze between Jacobsson and Knutas, as if trying to convince them of her own bewilderment. Jacobsson sat motionless, her hands cradling her coffee cup. Elisabeth continued her diatribe, as if a dam had burst.

'And he wanted to destroy everything, tear it all down. He cared nothing about me, or the fact that he was about to shatter my whole life. And he had no consideration for the children. No, he was thinking only about himself. It was a week before my birthday when he told me that he wanted a divorce. Just like that. And this summer we were supposed to spend a month in Italy, the whole family, and rent a villa in Tuscany. That might have been the last summer the four of us spent together, since the children will probably have their own families soon. Our friends couldn't understand it either. They couldn't fathom why he'd want to leave me and everything we had together. They thought it was just a whim, a mid-life crisis. But I'm not so sure . . . And then what happens? He goes and dies only weeks later. So much for focusing on his own life. If it wasn't so sad, I'd probably laugh myself silly. Yes, I would. The whole situation is utterly absurd.'

At last she fell silent and paused to drink her coffee. Elisabeth Algård was not behaving at all the way Knutas had expected. He'd pictured a grieving widow overcome by despair. Instead she mostly seemed filled with rage. He realized that she must have spent the past two weeks brooding about the collapse of her marriage.

'Did he have any enemies that you know of?' Knutas asked. 'Anyone who might have wanted to harm him?'

'Of course he did. After that sixteen-year-old boy was beaten up outside the club, half of Gotland was angry at Viktor. Plenty of people even thought that he was to blame for the boy nearly getting killed. And then there's the divorce. All of our relatives and friends were surprised by his decision. Nobody understood why he was doing this. But of course it's ridiculous to think that someone would murder him for that reason.'

'What was Viktor's attitude towards the assault?'

'Naturally he thought it was a horrible thing to happen. He was truly shocked and blamed everyone except himself. He said that it was the parents' fault for not having better control over their kids; that the bouncers should have stepped in sooner and with greater force when they saw what was going on; that the police should have had a greater presence outside the club, since they knew about all the drinking and fighting that went on. Viktor was devastated and went over to visit the boy's mother, but he was thrown out on his ear. She blamed him. She runs the Kloster Restaurant, which is near the club. Viktor claimed that in addition to being upset that her son had been assaulted, she was also mad at him for chasing away her customers with his rowdy club parties.'

'Are you talking about Ingrid Almlöv?'

'Yes. And I know that Viktor was very upset about the fact that she refused to see him. He tried several times.'

'Are there other enemies your husband might have acquired because of the assault incident? Or simply because he ran the club the way he did?' asked Jacobsson.

'Of course. The bouncers were mad at Viktor because he accused them of shirking their duties. Now they're at risk of losing their jobs altogether. And just think about all the parents and others who have been complaining ever since the club opened.'

'But as far as you know, he never received any sort of specific threats?'

'No.'

Knutas thought about what the widow had told them. They were going to have to thoroughly investigate the whole story about the assault and Viktor's club. He decided to phone Ingrid Almlöv later in the day. He'd talked to her a number of times since her son had been beaten, but their conversation had never touched on any of these issues. He felt sick at the idea of having to broach these topics with her when her son was hovering between life and death.

'Think very carefully,' Jacobsson said now. 'If we disregard everything having to do with the assault and the divorce, was Viktor on bad terms with anyone else? It might be related to something in the distant past. It doesn't have to be something current.'

Elisabeth took a bun from the plate and slowly chewed on it as she considered the question.

'In that case, the only person I can think of is Sten Bergström, who lives out near Holmhällar down the road. Several years ago he started a company similar to Viktor's. In the beginning it was just a matter of a few events. The first thing he did was handle the arrangements for a big wedding here in the area, and it was a huge success. We were even invited. After that he got so many requests to arrange weddings and other types of celebrations that he started his own business, specializing in local parties. Slightly smaller events than those Viktor handled. But the problem was that he gave his company a name that was ridiculously similar to Viktor's, which is called "Go Gotland". Sten Bergström called his firm "Goal Gotland". Gradually Sten began getting requests from customers who had previously hired Viktor's company. His business grew. Viktor got more and more unhappy and even alarmed over the competition. After a while rumours began to spread that Sten's events were marred by drunkenness and brawls. I think he lost his licence to serve alcohol, and eventually he went bankrupt.'

'When did all this happen?' asked Jacobsson.

'Maybe three or four years ago. After the bankruptcy, Sten and Viktor never spoke to each other again. He's the only real enemy that I can think of.'

Knutas made a note of the name. Jacobsson decided to change tack.

'And your children – what did they think about the fact that you were getting a divorce?'

'It's hard to say. They're both adults now, you know. Fredrik is twenty-eight and Sofia is twenty-six. Both of them live in Stockholm and have their own lives. Neither of them seemed particularly upset by the news, although they might not have wanted to tell us their true thoughts or feelings. Children end up with conflicting loyalties, not wanting to side with one parent or the other.'

Elisabeth Algård gave a heavy sigh and then refilled their coffee cups.

'What was your reaction when you heard about Viktor's death?' asked Jacobsson.

'When the police came here the first time, I had such a migraine that I hardly reacted at all when they told me that Viktor was dead. And to cap it all, that they suspected it was murder. When my headache finally began to subside, I had a hard time taking in the news. As I began to comprehend fully what had happened, I felt angry. Because he was dead and I could no longer talk to him. Because I still couldn't work out why he wanted a divorce. Or what had made him come up with such an idea. I'm angry because I never had a chance to find out. I feel cheated. It's as if I'm living in a vacuum, and I can't seem to get anything done. But there are a lot of things I need to deal with: the funeral, the estate, his will and our finances. I need to decide what to do about the farm, and whether I can even afford to live here any more. Then there's Viktor's business – and everything else. I feel like there's no room for grief. Just a lot of practical matters that need to be addressed, along with my own anger, and I have no idea what to do about that.'

Knutas felt genuinely sorry for Elisabeth Algård. So far he had deliberately put off asking her about her husband's purported love affair.

Jacobsson made it easy for him by broaching the sensitive topic herself.

'There's one more thing that we have to ask you,' she began. 'Do you know whether Viktor had met someone else? Another woman?'

The widow's eyes narrowed.

'What do you mean?'

Jacobsson nervously shifted position and cast a quick glance at Knutas, as if asking him for help. But he had none to offer.

'Certain people we've talked to claim that they suspected Viktor had a mistress.'

Elisabeth got up and went over to look out of the window, with her back turned to the two officers. When she spoke, her voice was dry and composed.

'Who told you that?'

'Several witnesses have said that they recently started

to suspect that he had fallen in love. This could be of great importance to the investigation. Think carefully. Did you notice any change in his behaviour? Some small sign that might indicate he was having an affair?'

'No, nothing. I didn't notice anything like that.'

'Did you ever spend the night in Viktor's flat in Visby?'

'No.'

'When was the last time you were there?'

'Good Lord, it must be at least a year ago. I've never had any reason to go there.'

'So you didn't keep any personal belongings in the flat? Clothing or toiletries?'

'No.' Elisabeth turned around and gave the officers a resigned look. 'Is that what you found there? In Viktor's flat?'

Knutas had no option but to nod.

Yet another night when Johan had slept very poorly. Elin woke up at least ten times, coughing so hard that it sounded as if her lungs would burst. He'd phoned both the doctor on call and the paediatric hotline, but both times he was advised to remain calm, give the child some cough syrup and keep an eye on her. How typical, he thought with annoyance. *Just because they don't want to use any of their sodding resources to make a house call.* He deeply regretted that he and Emma had decided not to vaccinate their daughter against whooping cough, but they had both judged the vaccine to be too new and unproven.

Around 4 a.m. Elin finally fell asleep, and she was still sleeping soundly when he got up. Emma would stay home with Elin as long as necessary. Johan had taken care of their daughter the previous week, but now he was swamped with work because of the Algård murder case. Besides, Emma was feeling generally worn out, so she candidly admitted that she was more than happy to stay home from work. She was a primary school teacher at the small Kyrk School in Roma. Right now the pupils were bubbling over with spring fever, which made them even more rambunctious than usual.

Luckily, Johan and Pia had agreed that he didn't need to drive into town to the editorial office. She was going to pick him up in Roma on her way south. As expected, the murder in the conference centre had prompted big headlines in the local morning papers. It was front-page news, with other related stories inside as well. None of the papers mentioned the victim's name, merely speaking of 'a well-known individual in Visby's hospitality industry'. When Johan carefully read through all the articles about the murder, he happened to notice a brief story in *Gotlands Allehanda*. It was about the case of the sixteen-year-old boy who had been assaulted. Shit. He'd completely forgotten about that because of everything that had happened yesterday. The boy's condition was still serious. I need to remember to check up on the case sometime today, he told himself.

Pia turned up at nine o'clock sharp, as agreed, and then they headed south.

'I think we should start with Birgitta Österman. She's the one who usually takes care of the Algårds' dogs.'

'Do you think she'll talk to us?'

'I've already phoned her,' said Pia with a grin.

'Of course you have. I should have guessed.'

The farm they were headed for was located a short distance before the road ended at the Algård farm and on the opposite side. The farmhouse was an impressive limestone building with barns forming separate wings on either side and a horse pasture where a colt was restlessly trotting back and forth. The front door opened even before they could get out of the car. Birgitta Österman was a stout woman in her sixties. She gave them a friendly smile when they introduced themselves and then invited them in, but they politely declined the obligatory offer of coffee. Instead, they all sat down outside in the comfortable patio chairs. The yard was warm with sunshine and there was no wind.

'What do you think about the news of the murder?'

'Well, I was certainly shocked.' Birgitta Österman shook her head. 'Even though it happened up north in Visby, it still feels so close, since he was a neighbour and all.'

'What was Viktor like?'

'To be honest, I really couldn't stand the man. There was something fishy about him. I could never figure him out. He was perfectly nice as a neighbour, but he always seemed wound up somehow, as if he could never relax. I always had the feeling he was hiding something, but I don't know why. That's just how he seemed. He was that way from the very beginning.' She paused to look towards the Algård farm. 'And it turned out that he wasn't the reliable sort after all, since he suddenly wanted a divorce. Elisabeth told me about it just last week.'

Johan gave a start. This was something new, but he didn't let on that he hadn't known about it.

'Do you know why he wanted a divorce?'

'She had no idea. Nobody did. Everyone thought he must be having a mid-life crisis. But I knew that he'd found someone else.'

'Really? What makes you think that?'

'It's not something I "think". I know it for a fact.'

'How can you be so sure?'

'Because I saw them. Not here – oh no. It was in Stockholm. I went there one weekend to visit a friend who lives in Vasastan. It's something I do a few times a year. We were on our way to a restaurant, but stopped for a glass of wine at a pub first. And who do you think I saw? Viktor. With another woman! I just about had a heart attack, and I had no idea what I was going to say to him. But they were sitting at the very back of the pub, and they were so wrapped up in one another that they didn't have eyes for anybody else. They had their heads close and were practically cooing to each other. There was no question what was going on. They left soon after, and he didn't see me. If he had, he probably would have fainted.'

'What did she look like?' asked Johan, trying hard not to sound too eager.

'She was petite, with blond hair to her shoulders, in a pageboy style. Thin and expensively dressed. I never saw her face.'

'How old?'

'I'd guess about forty-five, maybe fifty.'

'Have you told this to the police?'

'No, I wasn't home yesterday when they came around to talk to the neighbours. They left a note asking me to contact them, but I just haven't had time yet. I've been out feeding the livestock this morning.'

'When did you see Viktor in Stockholm?'

'It was exactly one month ago.'

'Did his wife know about this other woman?'

'I have no idea. But she didn't mention it to me. On the other hand, it's not really something that you go around talking about, and we're not exactly close friends. More like acquaintances. And I didn't want to say anything. I'm not the sort who goes running about spreading gossip.'

The first thing that struck Knutas when he met Viktor Algård's children at the police station was how astonishingly different they looked.

Fredrik was relatively short and robust, with an olive complexion, and he had his hair combed back, just like his father. He wore a white cotton shirt with a green-checked pullover, a preppy look that reminded Knutas of an American college boy.

His sister, Sofia, was tall and fair. She was dressed in an oversize lilac shirt, black tights and patterned canvas shoes. She also wore enormous silver earrings and a checked Palestinian scarf.

Silent and tense, they sat next to each other on a bench in the corridor outside the interview room.

Jacobsson and Knutas chose to start with the son.

The minute they all sat down, Fredrik asked for a glass of water. Knutas switched on the tape recorder.

'I'd like to begin by expressing our condolences. As you no doubt realize, we need to ask you a number of questions.'

'Of course.'

The young man looked at him attentively. Knutas was again struck by how much he resembled Viktor.

'When was the last time you saw your father?'

'On his birthday, a couple of months ago. He was born on the twenty-eighth of February.'

'What sort of impression did he make on you at the time?'

'He was the same as always. We were at the house in Hamra. It turned out to be quite a bash, with about fifty guests. Pappa loved to celebrate on a grand scale.'

'What do you mean?'

'Well, he was a real party-person, even outside of his job. That was probably why he enjoyed his work so much. Pappa loved parties, and he was always ready to organize one at the drop of a hat.'

Knutas discerned a trace of scorn in the young man's voice. Jacobsson came back with a glass of water and then sat down on a chair at the other end of the room. Her presence was needed as a witness to the interview.

'And what did you think about that?'

'It didn't bother me. I didn't care.'

'What sort of relationship did you have with your father?'

'We didn't really have one. He was always working when we were growing up, and he was almost never home. So we didn't really know each other very well. I'm much closer to my mother, as you can imagine.'

'How did you react when you heard that your parents were getting a divorce?'

'I thought it was about time.'

'Why's that?'

'They were miles apart, in almost every way. They had completely different interests and never enjoyed doing the same things. Even politically they were mismatched – well, actually I don't think Pappa even had any political opinions of his own. He was simply ignorant. Mamma devours books, while Pappa never read anything except the evening paper and glossy magazines about celebrities. They had different views about nearly everything. They didn't even like the same kind of food. Mamma is a vegetarian, while Pappa loved rare steaks. Mamma got involved with the Red Cross and other charitable projects, while Pappa didn't give a damn about the problems of the world. I remember once when he yelled at my mother because she'd decided to sponsor a child in Guatemala.

'Mamma cares about her family far more deeply than he ever did. She often comes to Stockholm to visit us, but he never came with her. She has her friends and colleagues, and they like to travel together and go to the theatre. Mamma reads a lot and keeps up on social matters. If we ever wanted to discuss a current issue in world politics or some hot topic in general, Pappa never had anything sensible to say.'

Crimson patches had appeared on Fredrik Algård's throat. He took several sips of water.

'Do you know whether your father had any enemies?'

'I'm sure he'd managed to collect quite a few over the years. You know how it is in the hospitality business and the world of celebrities. Pretty on the outside, but lots of shit underneath.'

'What do you mean?'

'Pappa only cared about people who could be of benefit to him at that moment. People who were rich, successful and famous. If an artist who counted him as a true friend happened to lose the spotlight, he was suddenly of no use to Pappa. If a well-known author's books stopped selling, or if a top politician was found to have a drinking problem, or if an actor began to slide downhill, they no longer existed as far as Pappa was concerned.'

Knutas was surprised at the way this young man expressed himself. There was no mistaking the sarcastic tone.

'In other words, I think there must be plenty of people who were disappointed in Pappa. But whether they would go so far as to kill him, that's a whole different matter.'

'And what about you? How did you feel about him?'

'To be perfectly honest, I didn't care much for him. To win someone's trust and respect, you have to show the same in return. Don't you agree? You get the relationship with your children that you deserve. Everything depends on how you behave as a parent.'

For an instant, his words prompted Knutas to look inside himself. And he was frightened by what he saw.

He shook off his personal unease and went on: 'It sounds as if you actually hated your father.'

'No, I wouldn't say that. He had his good sides, just like everyone else. But who says that you have to love your parents? That's not a law. Honour thy father and mother? What kind of shit is that? Am I supposed to love him just because of a few seconds of orgasm when he impregnated my mother and I was conceived? He never gave a damn about me. We just ended up having to live in the same house.'

Knutas cast a glance at Jacobsson. The conversation was getting more and more unpleasant. Fredrik Algård's anger seemed to fill the whole room.

'Do you know whether your father ever received any threats?'

'No, I don't think so.'

'Did you notice anything different about his behaviour lately?'

'No. As I said, I saw him at his birthday party in February, and before that at Christmas.'

'But not for your mother's birthday? Wasn't that very recent?'

'Yes, but she came to Stockholm. She was angry and upset with my father because he wanted a divorce. We celebrated her birthday at our place instead.'

'So you live with someone?'

'Yes, my girlfriend Sanna. We live in Söder, near Mariatorget.'

'And you're studying at the university?'

'Yes. Political science. I also have a law degree, but I wanted to expand my interests. This is my last term, then I'll be finished.'

'How long are you planning to stay here on Gotland?'

'I have a breathing space in my studies at the moment, so I can stay at least a week. Mamma needs all the help and support she can get.'

A glance in the mirror inside the lift is enough to remind me of my sorry state. I've lost weight and look ghastly. But I'm in one piece and clean. That ought to be sufficient. Today I'm going out, which demands a great deal of mental concentration.

Life nowadays is a struggle, periodically marked by a lull and a vacuum. I have to think in small steps. Cleanse away everything else. The dreams I may have had, the goals and ambitions, no longer exist. I can't even remember what they were. Or whether I ever really had any.

The next test comes when I open the heavy front door to the street. Like a stinging slap in the face, I'm confronted with all the traffic noise of the city, the people and the smells. I hadn't noticed that it was raining and I'm freezing in my thin jacket. I refuse to meet anyone's eye as I walk along the pavement. I shut everyone out, pretending that they don't exist: all those poplin coats, jackets and sweaters, the ribbed umbrellas, the briefcases and the shoulder bags made of brown leather. Rubber galoshes and walking shoes.

The blurry faces that I glimpse passing by are nothing but hazy masks.

Finally I arrive. A moment of panic because at first I can't remember the door code. I rummage around in my pocket for the slip of paper and breathe a sigh of relief when I find it. I can't handle any setbacks right now.

It's a square room, with one window facing the street, a bed along one wall, and a small table and two arm-chairs.

'I had a bad dream last night.'

'Tell me about it.'

'I dreamed that all of my teeth turned black and became porous bits of coal. One by one they came loose and then fell out into my cupped hands. Soon my gums were bare and my hands were full. I was heartbroken and thought to myself: But I'm so young. I woke up screaming, and after that I couldn't go back to sleep, as usual.'

'What did you think about while you were lying there awake?'

'Those horrible years when I was a teenager. I haven't had that dream in a long time, but back then I had it all the time, when I was in my early teens.'

'It sounds like you were suffering from anxiety.'

'I was. It lasted three years.'

'Can you tell me about it?'

I shake my head. I don't really want to. I know that

whenever I dredge up memories, I feel as if I'm transported back to that time for a moment. And it's too painful. I'm overwhelmed by the same abysmal sense of despair. It has taken up residence inside my body, and it will always be there. For as long as I live.

'Try.'

'It doesn't make any sense. For example, I still have a hard time taking a shower.'

'Taking a shower?'

'Yes. Ever since my schooldays. I can't believe I can't get over it. During my first years I was very popular. In photographs from back then, I often looked happy. My classmates thought I was fun, sort of the class clown. Plus I was a good football player. I liked sports and music. Those were my two main interests. But when I started secondary school, everything changed.'

'In what way?'

'I still have no clue what happened, but it had something to do with my father dying in a car accident that summer before secondary school. Mamma and Pappa had already been divorced for a long time, but we lived in a small town and everyone knew everything about everyone else. There was something about that accident . . . My siblings and I spent nearly the whole summer holiday at a camp for kids. When I got back, my old friends' attitude towards me had changed. They avoided me. No one wanted to be around me any more.

'I started at a new school, with new classmates,

and suddenly it was as if I didn't exist. The other kids treated me like air. No one said a single word to me; they hardly even gave me a glance. For the rest of my schooldays I never talked to anyone in my classes. I was alone during breaks and at lunchtime in the cafeteria. I was never chosen for any sports teams; I moved like a shadow along the walls. Frozen out.'

'What about the shower?'

'The shower?'

'You said something about having a hard time taking a shower.'

'Oh, right. PE lessons were the worst. I was the smallest boy in my class, a late bloomer, and I looked like a child. One after the other, they all entered puberty. Lots of the boys were more than a head taller than me. They had broad shoulders, and their voices were changing. They had peach fuzz on their upper lips, hair on their legs and in their armpits. Their Adam's apples were as big as ripe plums. Before games I used to try to hide in the changing room. It was a torment to have to undress in front of the others. I always claimed the shower in the corner and stood with my back turned, washing as fast as I could.'

I close my eyes. These memories are painful. My eyes are stinging. I don't want to cry right now. I'm feeling a little sick, but I go on: 'Even today I can still hear the sound of the spraying shower water, the rough voices, the joking and teasing. The snap of towels slapping bare skin. Water fights, towel fights. And the whole time I'm standing in the corner with my back turned to all the other boys. It was pure hell. PE lessons were too. I was always the last one to be picked. Everyone sighed if they were forced to have me on their team. They never passed the ball to me. When I lie awake at night, I can still see their faces and hear their comments.'

'How did you get through it?'

'I didn't. Finally I asked the teacher if I could practise discus throwing instead. Can you imagine that? The discus, of all ridiculous ideas. And the teacher went for it. So instead of playing basketball and football with the others, which was actually what I loved most, I would stand all alone on the grass behind the sports hall and throw the discus. Lesson after lesson. The teacher didn't care. He just let me keep practising. That was probably a lot easier for him.'

Silence settles over the room. I down the rest of the water in the glass on the table in order to stave off the feeling of nausea. I'm about to fall into the darkness, and I don't want to go there. I clutch the glass tight, holding it with both hands. I need to concentrate. How am I going to make it home? I'm on the verge of collapsing. I open my mouth again and the words automatically spill out. I listen to the voice, which sounds unfamiliar, as if it doesn't belong to me.

'If only I'd known what was ahead of me when I

entered that classroom. A darkness that would last three years. And that's an endless number of dark days. A feeling of dread would fill me each morning when I forced myself to get out of bed. Three years of humiliation and annihilation. Do you know what that does to a person? I've never understood why they hated me so much. I was completely alone.'

The memories are still buried in my body. My hands are shaking so badly that I have to put down the glass.

'But what about at home? During all those years when you were having such a bad time, didn't your mother notice anything? What did she do?'

I can hear the bitterness in my voice as I say: 'Nothing. She never did anything.'

'Nothing?'

'It must have been obvious that I was having a bloody awful time of it. I never wanted to get out of bed in the morning. After school and all evening I would lie on my bed, alone in my room, and listen to music on my headset. Do you understand? Every night! Weekdays and weekends. Year after year. For three years not a single friend ever came home with me. No one ever phoned. And what did my mother do? Nothing.'

'And you never talked about this with her? Didn't she ever ask you what was wrong?'

I can't bring myself to answer. Nausea has taken hold of me full force, and I feel as if I'm going to throw up at any second. My vision blurs. I see that the person across from me is leaning forward and saying something, but I no longer hear the voice.

I can't stay here. I pick up my jacket and rush out of the door, then set off running for home. Along the way I bump into a pram, almost toppling it over. A woman screams abuse after me. Outside of the Konsum supermarket I knock over a bucket of tulips.

I manage to stay in control as I ride up in the lift. As soon as I get my door open, I dash for the toilet.

I lift the lid just in time.

Johan had never received so much criticism for a story as he did after his report on the murder at the conference centre, which was broadcast on Monday evening. *Regional News* was the only programme to reveal Viktor Algård's identity and the first to mention his pending divorce, as well as the possibility that he was having a love affair. All of this provoked a heated discussion about journalistic ethics.

After every broadcast Johan and Pia had a teleconference with the head office back in Stockholm. This time both were harshly reprimanded, primarily for choosing to publicize the information about Viktor's mistress. It didn't help that the neighbour's speculation about Algård's dalliances had been confirmed by his employees.

Several managing editors also found it appalling that *Regional News* had revealed the victim's identity only twenty-four hours after he was found murdered. Johan defended his decision by saying that there was enormous interest in the case on Gotland, since Algård was so well known on the island. Besides, they had checked with the police to make sure that all family members had been informed about the death.

Johan, together with Pia and their boss Max Grenfors, had thought the information sufficiently relevant to make it public, given that this was a high-profile homicide. It might also provide an important clue to the motive.

Even though Johan defended himself fiercely and certainly presented a convincing argument, doubt was gnawing at him as he drove home to Roma in the dark.

He hoped to find Emma still awake. What he needed right now was a glass of wine and a chance to talk.

And Emma. He was longing for her. He was always longing for her. Finally they were able to be together, all the time. They could fall asleep together every night, and wake up together every morning.

Their relationship had definitely had its ups and downs since they'd met five years ago. Back then, Emma was married to Olle, she had two children in primary school, and she was living a quiet life with her family in Roma.

Then she met Johan. He happened to interview her in connection with a murder case, and they instantly fell in love. Eventually she divorced Olle and gave birth to Johan's child. Their relationship had been stormy ever since. Against all odds, they had decided to get married during the previous summer. Johan had begun to doubt that they'd ever become husband and wife, when

Emma had suddenly accepted his marriage proposal. On the day of the wedding, she kept him nervously waiting outside the church. Fårö Church was filled with guests, the time for the wedding came and went, and the pastor was wringing her hands. Johan's best man, Andreas, started looking worried, while all the groom wanted to do was run away. Half an hour late, Emma and her maid of honour had finally appeared, both of them out of breath. They'd had a flat tyre and had left their mobiles at home.

For the past six months they'd led a normal family life with their three-year-old daughter Elin. Every other week the family expanded when Sara and Filip, Emma's children from her first marriage, now eleven and ten, came to stay. Johan had moved into Emma's house in Roma and sublet his flat in the Södermalm district of Stockholm.

His routine of buying fast food at the local 7-Eleven had now been replaced by major shopping expeditions at Willy's supermarket. Takeaway pizza had been replaced by home-cooked meals served at specific times of the day. He'd become an expert at making sausage stroganoff, mincemeat sauce and pancakes. Instead of sleeping late on the weekend, he now got up to fix porridge for the kids in the kitchen. The days were filled with playing with the doll's house and plastic cars, watching children's programmes on TV, Parcheesi, football and sledding.

Instead of spending late nights at the pub, Johan would fall asleep by ten o'clock in front of the TV, with Emma leaning on his shoulder and sometimes one or two of the kids on his lap. His job didn't claim all his attention the way it used to do. Sometimes in the middle of editing a story he'd find himself suddenly wondering what Elin was doing at the day-care centre. And an interview that unexpectedly ran late could make him start to fret because he'd promised to take the children swimming or to football practice, or he was supposed to attend a parents' meeting at school. Previously he'd been the type of person who more or less lived for his job, endlessly on his computer or discussing work with colleagues. But now he was always in a rush to get home. His family was waiting for him. They needed him. And he loved that.

It was dark by the time he parked outside the house, but there were lights on in all the windows. Emma was awake.

'Hello,' he called as he went in, pushing aside ten pairs of shoes and some little rubber boots decorated with flowers.

'Hi,' he heard her reply from the kitchen. She was sitting there, clad in her usual grey jogging suit, with her long, sandy-coloured hair hanging loose down her back. Her eyes looked tired.

He gave her a hug.

'Hi, sweetheart. How are things?'

'OK. Elin's cough is better. She's asleep now, thank God.'

Johan went upstairs and opened the door to Sara's room. Her breathing was slow and regular; she always slept so soundly. He gently touched her cheek, and then turned off the light next to her bed, which was shining right in her face.

In the next bedroom Filip was asleep with his arms stretched over his head and his mouth wide open. He had kicked off the covers. Johan stood there looking at the boy for a moment. He almost thought of Filip as his own son. Lately they'd had such good times together. They shared a passion for football and a week ago Johan had gone to watch Filip play in a match. The boy had scored his first goal and they'd celebrated afterwards with hamburgers for dinner.

Then he went to look in on Elin. Her room was next to the bedroom he shared with Emma. All of her stuffed animals were lined up in her bed, barely leaving any room for the little girl. There she lay, squeezed in between the dolls, rabbits, teddy bears and shaggy dogs, a monkey with long arms and a cuddly elephant. All of them had names, and whenever Johan or Emma kissed their daughter goodnight, they also had to kiss all the animals, one after the other, and in the proper order. He smiled and kissed Elin on the forehead, prompting a little sigh. She turned on to her side and hugged one of the rabbits even closer.

After completing the interviews with Sofia and Fredrik Algård, Knutas felt utterly confused. Never had he met two children from the same family who had such vastly different attitudes towards their father. While Fredrik's feelings bordered on hatred, his sister Sofia had praised her father to the skies. She said that he'd been her best friend, always available and ready to help. She was devastated by her father's death, completely undone, and she burst into tears several times during the interview. According to her, Viktor had been the best father in the world.

Knutas yawned, rubbing his tired eyes, and went to get a cup of coffee. He also bought a dry sandwich from the vending machine. He hadn't made it home for dinner today either. He was lucky that Lina was so understanding. After all these years she had become used to his erratic schedule, and she almost never complained. Besides, as a midwife, she often had to work late herself. Things were easier now that the kids were older. Knutas suddenly pictured his son's face. He would just gather up a few documents and then head for home before Nils went to bed.

He thought about Elisabeth Algård. Apparently there had been another woman in Viktor's life. Who was she? It was absolutely essential that they find her. He wondered why she hadn't come forward, especially now that the victim's identity had been revealed on TV. On the other hand, that had happened only a few hours ago. Did she even know about the murder?

Knutas had talked to the technicians who had examined Viktor's phones and computers. There were no text messages or emails with any woman who might be the person they were looking for. And of the friends and colleagues that the police had interviewed so far, not one had any idea who the event planner's new love interest could have been. The only clues they had were the items that had been left behind in the flat in town.

The box was sitting on Knutas's desk. It contained an ordinary bra, a pair of white cotton knickers, a cotton shirt, size medium, and a pair of linen trousers. A small bag held make-up and toiletries. The police had also found a handwritten note among a stack of old newspapers: 'Thanks for yesterday. Love you. Your sweetie-pie.' With a drawing of a flower at the bottom.

Knutas tapped the note. *Sweetie-pie.* What a thing to say.

According to his wife, Viktor Algård had planned to

stay in town after the party at the conference centre, which seemed perfectly natural. No one had questioned his decision. That was what he usually did whenever he had to work late.

What puzzled Knutas was the fact that Algård and his mistress never seemed to have phoned each other or corresponded by email.

The police had talked to the other tenants in the building. No one had ever seen Viktor enter or leave his flat with a woman. Either the relationship was very new, or the couple must have met somewhere else. Which meant that the investigative team would have to contact all the hotels and bed-and-breakfast establishments that were open during the wintertime. Knutas wrote himself a reminder to do this.

He went back to studying the note, turning it first one way and then the other. Why hadn't the woman come forward? He felt restless with frustration. The techs had lifted fingerprints from the flat, but found only three different sets. One belonged to Algård, the second to the building custodian who had recently repaired the window. The third set of fingerprints most likely belonged to the unknown woman.

How had they managed to keep their relationship so secret? On Gotland Knutas could hardly step outside his front door without running into someone he knew.

Maybe she lived on the mainland. Viktor Algård was a very fit fifty-three-year-old who was extremely fastidious about his appearance. Men in that time of their life – and Knutas was actually the same age – often sought out younger women. Maybe because they were afraid of growing old, or simply because they were feeling randy. A man like Viktor would certainly have had no problem attracting women. He had money and status, and plenty of women would have enjoyed basking in the spotlight that focused on him.

Knutas puffed on his pipe. They had met somewhere. The question was: Where? And how did they keep in touch?

Then, seemingly out of nowhere, an idea popped into his head. Could it be that simple?

Suddenly he was in a big hurry.

Algård's pied-à-terre was located on Hästgatan in the centre of downtown Visby, in a whitewashed two-storey building that housed four flats. The building was surrounded by a high wooden fence that prevented passersby from looking in. To Knutas's surprise the gate in the fence was unlocked, so he was able to simply step inside. The courtyard was exceptionally beautiful with resplendent flowerbeds, lilac bushes and a bubbling fountain in the middle. On the other side of the courtyard was an artist's studio. Knutas walked across to the studio but found it closed and shuttered. On the door hung a hand-painted sign showing a flock of sheep grazing in a pasture. Also on the sign was a name painted in ornate letters. It said 'Veronika Hammar'.

Knutas read the name several times as his heart began pounding faster. He took a few steps back to look at the studio's façade. Veronika Hammar was a well-known artist on Gotland. Her speciality was painting sheep in every possible and improbable guise and setting. Her paintings were not highly regarded by the local citizens, but they were certainly popular among tourists.

He had seen her in photographs from the dedication of the conference centre. Veronika Hammar had been one of the guests. And her studio shared the courtyard with Viktor Algård's pied-à-terre. Could that be the explanation for the absence of emails and phone calls? Because they were unnecessary, given the close proximity of Viktor and Veronika? Wouldn't the neighbours have noticed? Maybe not if they were sufficiently discreet. Knutas pictured Veronika Hammar's face. An attractive woman, about fifty, he would guess.

Knutas turned on his heel and quickly made his way back to the police station.

Veronika Hammar looked nervous as she sat on the very edge of the chair in the small interview room. As if she might take off at any moment. Calm down, thought Knutas. Just stay calm. This is going to take a while.

It was almost midnight, but the fatigue he had felt earlier was completely gone. Jacobsson took the lead in the interview.

Knutas studied Algård's lover sitting on the other side of the table. She looked younger than her fifty-six years, but he suspected that she'd had some work done to hide her age. The smooth, taut skin on her face hinted at Botox treatments. Her breasts seemed unnaturally full and positioned too high for a woman her age.

She was a striking woman, her blond hair pinned up under a colourful scarf wrapped around her head. She was petite and slender, clad in dark trousers and a dove-grey polo-neck sweater. Her lips were painted bright red, and the mascara and eyeliner had been applied with a heavy hand.

As Jacobsson made the usual introductory statements

for the tape recording of the interview, she leaned back in her chair and gave Veronika Hammar a friendly look. She wanted the older woman to relax. Her voice was gentle when she asked the first questions.

'Do you understand why you're here?'

'Yes,' Veronika replied. 'I suppose it's because Viktor is dead.'

'What was your relationship with him?'

'What do you mean?'

'How did you know him?'

Veronika's gaze shifted.

'Viktor and I got to know each other a couple of months ago.'

'Surely you must have met before then. You're a well-known artist, after all, and he was Gotland's most important event planner. You were also about the same age, weren't you?'

'Well, yes. And of course we'd met before. We knew of each other's existence, but that was about all. I've been invited to a lot of events, but . . .'

'But what?'

'It was only recently that we really got to know each other. I mean, we started spending time together.'

'As a couple?'

Veronika Hammar looked down.

'We were in love. Actually, it was more than that. We were thinking of getting married. He had even proposed.'

'But Viktor was already married.'

'He and his wife had split up. They'd already filed for divorce and everything.'

'Why didn't you get in contact with the police?'

Veronika nervously ran her fingers over the tabletop.

'I'm not feeling very well,' she murmured. 'Could I have a cigarette?'

Jacobsson got out her pack and handed it across the table. Then she leaned forward and lit the cigarette for Veronika. Smoking was not permitted inside the police station, but the interview room was exempt from the rule.

'The thing is, I was at the party and late in the evening Viktor finally decided to take a break. He asked me to come with him.'

'What time was that?'

'A few minutes after midnight, I think. The show had just started.'

'Where did the two of you go?'

'Viktor told me to meet him downstairs. There was supposed to be a lounge area where we wouldn't be disturbed. It was closed off for the evening.'

'And?'

'Well, I agreed to go with him, but I needed to use the loo, so he went first. Then I ended up being delayed because I met some friends. When I went downstairs, the room was empty. He wasn't there.'

'Are you sure?'

'Yes. It was dark and there wasn't a sound. But I didn't go inside or look around. I called his name, but he didn't answer, so I thought he must have grown tired of waiting for me. I was very disappointed, as a matter of fact.'

'Then what did you do?'

'I went back to the party.'

'Which route did you take?'

'Up the main staircase, like everybody else.'

'And you just glanced inside the room?'

'Yes.'

'Where were you standing? You didn't go in?'

'No. I stood in the doorway. I could see at once that the room was empty.'

'Do you remember noticing anything at all inside?'

'One of the bar stools was lying on the floor, but I didn't give it much thought.'

Jacobsson cast a quick glance at Knutas. If what Veronika Hammar had just said was true, they had now established an almost exact time for the murder.

'What did you do next?'

'Just what I told you. I went back to the party. I looked around for Viktor, but I didn't see him. Then someone asked me to dance, and the rest of the night just flew by.'

'And you didn't see him again?'

'No. We were supposed to go home together, but I couldn't find him anywhere. I didn't want to ask too many people, since we were trying to be discreet until his divorce went through.'

'And then you went home?'

'Yes.'

'What time did you leave the party?'

'When they closed up the conference centre.'

'What did you do during the last hour or so of the party?'

'I sat on the veranda, talking to a doctor.'

'Who was that?'

'His name is Gunnar Larsson.'

'Where can we get hold of him?'

'At the hospital. I don't know where he lives, but he works there as an anaesthetist. We sat outside on the veranda and talked for a long time.'

'Did you leave the conference centre together?'

'Yes, but then I decided to wait for Viktor outside the front entrance. I still thought he would turn up. I waited maybe half an hour, but he never came.'

Her voice quavered and tears came to her eyes.

'So you went home alone?'

'Yes.'

'What time was that?'

'Probably close to three.'

Jacobsson gave her a searching glance.

'Is there anyone who could confirm what you've just told us?'

'Yes. There were a lot of people still there, standing

outside the conference centre and talking. I'm sure that some of the staff would have seen me. Why?'

'Right now I'm the one asking the questions,' said Jacobsson sternly. Her former friendliness was gone, and she paid no attention to the fact that Veronika Hammar looked as if she might start crying in earnest at any moment. 'By Sunday evening the media was already reporting that a man had been found dead in the conference centre, and had probably been murdered. You must have suspected that the man could be Viktor. The two of you were on intimate terms, so you're up to your ears in this case whether you like it or not. Why on earth didn't you contact the police?'

Veronika stared at Jacobsson in alarm.

'I didn't want to get involved.'

'Involved? Did you seriously think that we wouldn't find you? That no one had noticed anything? That you'd never been seen together?'

'Well no, but . . .'

'This is a murder case we're talking about. Don't you understand the gravity of the situation?'

Veronika bit her lip. Her hands shook as she put out her cigarette and then immediately lit a second one.

'I . . . I don't know. I had no idea what to do. I'm shocked and sad and upset. We were going to get married, you know. Victor and . . .'

'What were you thinking?'

'I was panic-stricken. I couldn't think clearly. I wanted to pretend that nothing had happened. I sat at home, hoping that he would come in the door.'

'Do you have any idea who might have done this? Who might have killed him?'

'I can only think that it might have been his wife. She doesn't seem right in the head.'

'What are you basing that on?'

Veronika took a deep drag on her cigarette before answering.

'She was furious when Viktor told her that he wanted a divorce. She went berserk and starting throwing things around the house. She even hit him. She was rabid, and refused to accept the situation. She did everything she could to stop him from leaving her. She even booked a holiday in Italy for the whole family this summer after he said he wanted a divorce. She tried to force him to stay, the poor man. She acted like a crazy woman, without an ounce of shame.'

Abruptly she fell silent and looked down at her hands. Then she asked faintly: 'How did he die?'

The question echoed in the small, cold room.

'He was poisoned.'

'But how . . . ?'

'That's all we can tell you right now. I'm sorry.'

*

Jacobsson glanced at her watch and saw that it was very late. She leaned towards the tape recorder on the table.

'The time is one fourteen a.m. That concludes the interview with Veronika Hammar.'

It was Tuesday morning, and the first thing Knutas thought of when he woke was that he hadn't managed to talk to Nils the previous night. He turned on to his side and looked at Lina's freckled back. Cautiously he ran his fingertips over her smooth skin. He didn't want to wake her. She had worked the night shift at the hospital and had probably fallen asleep only a short while ago. As usual, she was sprawled across the bed so that there was hardly any room for him. When he moved her over so that he could get up, she grunted and then put her arms around him.

'Hugs,' she whispered.

'Sorry. Did I wake you?'

'Not at all. I'm sound asleep.'

She burrowed her head against his chest. Her hair spilled out across the covers.

'How was Nils feeling last night?' he asked.

'Good. Fine. His stomach ache was gone. We had lasagne for dinner before I left for work. It's Nils's favourite, as you know. We had a nice time together.'

Lina had a much better relationship with their son.

Towards her Nils was as sweet as could be, and he almost never snapped at her. Knutas felt a pang of jealousy.

'I was planning to have a talk with him last night, but then I got home too late.'

'Do it tonight instead. I have the night shift again and start work at nine. Maybe it would be better if I'm not home. Then the two of you can talk in peace.'

Knutas looked in on the children before he went downstairs to the kitchen. It was only six o'clock. Too early to wake them. Petra was tangled up in the duvet with only her hair showing. Her room was crowded with so many things, but it still had a certain sense of order. Her desk and the shelves above were cluttered with hairspray, perfume, various containers and bottles in garish colours. There were dozens of little notebooks, stacks of notepads and scraps of paper covered with handwriting. He wondered what it said. Heaps of clothes, belts, various small purses and shoes were scattered about. The walls were covered with pictures of different pop stars, but he didn't know the names of any of them.

What did he really know about his daughter and the thoughts that whirled about in her head? How many genuine conversations had they had lately? When did they ever talk to each other, and what did they say? Feeling dejected, he realized that they mostly discussed practical matters: what they should cook for dinner, whether she had to go to practice or not on a specific evening, and how things had gone at school.

And then there was Nils. He was lying in bed with his back turned to the door, and he'd forgotten to turn off his desk lamp. Nils had inherited his mother's thick red hair. The room seemed naked, stripped bare. Nothing on the walls, a few schoolbooks on the desk, otherwise just the computer, which he spent far too much time staring at, in his father's opinion. Nils was sleeping calmly.

How well do I really know my own children? thought Knutas. He felt an uneasy churning in his stomach, out of fear that they were slipping away from him. If he didn't do something about it soon, it might be too late. We should take a trip somewhere, he thought. Just me and the kids. Lina often spent time alone with them at their summer house out in the country when he had to work at the weekend. Why shouldn't he spend time with them too?

Quietly he closed the door to Nils's room. He needed to think of something: maybe a week's holiday on the Canary Islands or a long weekend in a big city. London, Paris, New York? The kids could choose where they wanted to go, within reason, of course.

Maybe sharing some experiences with them away from home would help.

I wander through room after room and pull down the blinds on all the windows. It takes a while. The flat may be a free zone for me just now, but I'm actually trapped in here, like a prisoner in a cell with too much space. Taking the lift four floors down seems, as usual, practically insurmountable, even though I need to buy groceries. I have no desire to go out in the street, among all those people who are always racing along in every direction yet going nowhere. I'm no longer part of any of that. I feel as if I'm looking down on a gigantic anthill. People and cars rush aimlessly through their daily lives, like hamsters in a wheel. To what purpose?

In the bathroom I take my medicine, though with some hesitation. I shake out two capsules and a little round tablet. Then wash them down with several gulps of water, shuddering. I've always had trouble swallowing. I avoid looking at myself in the mirror, fully aware of what an unpleasant sight it would be. My stomach is empty, but I'm not hungry even though I've hardly eaten a thing in days.

I go back to the sofa and curl up in a foetal position

with my back to the room. My eyes are dry and open wide, staring without seeing at the white upholstery of the sofa cushion. I know that I won't be able to sleep. I just lie there, mute and motionless. Like part of the furnishings. That's precisely what I am.

Again I start thinking back.

To one of those Sundays. We were going to visit Aunt Margareta and Uncle Ulf, who lived inside the ring wall, very close to the church. Their eldest son, Marcel, was the same age as me. We went to the same high school but pretended not to know each other. I always looked away whenever I saw him in the corridor. I suspected Marcel of making jokes about the fact that we were cousins.

He was named Marcel because his mother loved the Italian actor Marcello Mastroianni. We might have been friends, if only circumstances had been different. If it weren't for the fact that I was regarded as a wimp. And the fact that we were always being compared to each other. By our mothers.

Marcel was already six foot one, with hair under his arms and a moustache. He had dark hair and doe eyes. He was well built, with attractively muscular arms, which he was happy to show off, evoking delighted giggles from both his mother and aunt.

The living room smelled like a shoe shop, maybe because of the white leather sofa in the corner. A pair of porcelain dogs six feet tall guarded the front door. The obligatory coffee was served at the obligatory time – always two o'clock. The leather sofa creaked as I sank on to it. The biscuit crunched between my teeth, the juice I was offered was a tad too strong. Aunt Margareta and Mamma chatted about one thing or another – the weather and other meaningless small talk. Paying no attention to any of us children, as usual, as if we didn't exist. We were their audience. Uncle Ulf mostly sat in silence, slurping his coffee and casting resigned glances at the two gabbing women. Marcel stuffed his mouth with the biscuits piled on his plate and then left to visit a friend. As soon as he disappeared through the door, the boasting began.

'Marcel is so popular, you know. He's always surrounded by friends. We hardly even see him these days,' Aunt Margareta clucked, looking immeasurably pleased. 'The girls just keep phoning and phoning him, one after the other. He went steady with a girl for almost two months. Helena, so nice and sweet, a real gem, but he broke up with her, and I can't tell you how much time I've spent on the phone talking to that girl. She's completely devastated, the poor thing. But now he's met someone else. Isabelle. And to top it all, she's two years older than him. That worries me a bit. She's not content just to hug and kiss, if you know what I mean. I've talked to him about contraception, of course, but it still makes me nervous. We don't want him to get anyone pregnant. That would be terrible. And he's out every weekend, every Friday and Saturday. Going to parties and dances and God only knows what else. But as long as he tends to his schoolwork, we let him be. He's so smart, gets top marks in almost everything. He talks about wanting to be a doctor. Can you imagine that? But I'm sure he'd be good at the job, he's so warm and open and outgoing. I think he really should work in a profession dealing with people. Although I don't know how he does it, what with ice hockey taking up so much of his time. They practise three times a week, and then there are matches at the weekend. By the way, did you know that he was chosen as the best player of the year by his hockey team? Yes, he's really incredible. I have no idea who he gets it from. Ha, ha, ha. Ulf has never been interested in sports, have you, dear?'

She stopped talking only to take a sip of coffee. Mamma smiled appreciatively and nodded encouragement as she stirred her coffee and murmured an occasional admiring remark. Aunt Margareta chattered on and on, talking only about Marcel, as if he were God's gift to humanity.

The biscuit seemed to swell inside my mouth. With every word I felt smaller and smaller. Suddenly my aunt turned to look at me, as if she'd just discovered that I was in the room.

'And what about you? Do you have a girlfriend?'

The question was so unexpected that it took a moment for me to respond, shaking my head.

*

I wanted to sink into the green carpet. Allow myself to be swallowed up.

In the car on the way home, Mamma kept on raving about how great Marcel was.

'And just think – Margareta told me that he has already started shaving,' she exclaimed. 'He even has to do it every day!'

I didn't say a word.

My siblings didn't either.

The rain was pouring down, so Knutas drove his beat-up old Merc to work. He still couldn't get himself to part with the car, despite pressure from Lina to sell it. He let her take the new car, since he assumed she wouldn't want to walk either, if the bad weather continued. He remembered her saying that they'd had lasagne for dinner the night before. Was that really part of a low-glycaemic diet? He smiled to himself. It was always the same thing with Lina. She would start out so enthusiastic and with lots of big plans whenever she decided to lose some weight. She would collect a whole bunch of information, buy exercise equipment and fill the refrigerator with the proper food. The diet usually lasted no more than two weeks.

When Knutas entered the conference room for the meeting of the investigative team, he was eager to get going.

'Good morning, everyone,' he began.

He raised his hand to quiet the usual morning buzz of conversation. Sometimes he felt like a schoolteacher in a classroom. Right now he wanted to tell his colleagues about what he'd discovered the previous evening. He briefly described how he happened to find Veronika Hammar's studio at the same address as Viktor Algård's flat.

'But isn't she at least sixty?' Wittberg interjected. 'I thought he'd go for a young hottie.'

'Not every man shares your preferences,' Jacobsson teased him.

Thomas Wittberg's numerous love affairs were legendary among his colleagues. They often involved twenty-year-olds who were infatuated with Wittberg because of his status as a police detective and his wind-surfer good looks. Jacobsson regarded his style as hopelessly out of date and usually made some remark about him being stuck in the eighties. But that sort of criticism rolled right off Wittberg's back. He continued to show off his biceps in tight T-shirts, regularly went to the tanning salon close to his home, and stubbornly refused to cut his long blond hair.

'She's actually fifty-six,' said Knutas. 'Viktor was fifty-three. So there was only a three-year age difference. We got hold of her last night and during the interview she confirmed that she'd had a relationship with Algård. She told us that she was at the party at the conference centre, but she couldn't find Viktor when she was about to leave, so she went home alone. At one point during the evening, they had intended to withdraw to the room downstairs where the victim's body was eventually found. Viktor went on ahead, while Veronika made a detour to the ladies' room. She ended up being delayed because she ran into some friends. When she finally went downstairs, Viktor wasn't there. She assumed that he'd grown tired of waiting for her.'

'What time was that?'

'Just after midnight, sometime between twelve and twelve thirty.'

'So she went down to the closed-off lounge area, with the bar and the sofas?' asked Wittberg.

Knutas nodded.

'Did she see anything?'

'No. Apparently she didn't actually enter the room because the lights were off. On the other hand, she did notice that a bar stool had toppled over on to the floor.'

Prosecutor Smittenberg looked puzzled as he pensively tugged at his earlobe.

'That means the murder must have been committed while Veronika was in the loo.'

'Provided that she didn't do the killing herself,' Jacobsson countered sagely.

'It does seem strange that she made no attempt to contact us. It's frankly incomprehensible,' said Wittberg. 'What was her explanation?'

'She said that she was overcome with panic.'

'That's not really credible. What was she afraid of? But

I assume that's not enough to arrest her, is it, Birger?' Wittberg turned to the prosecutor.

'No, it's not. She was shocked and upset. They were conducting a secret love affair, and she didn't want to get involved. We also need to consider that she's actually quite a well-known artist. Maybe not famous, but certainly well known,' he added dryly. 'That made the situation more sensitive, of course. The circumstances aren't sufficiently compelling to warrant an arrest.'

'Does she live on Hästgatan or is that just where she has her studio?' asked Wittberg.

'She lives on Tranhusgatan, over near the Botanical Gardens,' said Knutas.

'So who is she, actually? And what sort of life does she lead? The only thing I know about her is that she paints lousy pictures,' said Wittberg.

Knutas looked down at his notes.

'She was divorced years ago and now lives alone. She has four grown children. Her eldest son, Mats, lives in Stockholm. He didn't spend much time with her while he was growing up. He was born when Veronika was very young, so he was raised by a foster family. Then she had Andreas, who's a sheep farmer out in Hablingbo. A daughter, Mikaela, has moved out to the island of Vätö in the Stockholm archipelago. She and her husband own a riding school. The youngest son, Simon, lives on Bogegatan here in Visby.'

He was interrupted by Sohlman coming into the room. The crime tech looked tense.

'Sorry to be late, but we found a match on the fingerprints. Veronika Hammar's prints are on the handle to the terrace door near where the body was found. Meaning the door that the perp presumably used to escape.'

Utter silence descended over the room.

The hunt for Veronika Hammar began as soon as the meeting was over. The police quickly discovered that she wasn't in her house on Tranhusgatan or in her studio on Hästgatan. She had no other known residence, so they went looking for her at the homes of her children. The only one they managed to contact was the sheep farmer named Andreas in Hablingbo. He claimed to have no idea where his mother might be, but he promised to phone if he heard from her. According to the employer of her eldest son, Mats was on holiday on Mallorca. The daughter who lived on the island near Stockholm was travelling with the Red Cross in South America, and it was impossible to reach her. Her husband also told the police that Mikaela had broken off all contact with her mother ten years ago. When Jacobsson asked why, he said that she would have to ask his wife about that. The youngest son turned out not to be at home either, but no one knew where he was.

In the meantime, the investigative team worked on finding out who else belonged to Veronika Hammar's immediate circle of family and friends – a task which was quickly accomplished. She had two sisters, but both of her parents were deceased. And she seemed to have only a small number of friends.

At lunchtime the ME's preliminary post-mortem report arrived by fax. It confirmed that Viktor Algård had died as a result of cyanide poisoning. He had apparently caused the gash on his forehead himself. According to the ME, the wound occurred when Algård fell against one of the cocktail tables near the bar. The tabletop was made of marble, and Viktor's blood was found on the surface, as well as on the floor underneath. In her report the ME wrote that cyanide poisoning typically provoked convulsions, and that the victim, by all indications, had staggered around for several minutes before he ran into that table and then died. The time of death had to be between midnight and six in the morning.

Knutas leaned back in his worn old chair, gently rocking back and forth. The report largely confirmed what they already knew. The murderer had most likely exited through the terrace door, which faced the narrow side street. It was all so simple. And their suspicions about Veronika Hammar had been reinforced when her prints were found on the door handle.

In the conference centre just one floor above, Knutas himself had merrily partied away with all the other guests while the murder was being committed. That was a fact he was having a hard time digesting. There were no witnesses. No one had seen anyone leaving the building at the time in question, which would have been between twelve fifteen and twelve thirty. There were no residences in the area surrounding the conference centre.

Knutas felt overcome with restlessness. It seemed very likely that Veronika was the murderer. Maybe Algård had grown tired of their affair and wanted to go back to his wife. Jealousy was quite a common motive for murder.

They needed to find out more. Above all, they had to locate Veronika Hammar.

The shoreline near Holmhällar at the southernmost point on Gotland was covered with limestone. The kilometre-long *rauk* area had a very distinctive look to it. The stone formations were massive and strangely shaped, with the tallest nearly 5 metres high. Here the *rauks* were not isolated stone pillars; instead they stood in clusters. They clung to each other as if seeking shelter from the wind, the fossil-seekers and the ever-encroaching hordes of tourists. A short distance out to sea the little island of Heligholmen was visible – a nature reserve that was now off-limits to visitors. Out there the seabirds bred by the thousands.

Close to the water, at the very edge of the shore, stood the fishing village, a group of boathouses made of stone with slate roofs. They were several hundred years old, remnants of the era when the island's farmers were forced to supplement their livelihood by fishing. Back then they would arrive from their inland farms to fish for several days, staying in the cramped boathouses, which had only small slots for windows facing the sea. The quarters stank of tar and kelp.

She walked along the rocky shore, taking care not to stumble on roots or loose stones. The sea was grey, and a strong wind was blowing. Above the *rauk* area stretched an expansive plateau with a meadow of billowing grasses filled with the bright yellow flowers of pheasant's eye, which looked like little suns, and dark violet pasque flowers. A few juniper bushes and gnarled trees stunted by the harsh storms continued to defy the wind, stubbornly holding on to the stony ground. The landscape was barren and desolate at this time of year, with not a soul in sight. The gusts brought tears to her eyes. She turned her face away from the sea and looked up towards the plateau and the woods beyond.

When she reached the other side of the *rauk* area, she saw the sandy beach spreading out before her. This was where she usually spent the summers. Now the water was icy cold after the long winter. It looked dark and inhospitable, with the waves restlessly rolling in and then retreating. She turned round and headed up towards the summer houses at the edge of the woods. There were about ten cottages scattered over quite a large tract and set at a discreet distance from one another. The bed and breakfast, which stood a bit further away, was closed for the season, and the other buildings were all empty as well.

Suddenly she jumped, startled by a rustling sound in the grass right behind her. For a moment ice-cold fear raced through her veins, until she realized that it was just a rabbit darting past. She watched it run off until it disappeared into a burrow in the ground. Her nerves were wound tight. The air was hazy and damp, and dusk had begun to close in around her. A flock of swans, flying in formation, streaked past in the dark sky. Echoing shrieks issued from their long necks. She found the sound sinister. Like death cries.

She didn't notice the man standing up on the plateau right above her, watching every move she made.

The man lowered his binoculars and started walking towards her summer house.

The members of the investigative team were giving top priority to finding Veronika Hammar, but that didn't mean that they had dropped all other avenues that might still be of interest. Knutas didn't want to focus on her as the only possible suspect. Even though it seemed unlikely, there might be an explanation for why she was at the crime scene but hadn't alerted the authorities. After nearly thirty years on the police force, he had learned that people were capable of behaving in the strangest, most irrational ways. Anything was possible.

For that reason, the police were working on other potential leads. One of them was Viktor Algård's former competitor Sten Bergström. Because he suffered from painful lumbago, he was unable to come to the police station, so Knutas and Jacobsson had decided to visit him at his home on Tuesday afternoon.

For the second day in a row they drove south towards Sudret and Holmhällar. Granted, several years had passed since Algård's biggest competitor had gone bankrupt, but old grudges might have resurfaced.

Bergström lived alone on a farm out in the country, close to the Holmhällar *rauk* area. After they passed Hamra, the houses became sparser as the landscape grew more rugged. The distance between farms increased. Most of the homes were used only during the summer holidays, so the area seemed even more desolate in the off-season. They'd been instructed to turn right at the exit for Holmhällar and head for Austre. The rain had stopped, but heavy clouds filled the sky, and it looked as if the downpour might start up again at any moment.

'Nothing but shuttered summer houses,' Jacobsson sighed wearily as they passed one empty cottage after another. They didn't see a living soul.

'I'm starting to wonder if we're going the right way,' muttered Knutas.

Jacobsson peered at the map.

'This is the only turn-off. We have to take another right when we come to a row of letter boxes, right across from the road leading down to the shore. There's supposed to be a sign.'

She had barely uttered these words before they reached their destination. Sten Bergström had sounded surprised when Jacobsson phoned him on the previous day, but he was cooperative and willing to meet with them. He lived in a two-storey, whitewashed wooden house that had definitely seen better days. There were also several ramshackle outbuildings on the property, along with a garage that had no door and seemed to hold nothing but junk, including a rusty old car. On the bonnet sat a black cat, watching them.

They rang the bell, but it didn't seem to be in working order. Knutas pounded his fist on the door. Nothing happened. They stood there, waiting. Knutas knocked again, while Jacobsson walked around the side of the house. Clearly no one was at home. Suddenly they heard a dog barking from the road. They turned to see a tall, lanky man walking towards them, his shoulders stooped and his back bowed. He seemed to be in pain. He wore a windbreaker, a cap and rubber boots. Trotting along beside him was a stately Afghan with beautiful golden hair. The man raised his hand in greeting.

'I'm sorry. I didn't know you'd get here so soon. Have you been waiting long?'

He shook their hands. The dog kept a wary eye on the officers, showing no sign of wanting to make friends.

'It's no problem,' said Knutas. 'We just arrived.'

Sten Bergström led the way into the house, ushering them into a living room with a huge bay window facing the garden. The wood floor was worn and bare of any rugs. The window had no curtains. The furniture was sparse but solidly built, the type that might have been bought at one of the countless farm auctions held at intervals on the island. Bergström offered his visitors coffee and homemade sponge cake. Knutas and Jacobsson sat down on the kitchen bench, but Bergström remained standing. He explained apologetically that his bad back prevented him from sitting.

Knutas was having a hard time forming a coherent impression of Sten Bergström. On the one hand, the man seemed to live a rather shabby and simple existence; on the other hand, he personally emanated style and elegance. His striped shirt and light cotton trousers were clean and freshly pressed, and his home was neat and tidy. His dog could have been photographed for the cover of *Castles and Manor Houses*, with a duke or baron holding the Afghan's lead.

'We're here with regard to the murder of Viktor Algård,' Knutas began after the coffee was served and a slice of sponge cake was sitting on the plate before him. 'It may seem strange that we're interested in talking to you, but we're looking into the victim's past and checking everything that might give us a lead in the investigation. Even though it might seem like a long shot.'

'I see.' Bergström smiled as he leaned against the door frame. 'I understand.'

'When did you last have contact with Viktor?' asked Knutas.

'That was years ago.'

'What sort of relationship did the two of you have?'

'It's no secret that we were bitter enemies. He ruined me and forced me into bankruptcy.'

'How did that happen?'

'I began arranging parties on a small scale about five or six years ago. They were very successful, so I started my own company. The first conflict we had was over the name. I called my firm "Goal Gotland", since I was planning not only to arrange events for local clients, but also to entice customers from the mainland to hold their weddings here, as well as birthday parties and so on. There are an awful lot of mainlanders who spend the summer here. Viktor thought the name was too close to his own company name, so he decided to sue me. But that was one battle he lost. There was nothing he could do about the name. At any rate, I continued doing event planning and gradually took over a significant number of his clients.'

'How did you do that?'

'I don't think they were dissatisfied with his efforts, and there was certainly no reason for complaints. He was highly professional. However, there were periods when he was booked up, which meant there was room for other event planners. I filled that gap. Plus my prices were lower, so more and more people chose my company instead, and then they became steady clients, returning whenever they needed my services. It's rather like when people change hairdressers. If their own hairdresser doesn't have time, they try somebody new. If they're happy with the results, they don't see any reason to go back to their former hairdresser. People are remarkably disloyal when it comes right down to it,' said Bergström pensively as he stirred sugar into his coffee. He never took his eyes off the officers, merely shifting his attention back and forth between Jacobsson and Knutas, with an interested expression on his face.

'What sort of contact did you and Viktor have with each other?'

'Nothing personal. Only by phone and letter. He accused me of stealing his clients. He ranted and carried on over the phone, and I'm sorry to say this, but he was extremely rude. I did my best to explain that the people in question had come to me on their own initiative. If certain clients preferred my services, there wasn't much I could do about it. But Viktor refused to listen. He was truly unreasonable, as a matter of fact. I must say that I thought his behaviour was uncalled for. He still had more clients than he could realistically handle.'

Jacobsson had to hide a smile. Sten Bergström seemed so out of place in this tumbledown house in the middle of nowhere. He had a bombastic way of speaking and carried himself almost like a nobleman. His surname ought to be something more aristocratic, such as Knorring or Silfversparre, she thought.

'So what did you do?'

'Nothing. I just let him scream and shout and contact various authorities while I tended to my business. And he couldn't touch me, which no doubt made the poor man even more frustrated.'

'Why did your company go bankrupt?'

Sten Bergström's face took on a distressed expression. 'Unfortunately a few parties got out of hand. There was a lot of trouble with drunken guests and brawls. It tarnished my reputation, and people began talking behind my back. My clients fled and my revenue dropped dramatically. Finally it all went to hell. It wouldn't surprise me to find out that Viktor was behind what happened. But I didn't have the energy to pursue that theory. And besides, I'd lost any desire to go on since I no longer had the confidence and trust of my clients.'

Bergström suddenly looked as if he were in terrible pain.

'I'm sorry, but I'm afraid I'm going to have to lie down,' he said with a moan. 'I can't stay on my feet any longer. Is there anything else you'd like to know at the moment?'

He pressed his hand to his lower back and then, with an effort, got down on his knees. The dog began whimpering.

'Would one of you be kind enough to bring over a chair?'

Jacobsson watched in astonishment as the elegant man lay down on his back on the floor and held up his legs. Knutas helped him to prop his feet on the chair so his legs were at a 90-degree angle to his body. Knutas knew exactly what was going on. Lina had suffered from intermittent back pain for years.

The dog eagerly licked his master's face, clearly happy to have him down at his own level on the floor. Bergström didn't share his enthusiasm. He ordered the dog away and the Afghan immediately retreated to his basket, curling up with a sigh of resignation.

'Thank you so much for your time,' said Knutas. 'We'll get back to you if there's anything more.'

'You're welcome,' said Bergström faintly. He closed his eyes. 'Goodbye.'

As they left, closing the door behind them, the dog stared after them.

All of Tuesday passed with no progress in locating Veronika Hammar. By the time it was six thirty and Knutas realized that he'd been on the job for twelve hours straight, he gave up.

There was nothing more he could do, and besides, he'd promised to take care of dinner. Lina was again working the night shift at the hospital and wouldn't be back until the early morning hours. He stopped on his way home to buy pizzas. The children had each requested a pizza topped with fillet of pork and Béarnaise sauce. He shuddered when he ordered the food. How could anyone come up with such a combination? Pretty soon they'll be serving pizzas with shrimp and sweet-and-sour sauce, he thought. Or a Thai pizza with chicken and red curry. And why not a dessert pizza with saffron in the dough, topped with almonds and raisins?

As soon as he stepped inside, he could tell that something was wrong. The house was dark, with not a single light turned on.

'Hello,' he called from the hall. No answer. He set down the pizza boxes and went upstairs.

'Hello,' he called again. 'Anybody home?'

He opened the door to Petra's room. The only light came from a pair of thick scented candles on a tray on the nightstand. Several sticks of incense in a porcelain jar were spreading a heavy musk fragrance through the air. On the computer screen he saw flickering images of scantily clad teenagers against the Manhattan skyline, while incomprehensible hip hop music thudded through the room. His daughter was lying on the bed with her legs stretched up against the wall, her eyes on the ceiling as she talked on her mobile.

'Shhh,' she hushed her father, gesturing with annoyance for him to leave the room.

'It's time for dinner and—'

'Shhh!'

Knutas closed the door. Feeling discouraged, he tried the next room. It was pitch black inside, but he could hear the crashing of hard rock music from his son's iPod.

'Hi,' he said, switching on the ceiling light. 'What are you doing?'

Nils quickly turned to face the wall, but not before Knutas saw that his eyes were red. It looked as if he'd been crying.

'What's wrong?' He took a few steps towards the bed.

'Nothing.'

'But I can see that you're upset about something.' Cautiously he sat down on the edge of the bed. Nils had his back turned and pulled away until he was even closer to the wall. 'What's wrong?'

'Nothing, I said. Leave me alone. Get out of my room.'

'But, Nils.' Knutas gently touched his son's head. 'Won't you tell me what's going on?'

'Cut it out.' He pushed his father's hand away. 'Just leave me alone,' he snarled, his voice cracking.

'But I bought pizza for dinner.'

'I'll be down in a minute,' said the boy, his tone now much less aggressive.

Feeling powerless, Knutas left the room. Pushed away again. Locked out. There was nothing he could do about it. He couldn't very well force Nils to open up to him if the boy didn't want to. That sort of thing had to be based on trust.

Disappointed, Knutas went down to the kitchen and began setting the table. He was so respected and decisive at work, but his teenage children regarded him as a pitiful old man. He really had no clue how to deal with them. At the same time, he felt hurt and sad. Don't they like me? he thought.

He heard the stairs creaking. Petra came into the kitchen. As if she sensed how he was feeling, she gave him a brief hug.

'Sorry, Pappa. But I was on the phone, and it was a really sensitive conversation.'

'Anything you want to tell me about?' he asked cautiously, encouraged by the meagre gesture of affection that she'd shown him.

'Alexander died.'

'What did you say?' Knutas felt an icy stab in the pit of his stomach. He stared at his daughter, uncomprehending.

Slowly it sank in that what she had said was true. All hope was gone. Then his brain began whirling like a centrifuge filled with questions. He immediately thought about Alexander's mother, Ingrid, and his sister, Olivia.

'I was talking to Olivia on the phone,' said Petra, her eyes brimming with tears. 'They just found out. She's completely devastated. I promised to go over to see her after dinner.'

'I didn't know you were such good friends.'

'We are now. After what happened over the past few weeks.'

Again it occurred to Knutas how little he knew about his children these days.

Nils came into the kitchen to join them.

'Do you know what's happened?' Knutas asked. 'Do you know that Alexander is dead?'

Nils and his sister exchanged glances.

'Yes,' said Nils without looking at his father.

They ate dinner in silence. Knutas didn't know what to say, other than to reiterate how awful it was, and that he felt terrible for Alexander's mother and sister.

The case had largely been solved, with three sixteen-year-old boys under arrest, charged with aggravated assault. Now the charge would have to be changed. All three of the boys denied involvement, but the evidence was against them. Alexander's blood was found on their clothes and shoes, and a couple of witnesses among the crowd of kids that had been present at the time had dared to single them out.

It's not just the fact that assault cases are becoming more frequent and severe, and increasingly involve younger kids, thought Knutas. But people are also less willing to testify.

It was an alarming development.

After dinner both children left the table and went out to the hall to put on their shoes.

'Are you both going out?' Knutas asked as he filled the dishwasher.

'Yes,' they answered in unison.

'Where are you going?' he asked Nils.

'He's coming with me to see Olivia,' Petra said before her brother had time to answer.

'Why?'

'Oh, Pappa,' said Petra, giving him a look of pity as she shook her head.

The door closed after them.

Knutas took a deep breath, sat down at the kitchen table, and picked up his mobile to call Ingrid Almlöv.

The swimming hall was deserted when Knutas arrived the following morning. He was there at six thirty when the doors opened, and for the first fifteen minutes he enjoyed the luxury of having the whole pool to himself.

Nothing helped him to unwind as much as swimming. He powered his way through one length after another, his body moving mechanically as if steered by a robot. Clarity was restored to his brain in the calm water, in the silence whenever his head dipped below the surface. The news of Alexander's death had temporarily pushed aside the perplexities of the homicide investigation. He couldn't even begin to imagine what it must be like to lose a child. What if the same thing had happened to Nils or Petra? He hardly dared complete the thought. We need to take care of each other, he thought. While we're still here. Everything can change in an instant.

Knutas had talked with Ingrid, Alexander's mother, on the phone for a long time last night. Both of his own children had chosen to sleep over at the Almlöv home, mostly for Olivia's sake. He was touched that they cared so much and that they were capable of such empathy. At the same time, he was feeling guilty for having neglected Ingrid over the past few years. He hadn't been in touch with her except right after the events that had led to her husband's death. Then life had continued on. And now Alexander was also gone.

He came to the end of the pool and turned, realizing that he'd lost count of how many lengths he'd already swum. He glanced up at the clock and decided it didn't matter. Half an hour was enough. Two elderly women in bathing suits appeared at the edge of the pool and then climbed down the ladder, their legs dimpled and unsteady. They grumbled a bit and then with a titter sank down into the water, choosing the lane furthest away from Knutas, much to his relief.

His thoughts returned to Veronika Hammar. Was she still on the island? He cursed himself for not detaining her immediately after that first interview. From the very beginning her explanation for not coming forward had seemed like a feeble excuse.

They now had evidence that she had actually been at the crime scene, although she hadn't mentioned it during the interview. Veronika Hammar might well be guilty of murder. The important thing now was to find her.

Johan was sitting in the editorial office with a dull weight in the pit of his stomach. Over the past few days he'd been so focused on the murder at the conference centre that he'd put the assault case aside. Now that he'd received word of the boy's death, he felt ice cold inside, and his heart ached. The sixteen-year-old had lost his life because of a completely meaningless dispute. What a shitty deal. Something that had lasted only a few seconds had put a halt to his future and destroyed his family's life. The whole thing was the result of several kicks to the head. It was incomprehensible.

At that moment Johan decided to concentrate all his efforts on the series of reports that he and Pia had planned about the current state of youth violence in Sweden – its causes and consequences, as well as what was being done to stop it from getting even worse. Later in the day they were expected to deliver a news story about Alexander's death, along with a follow-up report on the Algård murder. At the moment talking about the boy's death seemed more urgent.

Johan was roused from his melancholy thoughts by

Pia's arrival. She didn't say anything, just gave him a sympathetic pat on the shoulder as she walked past and noticed what was on his computer screen.

They had coffee together and discussed the assault case.

Alexander had been in his first year at the Rickard Steffen secondary school in Visby. They decided to start there.

When Johan and Pia drove up to the school, they saw the flags fluttering at half-mast in the springtime sun. On the phone the principal had told Johan that the teachers would not be following the normal curriculum for the day. Instead, they would be talking about Alexander with their students. A memorial was planned for eleven o'clock in the school auditorium. They got there just in time. Every seat was already taken. It was clear that the students, teachers and other school staff members were not the only ones who had gathered. Parents and siblings were also present. Pia and Johan found room to stand at the very back of the hall. Traditionally the principal would have been the first to speak but, surprisingly enough, that was not what happened. When the lights went out in the auditorium, and a single spotlight shone on the stage, the audience saw a thin teenage girl standing there. She wore jeans and a black camisole under a pink hoodie. Her long dark hair fell loosely to her shoulders. Goosebumps appeared on Johan's arms at her first words.

'My brother is dead.'

In a low, carefully controlled voice, Olivia Almlöv then spoke about her brother Alexander and what he had meant to her. How they had grown up together and what sort of things they had done – ordinary, everyday events. About Alexander's interests and dreams for the future. How they had got ready for the party on that Friday evening, what they had talked of and what they had done when they arrived at the club. He sometimes liked to sneak a cigarette, she said, and the last she saw of him was when he went outside to have a smoke with a couple of his friends.

He never came back.

Half an hour later she saw her brother beaten beyond recognition and lying in a pool of blood on the ground.

That was how Alexander ended his days, and her own life would never be the same again.

Everyone in the auditorium was deeply touched by what she had said, and here and there people could be heard weeping.

Afterwards, the principal spoke about the importance of not allowing Alexander's life to have been taken in vain. About the necessity of regarding this as a wake-up call – for the young people, their parents and society as a whole.

Both Johan and Pia were deeply moved by what they'd heard.

'We need to talk to some of the parents,' said Johan.

'We haven't heard anything from them in a while.'

'Sure. How about that couple over there?'

Pia nodded towards a middle-aged man and woman leaving the auditorium hand in hand.

Johan cautiously tapped the man on the shoulder and then introduced himself.

'Why are you and your wife here?' was his first question.

It was the man who answered.

'Because our son was a witness to the assault, and we wanted to offer our support. To Alexander's family, but also to the boys who were responsible and to their families. They are victims too.'

'Why do you say that?'

'Well, who's the winner here? Nobody. Everyone loses. And what is the whole thing really about? A mere few seconds that have lifelong consequences for umpteen people. Anger sparked by an ill-tempered word, an obscene gesture, a nasty look. When I was young, these sorts of quarrels were resolved with a fist fight. In the worst-case scenario, it turned into a brawl that ended at the first sign of bloodshed or when your opponent fell to the ground. But what happens nowadays? The person on the ground gets kicked – in the head! Several boys gang up on an unconscious kid. Why aren't there any boundaries any more? Is a human life of no value to these kids? Do they think they have the right to kill someone just because they feel insulted or humiliated?

Why do our children have so much anger inside? Where does that come from? Those are the sort of questions we need to be asking.'

Johan simply held out the microphone, without saying a word, as Pia filmed. They were standing outside the auditorium in the schoolyard and, one by one, people stopped to listen to the man's tirade. A crowd started to form around them.

The man went on: 'And it's not a simple matter of putting all the blame on violent computer games and the brutality shown on TV and in films. That does tend to desensitize viewers, but it's not the core of the problem. No, it has to do with the whole structure of society. The grown-ups work too hard and are too stressed, so they don't have time for their kids the way they used to in the past. And don't misunderstand me – I'm not advocating that women should be forced back into the kitchen. But all parents, both men and women, need to spend more time with their children. Kids are too often left to their own devices; they have to manage too much on their own. And just look what happens.'

He threw out his arms in a gesture of helplessness, and then fell silent as he shook his head. After that he walked straight through the crowd and across the asphalt of the schoolyard.

Johan slowly lowered the microphone, watching the man and his wife, who was hurrying to catch up.

Everyone else was shifting nervously from one foot to the other, and a few slunk away. Others remained where they were, as if they didn't really know what to do.

I have to ring Grenfors, thought Johan. We need to interview an expert in the studio about this topic. Maybe several.

His thoughts were interrupted by someone tapping him on the shoulder. He glanced up to see a young, lanky teenage boy with curly red hair, peach fuzz on his upper lip and a spotty complexion.

'Are you the reporter called Johan Berg?' the boy asked.

Johan nodded.

'I think you know my dad. My name is Nils Knutas.'

I always bicycled home from school. Even in winter, when the snow was piled high in drifts. On that particular day in March, most of it had melted away, and crocuses and snowdrops were peeking up along the side of the road. Our class had been allowed to go home early because the woodwork teacher was sick, and we were supposed to have had an extra hour in that class at the end of the day. I was relieved.

As usual, I hurried to my locker before anybody else, got out my backpack, and then was the first to leave the school building. I headed straight for the bicycle racks and unlocked my bike. To my horror, I noticed that I'd forgotten my English textbook. I needed to take it home with me since we had a test the following day. Shit. The last thing I wanted to do was go back inside.

When I reached the break room where our lockers were located, Steffe and Biffen were both there. They were talking to some girls from another class. Everybody turned to look at me. I avoided their eyes and went over to my locker, fumbling with the keys. To my dismay, I dropped the key ring, which clanged as it hit the floor. In a flash, Steffe dashed over and grabbed it. He waved the keys in the air. Clinking and clanking. 'Come and get it, if you can.' He grinned wickedly, and the thick wad of snuff that he'd shoved under his lip made black streaks in the spaces between his teeth.

Scattered laughter from the others, along with remarks about the 'little guy', and 'that wimp'. My cheeks were flushed and my ears burned. Normally they paid no attention to me, didn't even give me a thought. And that's what I preferred. My mouth was dry and I couldn't manage to utter a single word. Just waited. The keys swung back and forth, right in front of my face, but just out of reach. I raised my hand, tried to grab them. Steffe, who was two heads taller than me, took a few steps back. He began circling around me. 'Come on, come on.' The others drew closer, forming a tight circle. I needed those keys. Out of the corner of my eye I saw a teacher in the corridor. But he merely rushed past.

Steffe held the keys above my head. The clinking sound echoed in the room as he swung them back and forth. My body felt as heavy as lead as I clumsily made several more fruitless attempts to grab the key ring. The girls giggled. 'Did you see his ears? They look like stupid wingnuts.'

Swoosh. The key ring sailed past and disappeared behind me to land in a wastepaper basket. 'Go get it, you worm. You worthless little vermin.' I ran over and found the key ring lying in the middle of a soggy mess of banana peels, wads of snuff and old chewing gum. I reached down to pull it out.

At that moment Biffen and Steffe were on top of me, pressing my head down. The edge of the metal container cut into my throat as they forced my head into the rubbish, and the smell of rotting food filled my nostrils. I tried to turn my head but I couldn't budge even an inch. I was locked into position as if held in a vice. I panicked. It was impossible to breathe. 'What a bloody retard you are.'

I heard the girls' voices behind me. 'Stop it, let him go. Take your sodding keys and run home to Mamma. Just don't pee your pants.' One last shove before they released their grip. 'You fucking weirdo.'

My legs were shaking as I cycled home. I refused to cry. I was never going back there. I'd kill myself first. A big lorry rumbled past on the wide road. For a few seconds I considered pulling in front of it, right in the middle of the street. Anything to avoid going back to school. To escape all that shit. And my worthless life.

When I parked my bike round the back and opened the door, I immediately heard the sobbing. I went into the living room, and there she sat. In a corner, with her legs pulled up, weeping.

'What's wrong, Mamma?' I asked. 'Did something bad happen?'

I knew perfectly well what her answer would be.

Nothing ever happened. She just cried all the time. She was always finding new things to cry about, new problems. A fuse might blow, she might drop a glass on the floor, or the car could refuse to start. It might be because a bill was more than she'd expected, or because she'd burned the dinner, or because she had lost her keys. There were endless annoyances every day. And they all represented a catastrophe. Nothing was allowed to go wrong.

I'd lived with her sobs all my life. I felt like a container filled with her tears. I was aware of them sloshing around inside me from the moment I got out of bed in the morning. I had no idea what I was going to do when they overflowed one day.

'No,' she whimpered. 'I'm just sad.'

A lump formed in my stomach; the black curtain descended in front of my eyes.

Cautiously I approached. She smelled of perfume and a slightly stale, stuffy odour. Her face was wet, swollen and bright red. She looked grotesque.

'Come here, my boy. Come here and comfort your mother.' Her voice was whiny.

I bent forward but avoided looking her in the eye. She stretched out her arms and pulled me close. As usual, I didn't know what to say to make her stop crying. I couldn't think of any words. She was sniffing and snuffling. Her tears ran down my shirt.

'Oh, it's all so awful. I work so hard, you know. It's

not easy being a single mother. I'm so lonely. And I have to do everything myself. I just can't handle it any more.'

She began sobbing loudly, howling and wailing, making no attempt to restrain herself in front of me.

I was filled with both disgust and sympathy. I didn't know what to feel or say.

'Now, now, Mamma. You have us, you know,' I ventured.

'Yes, I know, and I'm so lucky,' she sniffled. 'What would I do without all of you? I'd fall apart. You're all that I live for.'

She didn't notice the bruise on my forehead or the smell of rotten banana peel in my hair.

She had enough to do just taking care of herself.

The death of Alexander Almlöv turned the focus away from the homicide investigation on Wednesday.

Even though Knutas wasn't in charge of the assault case, all the journalists wanted to ask him questions, since he was head of the criminal police. The story of the close friendship that had once existed between Knutas and Alexander's father just added to their interest. He spent the entire morning on the phone.

At the same time, one question kept nagging at the back of his mind: Could the motive for killing Viktor Algård be found in the case involving the assault on Alexander? The interviews the police had conducted at the club had produced very little, although it was likely that there were more witnesses to the beating who hadn't yet come forward.

Could someone close to Alexander have exacted revenge on the club owner? Knutas had seen Algård speak to the media several times about whether he considered himself responsible for some of the out-of-control behaviour among local teenagers. Each time he had brushed aside all criticism. That sort of thing might really infuriate people. Maybe somebody had finally had enough.

Knutas still hadn't paid a visit to the club in person after the incident. He needed to do that soon. Possibly even this afternoon.

He went over the latest findings with Rylander, his colleague from the NCP. The skinny detective folded his lanky body into a chair in front of Knutas's desk, holding a thick file folder containing a stack of documents. He placed the folder on the desk.

'This isn't an easy task, let me tell you. Not with so many damn people involved.'

'I know,' said Knutas sympathetically. 'We have two murders now, with no obvious connections, other than the fact that they were both committed brazenly in the midst of a crowd of partygoers. It's one of the hardest things for the police to handle – having to interview people who were more or less drunk when a crime was committed.'

'You're right about that,' Rylander agreed. 'We just have to do the best we can. So far, the interviews that we've conducted haven't brought us much further. This is the most interesting of the lot.'

He pulled a page out of the folder.

'One of Algård's closest colleagues, the pub manager called Rolf Lewin, was also at the dedication festivities at the conference centre. He was helping out at the bar.'

'And?'

'Maybe that's not so strange. Viktor usually brought in the same staff for his events. But during the interview it came out that Rolf and Viktor had had their differences. It might be worthwhile having another talk with the pub manager.'

'What else do you know about him?'

'A typical superannuated biker, if you want my honest and highly biased opinion. Lives alone in a two-room flat in Visby. Unmarried. No children. He's about forty-five, with straggly hair that sticks out in all directions. Wears an earring and always has a cigarette between his lips. From the broken blood vessels on his nose I'd assume he drinks too much.'

'OK, I guess I'll go out and see him,' Knutas muttered. 'Anything else?'

'Not much. The two bouncers don't exactly have a spotless past, but there's nothing to indicate that they had anything to do with Algård's murder. Besides, both of them have watertight alibis.'

'Which are?'

'That they were at home with their wives and kids on Saturday evening. They didn't set foot outside their houses all night.'

By the time they finished, it was one o'clock and Knutas could feel his stomach growling. After his morning swim he was extra hungry. He knocked on the door of Jacobsson's office and asked if she'd like to go out for some lunch. He needed fresh air and wanted to stretch his legs. The noisy lunchroom at police headquarters didn't seem very appealing.

There weren't many lunch places to choose from in Visby during the winter, but the Café Ringduvan, located near the eastern gate in the ring wall, was a pleasant place. At the counter they each ordered the special of the day and then sat down at a table outside. The sun felt gloriously warm. Jacobsson lit a cigarette.

'Have you started smoking again?' asked Knutas.

'You should talk. You with your pipe.'

'But I never light it.'

'Of course you do.'

He was well aware that Karin smoked only when she was worried about something.

'By the way, you said that later on you'd tell me what's been bothering you. Is this a good time?' asked Knutas.

'Definitely not. We need to talk about work. And besides, I don't know whether I'll ever be able to talk to you about this particular problem. It's way too serious.'

Knutas placed his hand on top of hers. 'I'm your friend, Karin. Don't forget that.'

'But just how good a friend are you?'

He looked at her in surprise, startled by the question. 'A very good friend. Probably much better than you even know.'

'OK. I'll think about it.'

'Do that.' Knutas sighed. 'It feels like we're just treading water. With the homicide case, I mean,' he clarified so that she wouldn't think he was talking about their personal relationship. Although in some ways he actually was.

'I know,' Jacobsson agreed. 'The investigation into the assault hasn't produced much yet. There's nothing to indicate that it has anything to do with the murder of Viktor Algård. It's just so awful that the boy died.'

'I've been thinking a lot about his poor mother, Ingrid. I talked to her on the phone last night. She was completely beside herself, of course. Losing a child must be the worst thing that can happen to a person.'

Knutas shook his head. He took a sip of his light beer and looked at Karin. She was staring straight ahead with a blank expression.

'What is it?'

'I'm not feeling very good. I've got to go to the loo.'

She put out her cigarette, got up unsteadily and disappeared inside the café.

A frown of concern crossed Knutas's face as he watched her go.

The building housing the Solo Club, which was so popular with young people, was located on the edge of the harbour district, squeezed between a family restaurant and a bicycle-hire shop. Knutas had made an appointment to meet the pub manager there at three o'clock, but he was a little early. The bartender offered him a cup of coffee and invited him to sit down to wait.

After a few minutes Rolf Lewin arrived. He matched perfectly Rylander's description of him. He was tall with a boyish physique, dyed hair that stuck straight up and pierced eyebrows. He wore a black T-shirt with a drum set printed in gold on his chest and a long gold chain. On his feet he wore a pair of black Converse trainers, just like the ones that Nils owned. But Rolf had an open, friendly face, and he smiled as he introduced himself.

'As you know, we're investigating the murder of Viktor Algård,' said Knutas. 'Since a boy was assaulted here right before the murder and he has now died from his injuries, we consider the incident to be of interest to our investigation.'

'OK, but the police have already been here several times.'

Knutas held up his hands as if to ward off any further objections.

'I know. But right now we'd like to hear what you think about a possible link to the murder. Have you seen or heard anything suspicious? Have you noticed whether anyone has displayed a particular hatred for Algård?'

'Everybody liked Viktor. He was a cheerful guy. He had good intentions, but he really had no idea what he was getting into when he started arranging special evenings here at the club for the younger kids. That's when things went wrong. He refused to see that there were any problems. His only concern was the money he expected to make.'

'So what was his reaction to the problems?'

'There was trouble right from the start. There's no use trying to hide that fact. Lots of kids were stewed to the gills even before they got here. They also smuggled in booze and drank outside the club. The bouncers did the best they could, but it was impossible for us to control everything that was going on. So of course there was a lot of drinking and fighting. We had to deal with plenty of violent incidents even before Alexander Almlöv got beaten up. But Viktor just brushed it all aside. He thought things would calm down after a while.'

'What sort of violent incidents?'

'Fights between pumped-up boys who'd had too much to drink. Brawls. One time a chick claimed that she'd been raped in the ladies' room, but no one took her seriously. I wasn't on duty that night, but I heard about it afterwards,' Rolf hastened to add, giving the detective an apologetic look.

Knutas frowned.

'And it was never reported to the police? The rape, I mean?'

Rolf shook his head.

'I know this sounds strange, but nobody knew who she was. Not even her name or where she was from. She just came outside crying and talked to the bouncers. Her clothes were a mess and she had several cuts on her face, but she was really loaded, and then she left with a friend who was trying to comfort her. The bouncers thought the kids were just going around the corner and would come back, so they'd have another chance to talk to the girl. But she never returned.'

'And they just let her go, even though she said she'd been raped?'

'Afraid so. But like I said, there's been so much trouble here during these club nights for teenagers that we just can't control everything that goes on. It's too much. I tried to explain the problem to Viktor, but as I mentioned, he didn't want to hear it. We have three more of those kind of club events that were booked ages ago, but after that, it bloody well has to stop.'

'Are you the one who's in charge now that Algård is dead?'

'For the time being, yes.'

'And you've always been against holding these parties for teenagers?'

'Not at first, but I quickly realized that they were getting out of hand. Even though they brought in a lot of money, it wasn't worth the trouble. We've got to think of the kids too. We've got a responsibility, damn it.'

'So you and Viktor didn't agree about this?'

'That's putting it mildly.'

'When did this rape incident occur?'

'It was on Lucia evening, December the thirteenth. Almost four months ago.'

'And you still have no idea who the girl was?'

'No, I haven't got a clue.'

'You were working at the bar during the dedication festivities at the conference centre, isn't that right?'

'Yes.'

'Why?'

'They needed help, and I have nothing against making a little extra money.'

'Did you notice anything out of the ordinary during the evening? Anyone who seemed suspicious?'

'No, I don't think so.'

'We now know that Viktor was having an affair with Veronika Hammar. Did you happen to notice them together? She was at the party too.'

Rolf Lewin's face lit up.

'Actually, yes. They were standing at the bar, talking. Just briefly. I even served them drinks.'

'Is that right?'

'Well, to be precise, I mixed a drink for Veronika Hammar. I remember because it was at the request of a secret admirer.' He rolled his eyes.

'What do you mean?' asked Knutas.

'Well, there was this guy who came over and ordered an alcohol-free strawberry daiquiri, which he wanted to give her.'

'And you gave the drink to Veronika?'

'Yes.'

'This man who ordered it – what did he look like?'

'Hmm. I don't really recall. There wasn't anything remarkable about him. Tall, in his forties, wearing a grey suit, I think. Blond hair, a bit straggly. He wore glasses with black frames. They looked like Armani.'

'But you didn't recognize him?'

'No. I'd never seen him before. I don't think he was from around here.'

'Why do you say that?'

'I'm not sure. Just a feeling I had.'

Considering Rolf claims not to have remembered anything about the guy, his powers of observation are certainly impressive, thought Knutas. Then another thought occurred to him.

'What time was this?'

'The stage show had just started, so it must have been right after midnight.'

'Did you see whether Veronika drank the cocktail?'

'I don't think she did. She handed the glass to Viktor. Then he went downstairs, while she went off in another direction. There were so many people, and I was busy filling drink orders, so I didn't give it another thought.'

'Do you recall what the man said?'

Rolf paused to think.

'Let's see now. First he ordered the drink, without saying anything in particular. After I mixed the cocktail and served it, he paid with cash and gave me a big tip.'

'Try to remember exactly what happened,' Knutas told him. 'Did he give you exact change?'

'Good Lord, how in hell am I supposed to . . . Wait a minute. Now I remember. He paid with a five-hundred-krona note. The drink cost eighty-five, and he told me just to give him four hundred back. That's right. Fifteen for a tip.'

'Then what?'

'Well, when I handed him the change, he asked me to give the drink to Veronika Hammar.'

'How far apart were they standing? I mean, Veronika and the stranger?'

'They were at opposite ends of the bar, so maybe ten metres apart or so. And there was a big crowd there. I told Veronika that the drink was from an admirer, but when I turned to point him out to her, the guy was gone.'

Knutas had listened to Rolf's account with growing interest. He realized that the bartender's story meant that the murder investigation was about to take a new and surprising turn.

He thanked the man for his time and then hurried out of the club.

As soon as Knutas got back to police headquarters, he asked Jacobsson to come to his office. He explained his theory, based on what he'd just learned from the pub manager. Jacobsson sat in silence on his visitor's sofa, listening with an increasingly surprised look on her face.

'So you think that Algård was killed by mistake? That the cyanide wasn't intended for him at all?'

'Exactly. It was meant for Veronika Hammar.'

'So we've been on the wrong track the whole time.'

'The man who ordered that drink is the one we need to be looking for.'

'What about the glass?'

'We're going to have to search the entire building again. Look in every damn rubbish bin, and every nook and cranny in the vicinity of the conference centre. The perp obviously took the glass with him.'

'So how did the poison get in the cocktail?'

'Emptying a vial into the drink could be done in a flash. It wouldn't take more than a few seconds. He could have done it while the bartender was getting change for the five hundred kronor.'

'This turns everything upside down,' said Jacobsson. 'We're going to have to start from scratch.'

'Definitely,' Knutas agreed grimly. 'Let's get everyone together for a meeting.'

The cabin couldn't be described as luxurious. It was a typical weekend cabin from the sixties with dark brown wood panelling, a tumbledown chimney and spartan furnishings. The front door opened on to a narrow hallway. A row of hooks on the wall held jackets, coats and various bags and purses. On the floor underneath were rubber boots, wooden clogs and slippers. A couple of walking sticks leaned against the wall in one corner. The small kitchen had a window that faced the forested area on the hill. A cheap rug on the floor, wallpaper with brown flowers. A laminate countertop, a small sink and a stove that looked at least thirty years old. Further along the hall was a large bedroom with a double bed, dresser and photographs of several children on the wall. The living room had a hardwood floor and a simple fireplace. The furniture consisted of a sofa, coffee table, bookshelf and a spinning wheel.

It was getting cold. She had heated up some soup for dinner and eaten it with a couple of open sandwiches on rye bread. Outside the window, it looked as if a big lamp had been switched off over Gotland. It was pitch dark. At night, not a single light was ever visible over the countryside, except for the moon if the sky was clear. Then it would spread its bluish glow over the treetops, glinting on the wings of bats as they fluttered overhead whenever she made her way to the outside privy. Tonight she stayed sitting at the table after she finished eating. She was staring at the flame of the candle that she'd set in the wrought-iron candlestick.

All day long she'd had a strange feeling that someone was watching her, but she had no idea why she felt that way. At first she'd thought it was the cat. He'd been gone since morning, and he hadn't appeared when she called his name. Maybe he was staring at her from some hiding place, enjoying the fact that he'd managed to elude her. Letting her stand there and call his name in a vain attempt to entice him back inside.

She'd come out here to this isolated cabin even though she hated being alone. In the summer it was a paradise, when the other homeowners brought life to the area and the Swedish nights were bright. In the wintertime it was hell, with the darkness, solitude and strong winds. But she'd had no other choice. She had to get away, escape everything that had to do with Viktor and the police investigation. Not to mention everybody's prying stares.

Feeling on edge, she listened tensely for any sound, but she heard only the roar of the sea and the wind rushing through the trees. What could it be that was making her so uneasy? Maybe it was just her imagination.

She glanced at the doorway leading to the hall. Then she got up to make sure that she had locked the front door properly. Yes, it was locked. Even so, she stared nervously at the key sitting in the lock. How much would that really help? Any guy with sufficient muscle could easily kick in the flimsy door. She had to admit that she was completely unprotected, vulnerable to anyone who might decide to start breaking into the cottages in this remote area.

She made the coffee and switched on the TV. The programme *Ask the Doctor* was on channel 2, while channel 1 was rerunning a drama series that she'd already seen. A show for kids was on channel 4. She sighed and went back to channel 2 and a discussion about prostate cancer. At least it was reassuring to have some background noise, voices to keep her company and hold bad thoughts at bay. She went into the kitchen to pour herself some coffee. Then stopped abruptly. She had glimpsed something moving outside in the dark. Like a shadow slipping past the window. All of a sudden she was uncomfortably aware of how visible she must be from outside as she stood in the brightly lit kitchen. She fumbled for the light switch.

When the room went dark, she had a better view of the outdoors. She crept over to the small window to scan her surroundings, looking from one side of the property to the other. She saw the lawn, which was covered with withered leaves, pine needles and branches that had come down during the winter storms. She saw the toolshed, the playhouse and the privy. Nothing. She went back to the living room, turned off all the lamps and blew out the candle. If someone was out there, she didn't want that person to be able to see every move she made. She also turned off the light in the hall. The house had no curtains or blinds. She had decided that window blinds were unnecessary since she usually came here only in the summertime. She loved it when sunlight flooded the small cabin, both day and night. Curtains merely gathered mildew, and besides, they blocked the view. But right now she would have given anything for some sort of window covering.

Her heart was pounding hard. Who in the world could be after her? She'd never done anyone any harm. But she was starting to wonder if she might be wrong about that. She turned off the TV and listened intently, straining all of her senses. All she heard was the wind. She sat down on the sofa in the dark living room and waited. Half an hour passed. Then another. Nothing happened. She was growing more and more annoyed. Should she keep sitting here like a rat in a cage? To make matters worse, she badly needed to pee, but unfortunately she had no chamber pot. She refused to consider peeing into a bowl that was used for food. After yet another half-hour passed, she gave up. She couldn't hold it any longer. And by now anger had taken over. She wasn't about to let fear keep her trapped inside her own house. Well, it wasn't really hers, but the cabin had always been available to her because her friends who owned it lived abroad. They wanted to keep the summer place in the family, so they had let her use it ever since her children were small. She'd made it her own, and she loved the cabin more than anything.

She put on her jacket and pulled on her boots, hesitating a moment with her hand resting on the door handle.

Then she turned the key and opened the door.

The rest of the world faded away and then vanished entirely as Knutas watched the Regional News programme on TV in the police break room that evening. The top story wasn't about Viktor Algård but about the death that had resulted from the assault outside the Solo Club. He was deeply moved by the interview with the father of one of the witnesses, and the statements made by Alexander's sister, the school principal and a few students. When he suddenly saw his own son appear on the screen, his breathing faltered.

In a voice-over Johan Berg proclaimed: 'Several young people were witnesses to the drama. One of them was Nils Knutas. Out of fear of reprisals, he previously hasn't wanted to say anything about what he saw. But today he has decided to come forward.'

Nils was shown standing at the scene of the assault, pointing to show where he and his friends had been, only a few metres away. They had watched as Alexander was severely beaten. None of them had dared intervene. He talked about his sense of guilt and about how scared he'd been, how powerless he'd felt. When the assault was over and the perpetrators had fled, he'd gone over to Alexander. He'd felt how faint the boy's pulse was, and he'd seen all the blood. While his friends had phoned the police and the medics, he had simply walked away, leaving the scene without doing anything to help.

'Why have you decided to talk about this today?' asked Johan.

His expression sombre, Nils looked straight at the camera as he replied: 'Because of what Alexander's sister, Olivia, said in the auditorium. If she has the guts to stand up there in front of hundreds of people and say what she knows, then how could I remain silent?'

With that, the story was over. It was followed by a studio discussion with several participants. Knutas saw them through a fog, not taking in who they were or what they were saying. He sat on the sofa as if frozen, incapable of moving. Jacobsson, who was sitting next to him, patted him on the shoulder and got up without saying a word.

After she left the room and closed the door, something happened that hadn't occurred in years.

Knutas wept.

Knutas opened the door to his house on Bokströmsgatan, filled with a sense of doom. He was overwhelmed by despair. For weeks Nils had kept quiet about having been a witness to the assault. Knutas didn't know whether it was his role as a father or as a police officer that had prevented Nils from confiding in him. Or which was worse.

He had tried to phone Lina, but he got only a busy signal on the landline, and she hadn't answered her mobile.

He hung his jacket in the front hall without calling out his customary 'hello'. The TV was on in the living room. It was some kind of quiz show. Lina was sitting in a corner of the sofa with the reading lamp on, the newspaper spread open on her lap. She glanced up when he stepped into the room.

'Hi, sweetheart,' she said gently. 'Come over here and sit down.'

He realized at once that she'd seen the Regional News report.

'Where's Nils?'

'Upstairs in his room.'

'Have you talked to him?'

'No. I wanted to wait for you.'

Knutas shouted at the top of his lungs: 'Nils!'

'Calm down,' Lina urged her husband. 'This isn't easy for him either.'

Knutas chose to ignore her. He was glaring at the stairs. He heard a door slowly open, and then a voice said: 'What is it?'

'Come down here.'

'But I'm doing my homework.'

'Get down here this minute!'

Nils appeared at the top of the stairs. His face was pale, his expression serious, his curly red hair more tousled than usual. His T-shirt was wrinkled and there were holes in the knees of his jeans.

'What is it?'

'Don't play dumb with me. Come down here.'

Knutas immediately regretted the harsh tone he'd taken, but it was too late now.

Knutas led the way into the living room, turned off the TV and sank down on to the sofa next to Lina. He motioned for Nils to sit on the armchair across from them. Anger overtook the sorrow he felt at not having the right expertise to deal with the situation. He felt as if he were adrift on an ice floe, floating on some distant, ice-cold and bottomless sea.

'Can you explain to me and your mother why you

haven't said a word to us this whole time about being a witness when Alexander was assaulted? Yet the minute a reporter waves a microphone in your face, you spill out the whole story as if you were getting paid to talk.'

Nils gave him a defiant look. His eyes were filled with contempt.

'Neither of you ever asked me about it.'

The words were so unexpected that Knutas was left speechless. He cast a glance at Lina. She merely shook her head and then hid her face in her hands.

'But we're always asking you how you are and what's going on. You never want to tell us anything, but we keep trying—'

'You're always so busy with your own stuff. You don't really care how I am or what I have to deal with! You just pretend to take an interest, but the only thing that's important to you is that fucking cop job of yours!'

Knutas was shocked. He was utterly unprepared for such an accusation. He'd been naive enough to think that Nils would be remorseful and apologize.

'What do you mean?'

'You don't care about me. All you ever talk about is yourself and your sodding investigations, and I don't give a shit about them. Why should I tell you anything? You pretend to care about me and Petra, but the only effort you ever make is to drag us along once in a while to do something you think is fun. Like when we went to the golf course. We just went along for your sake, even though you acted like you were the best father in the world who was doing something really great for his kids.'

Knutas felt his cheeks flush with indignation, but he forced himself to remain calm.

'I think you have to agree that you're being unfair. OK, I admit that there are times when I talk a lot about my work, but that's only when I'm in the middle of an important case. And that's not really surprising, is it? And think about all the fun things we've done together over the years. You don't really think it was all for my sake, do you? All those excursions we've taken you on, ever since you and your sister were kids? I can't even count how many times we've been to Kneippbyn and Vattenland. We've gone to Legoland and to the Astrid Lindgren theme park, and I've even gone riding on Iceland horses with you and Petra – and you know how scared I am of horses. Have you really forgotten all those things? I think you ought to show a little gratitude once in a while and not be so bloody sullen and selfish all the time. Your mother and I are doing the best we can!'

Nils stared at his hands, not once looking at his father. He said in a low voice: 'It's not Mamma that I'm mad at. She has always come through for us. Unlike you.'

Knutas looked at his son in bewilderment. He couldn't believe his ears. He swallowed hard. No one else spoke as he searched for words.

'I really don't understand what you mean, Nils. I never come through for you? How can you say that?'

'OK, maybe once in a while. And more often when we were little kids. But nowadays you never have time.'

Knutas leaned back on the sofa. The room began slowly spinning around. He took several deep breaths, blinked away a tear. Lina was silent, her face still buried in her hands.

This conversation with Nils wasn't going to end with the family reconciliation that he had hoped for. He was shaken to the core by his son's scorn.

'But why didn't you say anything?' he ventured. 'Why didn't you tell us that you were there?'

'Because I didn't want to.'

'Didn't want to? Don't you realize how serious this is? You're a witness, for chrissake!'

'Take it easy,' Lina protested. 'You've been a police officer for seventeen years, Anders. You, of all people, should understand how hard it can be for someone to admit that he saw something but either couldn't or didn't dare intervene.'

Nils glared at his father.

'You've just made it horribly clear that the only thing you care about is your job. *You're a witness, for chrissake*!' he said, his voice filled with resentment as he repeated his father's words. 'You don't give a fuck how I feel, or how I'm doing after watching those pricks beat the shit out of Alexander.'

Nils's face was rigid with anger, and his eyes flashed as he looked at Knutas.

'Why should I tell you anything? Give me one good reason!'

He leaped up and ran out of the room.

A few seconds later the front door slammed.

In spite of the long workday, Johan didn't feel tired, and he had no desire to go home to the empty house in Roma. Emma had gone with Elin to visit her parents on the island of Fårö. They were sitting in front of the fireplace drinking Irish coffee when he phoned. Emma complimented him on his report, which she'd watched on the news, and hearing her praise made him happy.

Pia had left the editorial office right after they had finished, presumably to go and see her sheep farmer. The relationship seemed to be serious. Usually she wasn't so enthusiastic about her boyfriends.

Johan sat in front of his computer, spending the next few hours aimlessly surfing the Internet. Then he found himself pulling up the website for the Solo Club. They were open. Of course he'd already done several reports from there about the assault case, but he'd never visited the club in the evening when it was actually filled with young people.

It was just after ten o'clock when he left the TV building. He walked through town, heading for the harbour.

He found Skeppsbron swarming with teenagers, and many of them looked younger than eighteen.

A long queue had formed outside the Solo Club, where it had all happened just a couple of weeks ago. The guy at the door recognized Johan and waved him through. Inside, the noise level was deafening and the dance floor was packed. He was surprised to see what the young girls were wearing. Many of them were scantily clad, to say the least, in minuscule tops and shorts that barely covered their bottoms. Some of them wore only lacy knickers with a top, and one big-busted girl was dancing around in her bra. Johan could hardly believe his eyes. Was this the latest fashion for teenage girls? It was alarming, and that alone made it worthy of a news report. The boys wore more familiar attire, most of them jeans and a T-shirt. A few were going around shirtless.

Johan ordered a beer and stood at the bar. It wasn't long before several girls who didn't look older than fourteen or fifteen came over to order Cokes. One of them wore only a bra and a pair of mini-shorts. He leaned towards her, forced to shout to be heard over the music.

'Why are you dressed like that?' he asked.

She giggled and stared at him, uncomprehending. Her eyes were almost invisible behind a thick coating of mascara. Her face was covered with tanning cream, her lips were smeared with a white ointment, and her hair stuck out every which way, sticky with hairspray. A typical fourteen-year-old.

'What do you mean?'

'Why are you out in public in your underwear?'

She tittered uncertainly, and then moved away and went back to talking to her friends. Johan saw one of them take a little bottle out of her bag and pour something into her Coke. So that's how it's done, he thought. Lots of the kids in the club were noticeably drunk. He signalled to the bartender.

'Has this place changed since the assault happened?'

The bartender shrugged.

'Not really. The first couple of weeks it was kind of quiet, but now there are just as many people as before, and they're all just as drunk. As if it never happened.'

'How can you make sure that kids under eighteen aren't drinking?'

'We can't. All we can do here at the bar is ask for a valid ID before we serve anybody alcohol. But there's nothing we can do about it if the kids drink before they get here, or if they hide the booze in the shrubbery and then go outside, supposedly to have a smoke, or if people outside the club sell them alcohol.'

'There must be some kids who smuggle booze inside, right?'

'Sure. But we can't frisk everybody. That's just how it is.'

He shrugged again and went back to work.

Johan finished his beer and left.

Outside it was just as lively as inside. Teenagers stood around smoking. A bunch of boys were laughing loudly as they tossed around a beer bottle. One young couple was wrapped in a tight embrace, kissing and not caring who saw them. And a little girl sat a short distance away, her head in her hands. She looked as if she wasn't feeling well. Johan sat down next to her.

'How's it going?'

Cautiously he placed a hand on her thin shoulder. When she looked up, he gave a start. The girl wore dramatic make-up but she didn't look older than twelve or thirteen. Her eyes were half-closed, and her face was very pale.

'I feel sick.'

She didn't manage to say anything more before she threw up. He helped her clean herself up. She started crying, and he did his best to console her.

'What's your name?'

'Pernilla.'

'Where do you live?'

'Hemse.'

Good Lord, thought Johan. What kind of parents would let a young girl like this stay out late at night so far from home? And, to cap it all, drunk. He searched her jacket pockets and pulled out a mobile that showed several missed calls from her mother. He rang the number. He heard loud music in the background and a laughing woman's voice answered.

'Hello?'

'Hi, my name is Johan Berg, and I'm sitting here with your daughter, Pernilla.'

'Yes?'

'We're in Visby, and I'm sorry to tell you that your daughter is extremely drunk.'

The voice now sounded worried.

'What? Are you sure?'

'It would be best if you came to get her. She can't make it home on her own.'

Now he heard several agitated voices in the background.

Christ. Pernilla's drunk. Who can drive? We've all been drinking. Susanne, she's pregnant. She's the only one who could drive right now. We shouldn't have let them go into town. I told you we shouldn't let them go. Where are the others? Where did they get the booze from?

After a minute the woman was back on the line.

'OK, my husband is coming. Where are you?'

Johan gave her directions to the Solo Club.

The girl threw up a few more times. She had no idea where her friends had gone. When Johan asked her how old she was, she said she was twelve. Good Lord, he thought. That means she's just a year older than Emma's daughter Sara. Is Sara going to be sitting here like this a year from now?

He stayed for almost an hour, helping Pernilla vomit up all the alcohol she'd consumed. Finally a car pulled up and parked. A man his own age got out, dressed in jeans and a shirt, looking stressed. Right behind him was a very pregnant woman. She was the one who had driven the car.

'Oh, sweetie,' cried the man, taking the girl in his arms. 'How are you feeling? Come on, let's get you home. Where are Agnes and Mimmi?'

He got her into the car as he continued to ask questions. He briefly thanked Johan for his help before they sped away.

Feeling depressed, Johan walked back through town to the office. He pictured Sara's sweet, innocent face. She had already started to use make-up once in a while. Was this what awaited her, right around the corner? He shuddered at the thought. At the same time, it seemed disturbing that the partying at the Solo Club was going on as usual, only a day after Alexander Almlöv had died.

Exactly as if the assault had never happened.

She was awakened by a fit of coughing. A suffocating smell. Her eyes were running. She immediately jumped out of bed, realizing to her horror that she was surrounded by thick smoke. When she went to bed, she had deliberately closed the bedroom door since she had nearly scared herself silly imagining that someone was outside.

The smoke was coming through the gaps around the door, and the heat was unbearable. For a moment she closed her eyes as she shut her mouth tight. The bedroom was at the very back of the cabin, behind the kitchen. Her first thought was to tear open the door and get out, but as soon as she touched the metal door handle, she knew that the rest of the house must be in flames. Instead she picked up the floor lamp and rammed it against the window to break the glass. Her eyes were burning so badly that she could hardly keep them open. The smoke was making her dizzy. She tried to breathe in as little as possible. Then she plunged headlong out of the window and on to the lawn. Feeling sick and in shock, she began crawling away, trying to get as far from the fire as she could. She didn't dare turn around until she'd made it all the way over to the privy. She sat on the ground, leaning against the wall, and watched, dumbfounded, as the drama unfolded before her. The cabin was totally engulfed, the flames shooting high up into the air, an angry inferno against the night sky. There was nothing she could do but sit there as the house, in which she'd spent so many summers and which had given her so many good memories, burned to ashes before her eyes. She hadn't managed to take a single thing with her. Her mind and her body were both numb; she didn't dare allow herself to feel anything.

There was no one else around. It was just her and the fire. She had no means of communicating with the rest of the world. She had no mobile, and the nearest neighbouring farm was several kilometres away. For a moment she drifted off, feeling as though she might fall asleep.

Only then did she hear the sirens.

Knutas couldn't sleep. He tossed and turned in bed. After several hours of fruitless attempts, he finally gave up. He slipped out of bed and went downstairs to the kitchen where he poured himself a glass of milk and got out a packet of biscuits. With a sigh he sat down at the table. The cat hopped up next to his plate and rubbed his hand, wanting to be petted. At least you like me, he thought morosely. The argument with Nils had proved a brutal wake-up call. He'd had no idea that the distance between them was so great. He cursed himself. How could he have been so clueless? So selfish?

The children provided a crystal-clear mirror that ruthlessly exposed every flaw and defect that he possessed as a parent. The degree of trust, love and solidarity the children displayed was a manifestation of his success as a father. How did they behave at home? What were they willing to share without being asked? How much love did they voluntarily express? He had merely walked about, blind to what was going on around him. It was Lina who took the kids out to the country on weekends; she was the one who drove them to football matches and practice sessions; she was the one who did most of the cleaning and cooking. He had been so wrapped up in his job that he hadn't been paying attention.

The guilt that he felt was almost too much to bear.

Maybe it's the regular conversations that are causing the haze before my eyes to disperse. The fog is starting to lift. My vision is clearer, even though I feel worse. The headaches clamp even more tightly around my forehead.

We're sitting in that room, as usual, resting in the silence for a while.

If I turn my head and the light slants in from the side, the plaster rose in the ceiling looks like a person with a huge mouth. Maybe it's my mother's jaws that just keep getting bigger the more things you try to stuff inside. Her sense of dissatisfaction grows with each day, month and year that passes. She always has something new to complain about. New problems, new obstacles, new spanners thrown into the works. It's the end of the world the minute life doesn't flow smoothly. She's constantly searching for new sources of wood to throw on her bonfire of wretchedness. Hungrily she swings her axe at the smallest thing that might sustain her misery. Sometimes it feels as if my brain is about to boil over.

She takes up so much space. I can always feel her presence, whether I like it or not. She's been transformed into a thick pulp that has forced its way up inside me to settle in my throat. The only thing I want is to spit out that crap once and for all. To vomit her up. Make her leave my body, which she has invaded from the day I was born. It's sick. I know it is.

Now I'm back with the person I'm talking to.

The window is slightly open. The sun is shining, and it's warm outside.

'The last time we met, you left rather abruptly. What happened?'

'Sometimes I feel so filled with my so-called mother that I end up overflowing. Then I either have to throw up or take a shit, almost as if I'm a rubbish bin and she's the rubbish.'

'Can you describe what it feels like when that's about to happen?'

'Sometimes I just can't stand the thought of her, and then it feels like something takes me over.'

'What do you mean by that?'

'As if my body takes control. It reacts on its own, takes on its own life, and it's impossible to control. It's a form of protest. As if it's rebelling against the fact that she's eating me up from the inside, like a fucking parasite. Taking up residence and getting bigger and bigger until one day she'll be the death of me. Against my will, she's the first thing I think of when I wake up and the last thing on my mind when I fall asleep. There's nothing I can do about it, no matter how hard I try. She is always there, like my guilty conscience.'

'How does that affect you?'

'Well, all my life I've always felt guilty if I did anything fun on my own, without her.'

'Why's that?'

'The minute I decide to take a skiing holiday or go to a concert or do anything else fun, I hear her complaints about how she's longing to do exactly the same thing. *If only I could . . .* Even when I had a family, I would feel guilty when we sat at the table with the candles lit, having a pleasant dinner. And I'd think to myself that I should have invited my mother. Not that it was particularly nice having her visit. I remember when Daniel was a newborn and we had moved to the new flat. Mamma used to come over on Sundays. Even before she'd taken off her shoes in the front hall, she would ask: "Is the coffee ready?" in that shrill voice of hers. Then she'd sit down on the sofa and stay there, as if glued to the cushions, until it was time for her to leave again. The coffee would grow cold in her cup as she babbled about one thing or another. If I happened to mention that Daniel was having trouble sleeping or if Katrina said that he was suffering from colic, my mother would merely dismiss our concerns as unimportant. Then she would turn to Katrina and start telling her how wonderful her own children had been.

They'd never had any stomach troubles or problems with eating or sleeping. And the implication was: *You're a failure as a mother. My children were always perfect, but that's because I was their mother, of course.* I mostly kept quiet or tried to smooth things over, but that just made matters worse. It gave Mamma even more fodder for her criticisms, and her barbs were vicious. Usually Katrina would end up leaving the room to potter about in the kitchen until Mamma left. I'm ashamed that I behaved so spinelessly.'

'Why did you act that way?'

'I don't know. When I think back, I can't for the life of me understand why I allowed Mamma to have so much power over me. Even as a grown man with my own family to take care of, I acted like a frightened little boy. It's as if she always makes me feel guilty. As if I ought to be paying her back.'

'It must be a way of maintaining control. And continuing to stand in the spotlight.'

'And the gods only know that's what she wants. Whenever she comes to visit, all other activity has to stop. Everyone is expected to immediately drop whatever they're doing and devote all their attention to her. And after we're done with coffee, she has to have help with everything. *Do you have a phone book? A nail file? Can you help me book theatre tickets on the Internet? Do you have a sewing machine? I want to sew a pair of trousers. I need to dye my hair – can I do it in your bathroom? Can*

I borrow the phone? How does my mobile work? Can you read the instructions out loud so we can go over them, step by step?

'And she's completely oblivious to the fact that we might have other things to do. If I tell her I've had a tough day at work, she waves it aside. *Be glad you have a job,* she'll say. Or if, in a weak moment, I ask for her support because Katrina and I have quarrelled, she'll tell me: *Be glad you have a wife – that there are two of you. Just think about me. I've always been a single mother.* She forgets, of course, that she was always the one to dump every single boyfriend she ever had while we were growing up.'

The person I'm talking to is starting to look more and more puzzled. As if it's hard to believe that what I'm saying is true. But it is. Every word of it. And now I'm really getting started. Even though it hurts, it's great to say all this shit out loud. I've never done that before.

'The worst thing is that no matter what I do for her, she's never satisfied. If I help her with her shopping, then drive her home and unload all the groceries, she still asks me to stay and cook dinner. If I refuse, I know that she'll be unhappy with me when I leave. If I go to visit her and bring along a bottle of wine as a surprise, she'll curse me for not bringing a whole case. No matter what I do, it's never enough. The strangest part is that the more I serve her, the more dissatisfied she is.'

'Why's that?'

'The more she gets, the more she wants. Her demands increase the more effort I make. She doesn't think like a normal person would: OK, now I've received so much help that I can be content for a while. She just can't do that. As soon as one task is finished, you have to start on the next one.'

'Why do you keep on doing things for her? You're just encouraging her behaviour. Why don't you ever say no?'

'I don't know. That's just the way it's always been. And I've learned not to protest. The minute I disagree with her or offer any sort of objection, she gets furious. She can't stand to be contradicted. Then she raises her voice and gets more and more worked up. She talks non-stop, her voice gets louder and louder and she repeats herself like a parrot. It's so unpleasant and she's so unreasonable that I'd rather not have that happen. I learned that early on.'

'Can't you explain to her how you feel?'

'I've dreamed of doing that. Mamma's inability to listen has sometimes made me fantasize about tying her to a chair, taping her mouth shut and forcing her to hear me. Then I would tell her everything. What my childhood was like and how I felt about her behaviour. I would give her concrete examples so she would understand. She would have to sit on that chair, her hands and feet bound and with thick duct tape over her mouth, and she'd be forced to take in every word.'

'Why do you think you have this fantasy?'

'Deep inside I may still have a naive hope that everything will be OK. That she will finally see me, understand me, and show me some respect. That we will connect somehow.' I hear myself sigh heavily. 'Soon I won't be able to stand this any longer.'

'What do you mean?'

'Just what I said. I won't be able to stand it.'

'And what are you going to do about it?'

'I have to do something. That much I know.'

'What do you have to do?'

I see the nervous expression but choose not to answer.

The fire out in Holmhällar confirmed Knutas's suspicions. The perpetrator they were looking for was after Veronika Hammar and no one else.

The entire investigative team was present at the morning meeting, and there was a charged atmosphere in the room when Knutas began.

'At two fifteen this morning, a call came in, reporting that a cabin was on fire out near Holmhällar. It was a neighbour named Olof Persson who made the call. He has a farm a couple of kilometres away. He saw the glow of the fire in the sky and drove over to find the cabin completely engulfed in flames. One person was injured in the fire, and it was none other than Veronika Hammar, the very person we've been looking for. She was suffering from smoke inhalation and was taken to hospital. The reason we didn't track her down at the cabin is that she's not the owner. She merely uses the place, although apparently she's been going there for more than thirty years.'

'Has anyone interviewed her yet?' asked Smittenberg.

'Yes, but only briefly. She says that she was woken

by the fire. By then the whole cabin was in flames. She could think of only one thing, and that was to get out, which she managed to do, and without suffering any burns. She breathed in a lot of smoke, but apparently she'll be released from hospital later today.'

'How is she doing?' asked Wittberg.

'She's upset and in shock. She didn't manage to save any of her belongings, and she lost a lot of possessions that had sentimental value for her. She's also scared. She says that she saw someone on the property a few hours before the fire started.'

'Someone who didn't want to be seen?'

'Exactly. The techs are out at the cabin now, although it'll be a while before they're able to make a more thorough search. But they've already phoned to say that they found a petrol can and some rags, so we have to assume that it was arson.'

'Are there any witnesses?' asked Smittenberg.

'No, none so far, except for the farmer who called the police. And Veronika's cabin was the only one in the area that was occupied, at least as far as we know.'

'I'm going out there as soon as the meeting is over,' said Erik Sohlman. 'It's quite a big piece of land. It might be possible to find evidence scattered around, if it hasn't been destroyed by the firefighting efforts.'

For a moment no one spoke.

'OK,' Jacobsson said then as she looked at her colleagues seated around the table. 'Shall we focus our efforts on the theory that Veronika Hammar is the sole intended victim? That Viktor Algård died by mistake?'

'And we stop working on any aspects that only have connections with Algård, right?' Wittberg added. 'Including the assault at the club and the conference centre?'

'Yes, at least for now,' Knutas agreed. 'We need to concentrate on finding the person who seems to have some motive for harming Veronika Hammar.'

'What about the wife?' asked Wittberg. 'Elisabeth Algård. How should we deal with her?'

'She's still a person of interest, of course,' Jacobsson replied. 'She could very well be a prime suspect, trying to get rid of her rival.'

'Sure,' said Knutas. 'Let's bring her in for another interview, right after the meeting.' He turned to Jacobsson. 'Have you found out anything new about Veronika Hammar?'

'Not really, although we already know quite a lot about her,' said Jacobsson, leafing through her notes. 'As we found out before, she's been divorced for many years. Her ex-husband died in a car accident twenty years ago. They were already divorced by then. She has four grown children. Two of them live here on Gotland, and two of them live in Stockholm. She's friends with one of her neighbours, and she has two sisters, one on Gotland and one in Stockholm, whom she sees once in a while. She has a few colleagues who are also personal friends.'

'OK, we need to interview everyone in Veronika's family and social circle. Including neighbours and artist friends. She probably belongs to some sort of art society or association. Also the people who live in the summer-house area in Holmhällar. We may find an important lead out there. I'm planning to go and see Sten Bergström. He lives right nearby, so I want to talk to him again. As far as her children are concerned, we need to interview them as soon as possible.'

Johan was woken by someone shaking him. He blinked at the light, and at first he had no idea where he was. Then he remembered. Last night at the Solo Club.

Afterwards he'd gone back to the office and crashed on the sofa. He was staring up at a face black with soot. It took him a second before he recognized who it was.

'Wake up. I've been ringing and ringing your mobile. You'd probably just go on snoozing even if the sky was falling.'

'Calm down,' he groaned.

He sat up, yawned and rubbed the sleep out of his eyes. He had a terrible taste in his mouth. Then he stared in surprise at Pia.

'Have you seen what you look like?'

'Some people have been working while you've been lying here dreaming. Did you go out on the town last night? Or to some party?'

'I wish. No, I was at the Solo Club, taking care of drunk little girls. What's going on?'

Pia's face was as black as the eyeliner she used. Her

hair stuck out even more than usual, and her clothes were wrinkled and covered with black specks. The streaks on her neck matched her black mascara.

'A cabin burned down out near Holmhällar.'

'And?'

'It was arson, and a woman was injured. I thought we could at least get some pictures for the wire service. I was awake when the call came in, and I happened to be down by Sudret, so I managed to take pictures while the cabin was still burning, plus I interviewed the fire chief. Then I waited for the crime techs to arrive and got one of them to confirm that they'd found a petrol can on the property along with several rags. Unfortunately, I missed the ambulance that came for the injured woman.'

'Do you know how serious her injuries are?'

'The fire chief thought she was just suffering from minor smoke inhalation. I called the hospital, but they wouldn't tell me anything, of course. And by the way, it turned out to be a lucky break that I went out there.'

'Why's that?'

'The cabin doesn't belong to just anybody, let me tell you.'

'What do you mean?'

'Veronika Hammar was living there. You know – the artist who does those sheep paintings that they sell at Stora Torget? Sheep out in the pasture, back-lit sheep, sheep on the beach . . .'

'Oh, right. Sure, I know those paintings.'

'Well, she's the one who was injured. And do you know who she was having an affair with?'

'No.'

'Viktor Algård. She's the secret mistress.'

Johan slowly put down his coffee cup.

'Are you sure?'

'Yes.'

'How sure?'

'Absolutely positive. I have a reliable source.'

'We need two sources. Independent of each other.'

'I don't know whether that's really necessary in this case.' Pia had a sly look on her face.

'Why not?'

'My source is very close to the individual in question. I got the information from Andreas. You know – the sheep farmer.'

'So?'

'His last name is Hammar.'

Johan stared at his colleague, dumbfounded.

'You're dating Veronika Hammar's son?'

'Your powers of deduction are impressive.'

Johan turned on his computer and read the wire service news. All of the newspapers had printed pictures of the fire on the front page. Nowhere did it say that the cabin belonged to Veronika Hammar or that there was any connection between the fire and the murder of Viktor Algård.

'But if the cabin belonged to Veronika and she was his secret girlfriend, then it sounds like the fire could have been attempted murder,' said Johan. 'Which means that the person who killed Algård is now after Veronika Hammar.'

'Very smart, Sherlock. Now you get it.'

Pia turned to her computer to upload the pictures.

Veronika Hammar had a private room at the far end of the corridor. The ward nurse had warned Knutas that the patient was exhausted and would probably be kept in hospital another day for observation. He gently knocked on the door before entering the room. He gave a start when he caught sight of the woman lying in the bed. Veronika looked as if she had aged ten years since he last saw her. She wore no make-up, her hair was uncombed, and she had on a white hospital gown that was partly visible above the yellow blanket. She seemed to have shrunk even smaller, looking like an injured little bird with no strength left. Her throat was wrinkled, her lips chapped. She lay there motionless with her eyes closed as he came in.

'Hello,' he said quietly.

No reaction. He patted her hand. She gave a start and opened her eyes.

'I'm sorry to disturb you. My name is Anders Knutas, and I'm head of the crime division here. We've met once before.'

'I know who you are. I may be suffering from smoke inhalation, but I haven't lost my memory.' Her voice was sharp and dry.

Knutas pulled over a chair and sat down.

'Could you tell me what happened?'

The frail woman sighed and pushed herself up into a sitting position, motioning impatiently for him to help her put two pillows behind her back. Then she rang for the nurse and asked for a glass of water.

'The fire woke me up. It was horrible, just horrible. The room was very hot, and I saw thick smoke seeping in around the door. I broke the window and climbed out. After that, all I could do was sit and watch the whole house burn to the ground. With everything inside. All of my things, all of my memories . . .'

She didn't look at him as she talked. She kept her gaze fixed on the ceiling.

Tears began running down her cheeks. Knutas waited before asking any more questions. The nurse came in with the glass of water and then left again. He shifted nervously on the chair. This was an uncomfortable situation, but since Veronika showed no sign that she would stop crying, he continued with the interview.

'Did you see or hear anything suspicious? Did you notice any strangers in the area?'

'I went out to the cabin the day before yesterday. I was worn out after everything that had happened – with Viktor dying and then the police interview and all the neighbours staring at me and whispering. It was too much. I went out there to escape, and I didn't tell a soul where I was going. I don't usually set foot out in the country until Whitsun because I hate being alone, so I'm sure nobody thought that's where I'd go. But right from the start I had the feeling that someone was out there. Both when I took a walk and later when I went back to the cabin. Last night, before the fire started, I was convinced that there was a prowler on the property.'

'Did you see anything?'

'No, but it seemed that a shadow passed by outside the window. It made me nervous, and I know that I can always trust my intuition. Someone was out there. I'm sure of it.'

'What's your interpretation of what happened?'

'Some madman is out to get me. There's no doubt in my mind.'

'How can you be so sure about that?'

Finally the woman lying in bed turned to look at him. Her expression was incredulous.

'Surely it has to be obvious, even to the police,' she said caustically. 'Someone set the cabin on fire while I was inside. That means the arson was intended to kill me. I was supposed to die in the blaze. My first thought was that it had to be Viktor's wife, Elisabeth, who did it. First she killed her husband and then she tried to kill me.'

'That leads me to my next question,' said Knutas. 'During the party at the conference centre you were given a drink from an unknown admirer. Do you remember that?'

Veronika Hammar looked confused.

'Yes, I think so,' she said uncertainly.

'It was a strawberry daiquiri, non-alcoholic.'

'So?'

'Did you taste the drink?'

Silence filled the room as Knutas tensely studied the woman. She bit her lip and turned to look up at the ceiling again.

'I don't really remember . . . Did I? I had the drink in my hand, but then I had to go to the loo, so I gave it to Viktor. I don't think I even took a sip.'

'And then you parted and didn't see each other again. Is that right?'

'That's right. I . . . do you mean that . . . ?'

'The drink was probably poisoned.'

'So it was intended for me?' Veronika pressed her hands to her chest. She looked stunned, and her voice shook as she went on: 'So you're saying that the murderer was after me right from the start? That Viktor died by mistake? That's terrible!'

'Why didn't you tell us about this before, at the first interview?'

'It simply didn't occur to me. I'd forgotten all about it.'

'You said that the last time you saw Viktor was when he took your drink and you went to the ladies' room. Is that right?'

'Yes.'

'So you didn't see him again that night?'

Veronika shook her head. Knutas didn't take his eyes off her.

'Then can you explain to me why the crime scene is practically covered with your fingerprints?'

Veronika's reaction was instantaneous and unexpected.

She stared at him in dismay for several seconds before she shrieked: 'Stop it! I can't take this any more! I'm a fragile person. I can't handle this sort of thing!'

Tears poured out, and now she was wailing, not just crying. The woman's unexpected outburst nearly frightened Knutas out of his wits.

'All right, take it easy,' he urged her, sitting down on the edge of the bed. 'I'm not accusing you of anything. You must realize that we need to know exactly what happened.' He patted her clumsily on the back.

'First somebody kills the love of my life, then someone sneaks up and sets fire to my cabin, and now you're trying to make me a suspect! There bloody well has to be a limit to what a person has to endure. There has to be a limit even for me!'

'Come on now,' said Knutas in his gentlest tone of voice. 'I'm not accusing you, but you need to tell me what you were doing in that room. Did you find him there?'

Veronika sniffed and coughed. The door opened and a nurse stuck her head in.

'Everything all right in here?'

'Yes, we're fine.' Knutas waved her away.

The nurse cast an enquiring glance at Veronika, who nodded. That seemed to satisfy her, and she closed the door again.

Knutas refilled Veronika's glass with water from the small sink in the room. Then he tore off a piece of paper towel.

'All right now,' he murmured, as if speaking to a child. 'Dry your tears and then let's work this out, once and for all.'

'OK,' she whimpered. 'I didn't do anything. It's just been too much to take.'

'I understand.'

He handed her the glass and she drank the water greedily.

'Tell me what happened.'

'At the end of the party – at the conference centre, I mean – I went to get my coat from the cloakroom, and then I looked around for Viktor. I got lost in the corridors but finally I found the room downstairs where we were supposed to meet. I went inside and saw a light coming from the lift a short distance away. The doors were open.'

She covered her face with her hands, stammering out the words.

'And there he was. Lying on the floor. Not moving. I went over, thinking that he was alive. His face was turned away. But when I got closer, I realized that he was dead.'

'What did you do then?'

'I panicked. I yanked open the nearest door and rushed home. I was terrified. I thought the murderer might still be in the room and would come after me.'

'But you didn't think about calling the police?'

'I was drunk and exhausted. I wasn't thinking straight. No one knew about our affair, and I couldn't see why everybody should have to find out about it. And nothing could change what had already happened. My Viktor was dead.'

'If what you're telling me is the truth, it casts a whole new light on the case.'

'What do you mean?'

'The fire, your explanation of why your fingerprints were at the crime scene, and everything else. It strips away any suspicions we may have had about you.'

'What do you mean? That I'm no longer a suspect?'

'That's right,' said Knutas, puzzled to see that the woman lying in the bed suddenly seemed to cheer up. 'In fact, I'd say you're free and clear.'

'Are you saying that you seriously thought I was behind all this? Responsible for killing the love of my life? The man I'd finally met after an entire lifetime of dealing with miserable jerks? Because that's what you are, the whole lot of you! It's a chilling thought that the police would come to such an infantile conclusion: that I was a cold-blooded murderer who would kill my own dream. Unbelievable!'

Veronika Hammar was now sitting up in bed, shouting at the top of her lungs. Suddenly she didn't seem fragile at all.

'How dare you come here and accuse me of first one crime and then another! Here I am, suffering from smoke inhalation, the victim of arson, and I could just as easily have died in that fire. And you have the nerve to barge in here and accuse me of murder! Get out! I want you out of here! Get out, and I don't ever want to set eyes on you again! You fucking cop! Go to hell!'

Knutas was astonished not only by the woman's sudden outburst but by the strength of her voice.

Within seconds two nurses came running into the room and tried to calm their patient, who continued to scream and cry and wave her arms about.

They glared at Knutas but didn't say a word to him.

In the midst of all the commotion, he left the room, relieved to make his escape.

Elisabeth Algård was interviewed by the police on Friday, but nothing new came of it. She had an alibi for the night of the fire since she was in Stockholm with her children. They had gone to see a film, then to a restaurant, and she had stayed overnight with her daughter. Knutas had never believed that she had had anything to do with the murder; there was something about her that made him doubt she could be the killer. And his gut feeling was usually right. At least when it came to his work.

No one had witnessed the setting of the fire, but the techs found ignition points at several different places inside the cabin. They had also recovered a petrol can and some rags. A neighbour who was out walking his dog had noticed a motorcycle parked outside the Pensionat Holmhällar, which was just a stone's throw from the cabin. The bed and breakfast was closed at this time of year, and the car park was usually deserted. Unfortunately, the man couldn't identify the model of the motorcycle, nor was he able to recall the licence number.

Veronika Hammar had been discharged from the hospital and was given an escort to her home on Tranhusgatan inside the ring wall. The police had installed a security alarm and added an extra lock to her front door. For the next few days she would be under police surveillance around the clock. An unmarked police car was present at all times outside her home. The authorities were hoping that the perpetrator might turn up over the weekend when he realized that once again he had failed to kill her.

As soon as the meeting was over, Knutas and Jacobsson left to interview Veronika's son, Andreas.

Andreas Hammar owned one of the biggest sheep farms in southern Gotland. His property was on the road between Havdhem and Eke. His house wasn't built in the typical Gotland style; instead, it was a stone villa that looked more as if it belonged in Provence. The yellow stucco was flaking off in places, and the roof needed to be replaced. In front was a beautiful veranda with stately pillars and a flower garden. Two border collies were lying on the front lawn, keeping an eye on the chickens pecking at the ground.

Knutas had called ahead to tell him they were coming. Andreas Hammar said that he was very busy weighing the ewes, so they'd have to meet in the farmyard and talk as best they could while he continued to work. He didn't have time to take a break.

When Knutas and Jacobsson parked, the collies began barking and a large man appeared from around the corner of the house. He wore blue overalls and heavy boots. He peered at them from under the visor of his cap and gave them a less than enthusiastic greeting.

'Follow me in your car,' he told the officers.

They drove along a tractor path into the fields next to the house and then stopped near a gate. Hundreds of sheep were out in the pasture and they came trotting from all directions, making an enormous din. Knutas watched in fascination as the huge flock gathered in a matter of minutes and came running towards them en masse. More disciplined than soldiers, he thought. A lorry was parked near the field. Inside the pasture, two smaller areas had been fenced off. The two dogs helped herd the sheep into the first enclosure. Andreas then shoved one sheep at a time through a chute that was covered with chicken wire and into the next pen, which was so small that there was barely enough room for the single sheep with its thick coat of wool. On the floor of the pen was a scale. It was a matter of getting the sheep to stand still for the few seconds required to register the animal's weight. Jacobsson helped to steer the sheep into the chute and then hold them still while Andreas wrote down the weight in his notebook. Then he pushed the sheep back into the pasture. Some of the animals submitted to the procedure without protest, while others panicked and did everything possible to get away. Occasionally a sheep would go berserk and look as if it might break its spindly legs in a vain attempt to escape. Jacobsson had her hands full trying to help, and after a few minutes she was soaked with sweat.

'That's what happens,' Andreas explained. 'They panic as soon as they're alone. They're sensitive animals, highstrung, but smarter than most people think.'

Feeling impatient, Knutas began the interview.

'Why didn't you mention that your mother might be at the summer house when we told you that we were looking for her?'

'It never occurred to me. She never goes out there until the Whitsun holiday, because she's terribly afraid of the dark. She hates being there unless other people are around.'

Knutas cast a dubious glance at the farmer, who continued working unperturbed. For the moment he decided to accept the man's explanation and went on: 'What sort of relationship do you have with your mother?'

'Parents are parents.'

'What do you mean by that?'

'You don't have a choice who your parents are, do you? So there's really not much to think about.'

'And your siblings?'

'I hardly ever see them, and these days none of them spends much time with Mamma. Mats and Mikaela never see her at all, and Simon is depressed and has shut everyone out of his life. Including Mamma, as much as he's been able to. Mats grew up with a foster family and never had any real contact with Mamma. My sister Mikaela broke off all communication with her years ago.'

'That's what we heard. But why?'

'Hmm. I suppose she just couldn't take it any more. My mother is . . . how should I put it? Extremely demanding.'

'In what way?'

'She doesn't really have a life of her own, so she expects her children to fill the void. She phones every five minutes, asking for help with all sorts of things. As if she constantly needs to be acknowledged. But the problem is that even if you do a lot for her, it's never enough. She always wants more. She also interferes in our lives and has an opinion about absolutely everything, from what to name a child to which curtains are best suited to a kitchen. I think Mikaela finally had enough. It's as simple as that. Mamma takes up a lot of room and sucks up too much energy. My sister couldn't stand it any more. She has her own family to think about, her own children. She needs to spend her time and energy on them.'

Knutas was surprised at how well the farmer was able to express himself. The next second he was ashamed for having such a stereotyped view of the man.

'What about Simon?'

'Well, he has his own story. A while back he split up with his live-in girlfriend Katrina, and after that he sank into a deep depression. He's been living temporarily in a flat in Stockholm that belongs to a friend. I don't think he's capable of doing much of anything at the moment.'

'Do you know where he is right now?'

'I have no idea. Sometimes he disappears for a while. No one knows where he goes.'

'So what about you? How do you deal with your mother if she's so difficult?'

'Who said that I deal with her? I don't think anybody can handle that woman.'

He shook his head as he leaned forward to check the tag on the ear of the next sheep to be weighed.

'It's nothing but constant trouble with Mamma, and it never ends. Whenever one problem is solved, the next one arrives like a letter in the post.'

'How often do you see each other?'

'Every once in a while, usually only if I stop by to have coffee with her. We talk about meaningless things for an hour, and then I leave. I just let all her drivel run off me like water off a duck's back. Simon and Mikaela have had a harder time of it. They're like sponges, soaking up all her complaints. They end up feeling annoyed and insulted. They have a symbiotic relationship with her. If she feels bad, they do too; if she's happy, then they are too. It's never been like that for me.'

'Why do you think that is?'

'Maybe because I'm older and had time to get to know Pappa before my parents were divorced and he disappeared out of our lives. I managed to form my own impression of him, and of Mamma and their relationship. I've always known that things weren't nearly as one-sided as Mamma tries to make them out to be.'

'What do you mean?'

'I can't explain it. And I don't really want to talk about it.'

'Do you know whether your mother has ever received any threats, or whether someone would want to harm her?'

'Threats? I've never heard about anything like that. And she would have mentioned it, because she always wants to get us involved in the smallest details of her daily life. Like telling us that she burned the soup or that she can't find her slippers.'

'What about someone who might want to harm her?'

Andreas gave Knutas an inscrutable look.

'A person may have the will, but that's not always enough,' he said tersely.

Then he went back to his work. The next sheep was waiting to be weighed.

Walpurgis Eve was the most beautiful it had been in years. Usually the day was cold with a strong wind, but this time the sun was shining and it was so warm that it felt as if summer was just around the corner.

Johan had worked all weekend putting together reports for both Regional News and the national news broadcasts, so he'd been given the day off. It had been hectic for both Johan and Pia after Alexander Almlöv died. The outcry about the assault case had overshadowed the murder of Viktor Algård. Big demonstrations were staged in Visby, protesting against violence and the politicians' lack of interest in providing services for young people. Instead, they had voted to shut down recreation centres, lay off school counsellors and cut funding for education, after-school programmes and sports activities. The investment in the new conference centre had once again come under fire. How could anyone justify spending millions of kronor for that sort of building when the island's young people had nowhere to go when they weren't in school?

Johan and Pia had compiled reports that were broadcast as part of the national news seen all over Sweden. The series they had planned was now put on the fast track; at the same time, it was given much more space in the news programmes than they could ever have imagined. Johan noted with satisfaction that so much attention was being focused on youth violence that now all the editorial pages and news programmes were concentrating on how to deal with the problem. But everything came at a price. This time it had cost a sixteen-year-old boy his life.

Johan had hardly even had time to miss Emma and Elin. But now that he was on his way out to Fårö, he could barely contain himself. He stood on the deck of the ferry with the sea wind blowing in his face, finally relaxed enough that he could stop thinking about work. He was going to devote himself to what was most important – namely, his family.

Emma's parents lived at the northernmost tip of the island, near the great sand dune called Norsta Auren. Their white limestone house stood all alone, with only a low wall separating the property from the beach. On one side was a bird promontory, which attracted ornithologists wanting to study the enormous number of seabirds that occupied the spit of land. On the other side of the house was the long, sandy beach, which extended for several kilometres. The light-coloured, fine-grained sand on the beach, which was several hundred metres wide in places, reminded visitors of sun-drenched July days in the Caribbean or South Pacific. The shoreline curved in a gentle arc, reaching all the way to the lighthouse, which was Fårö's furthest outpost.

When Johan turned his car on to the bumpy, narrow road leading to the house, Emma and Elin came walking towards him, hand in hand. He stopped the car and jumped out. He saw Elin's joyous face and Emma's warm eyes. He pulled both of them into his arms, giving them a big hug.

After dinner with Emma's parents, they took a bike ride out to Ekeviken, a lovely beach and summer-house area about a kilometre to the south. All the preparations for Walpurgis Eve had been carefully made, and the bonfire would be lit at eight o'clock. During the past month, people who lived in the vicinity had gathered wood for the pyre, which now loomed, tall and stately, in the middle of the beach. The entire island was involved in the celebration. Small booths set up along the shore were selling sausages, coffee and Gotland specialities such as leg of mutton, saffron pancakes, honey and blue raspberry jam. The vendors were also offering lambskins, ceramics and other handicrafts made on the island. Children dashed about, tossing as many branches as they could find on to the pyre before it was lit.

A choir of young people wearing their white

graduation caps was singing 'Winter Spills Out of Our Mountains'. Not that there were any real mountains on Gotland. The highest point was Lojsta Heath, which was no more than 82 metres above sea level.

Johan squeezed Emma's hand. This holiday was something he sorely needed.

The last notes of the song faded, and then a former cabinet minister, who lived on Fårö in the summertime, climbed up on the improvised stage. He was a tall, blond and athletic man in his forties who seemed to have everything going for him. He was youthful, charming and also terribly handsome, at least according to the ladies, including Emma. The hundred or so people who had gathered fell silent, turning their attention to the stage. Even the kids who had been romping around with their dogs stopped to listen. There was something magical about the man; with his golden locks and hand-knitted sweater, he seemed the very epitome of the healthy, sporty and confident Swede. As if he'd stepped right out of the pages of a Dressmann catalogue, thought Johan sourly.

Of course his speech was a big hit, filled as it was with warmth and a sense of commitment. Johan was amused to see that Emma looked utterly enraptured as she applauded along with everyone else.

The former cabinet minister concluded his performance by tossing the first burning torch on to the pyre while the choir sang another rendition of their springtime song. Everyone joined in, and an enchanted mood settled over the crowd. The fire rose up towards the sky, which had now grown dark, and the flames glittered in the reflection on the water's surface. The words of the song drifted out over the sea, and Johan was again filled with the joy of being a family man. He hadn't been to a Walpurgis Eve celebration since he was a boy. He put his arm around Emma and kissed the top of her head.

Her hair smelled of shampoo and wood smoke.

Early afternoon. The rain is beating against the windowpanes.

I was woken a moment ago by the insistent beeping of a refuse lorry backing up. It was entering the ugly alleyway outside my bedroom window.

I have a merciless encounter with my reflection in the bathroom mirror. My face is mute and blank. I'm trying to spare myself. My eyes are two black stones, without intensity or life. My lips are dry and cracked from not speaking or having contact with anyone else. The pills I take dry out my body from the inside, and my skin feels more taut every day that passes. My hands are chapped. As my body dries up, my brain is also shrivelling. I'm finding it increasingly hard to keep my thoughts straight; they keep merging, creating incomprehensible patterns inside my head, impossible to dissect. In most cases, I just leave them there in a tangled heap, like a ball of yarn that has unrolled and then become hopelessly snarled. Impenetrable.

*

I've been sitting in the kitchen, watching the refuse lorry and all the activity surrounding that rumbling behemoth that is now blocking the entire street. The kitchen window faces the same alley. Sometimes it's liberating not to look at the view that's visible from all the other windows in the flat.

Two men in overalls come out of the back door of the restaurant. They fling big black bags into the maw of the lorry. Imagine if you could do the same thing with your own shit. Just dump it somewhere and then start over afresh. Shit you never asked for, which was simply foisted upon you. And there was nothing you could do to escape it.

On the other side of the alley I can see people in the windows. Office drones at their desks, staring at their computers. Every now and then they pick up the phone, lean back and stare listlessly out of the window. They drink endless cups of coffee, pick their noses, unaware that they're being watched. One man has a habit of sticking his hand down his crotch while he talks on the phone. Inside the waistband of his dapper-looking suit trousers. Then he holds his hand up to his nose. People are disgusting.

What sort of lives do they have, those people in that office? Who is loved or not loved? Are any of them happy? Do they like each other? I doubt it. People meet, have dinner together, go to various social functions, but how many of them really enjoy spending time with one another?

Like Mamma and my siblings. Birthday parties, Christmas Eve celebrations, the obligatory flower bouquets, comments, compliments. I used to think they were fun, but now I see things much more clearly. Do my siblings share my view? When I was younger, I took that for granted. Now I see reality differently. There are too many obstacles. We were never encouraged to take care of each other, to support one another. Instead, Mamma split us apart, making us feel like three isolated islands without any connection to each other, which made us all the more dependent on her.

Of course that was exactly what she wanted.

I don't know how many times she has told me how wonderful my sister is and how much she loves her. More than anyone else. 'She's the apple of my eye,' she once said to me, giving me an intent look. Then what does that make me? How does she expect me to respond? What does she want me to say, feel, think?

On the other hand, she doesn't hesitate to complain, loud and clear. 'I can't for the life of me understand how he could say something like that to me, his own mother. Can you understand it? When I went to visit him, at the dinner table I asked him for some pickles, and all he said was: They're in the fridge. Can you imagine that? I was supposed to get up and go and look for them myself in the refrigerator! I would never have treated my own mother that way. Another time I asked your sister to return the rug that I gave her because I decided it would look so nice in the living room now that I've had it repainted. But she got furious and told me it was hers to keep. Good Lord, after all I've done for her, and that's the thanks I get?'

One day I have to listen to how adorable my siblings are; the next day I'm expected to comfort my mother because they've treated her so badly. And worst of all, they show her no gratitude. The same story, year in and year out. It never ends.

On top of everything else, we're expected to put up with her constant reminders of what she has done for us. We're supposed to be so bloody grateful, because of all the sacrifices she has made.

Mamma has always made it perfectly clear that she could have been a big star if it weren't for us. She once sang on the radio, after all. If she hadn't given up her career for her children, she could have been another Birgitta Andersson or Lill Lindfors. She was so gifted when she was young. A great dramatic talent. And she could really sing. She was simply amazing – none of her siblings could measure up to her. She was special. But no one saw her greatness, and no one discovered her glory. She received no encouragement at home. And we felt sorry for her, of course. How awful that nobody realized what a promising artist Mamma was. What an awful fate to give birth to us and then be forced to live on a desolate island in the Baltic, far from all the glamour and opportunities in the capital. The fact that things had gone relatively well for all of us – meaning that we had jobs and hadn't ended up as drug addicts – was solely due to her efforts. If she hadn't sacrificed herself like a lamb on the altar and squandered her unique talents on three snot-nosed kids, well . . .

In spite of how self-absorbed my mother was, for years I felt a great admiration for her. I hate duplicity. Even today, it's not something I've been able to master.

I picture her in my mind. My beautiful mother who would hug me and kiss me and love me. And in the next second crush me. A remark, a glance, an expression of disapproval. She had dreams; she encouraged me to travel, to experience things and enjoy life. She was ill but she still helped me with my homework. Stroked my hair. Made me hot cocoa. What happened to all that?

We enjoying clowning around as we cleaned, and Mamma would laugh so hard that she had to double over when I teased her with the hose of the vacuum cleaner. I loved to play the buffoon for her. The best thing I knew was making her laugh.

She used to dance in the living room to Miriam Makeba's song 'Pata Pata'. Turning and spinning, her eyes closed as she twirled the skirt of her dress. She loved Mikis Theodorakis, Lill Lindfors and Gösta Linderholm. She sang loudly as she did the cleaning.

And she looked so cute with a chic scarf wrapped around her blond hair, with those dark eyebrows of hers, and those pink lips.

She was always short of cash, but she liked to set the table with nice things and make it cosy with lighted candles. She made pizza capricciosa, she baked rolls, and she booked a holiday in the mountains even though we really couldn't afford it. She wanted us to learn to ski, she said.

On Saturdays we would go into town to shop for groceries and buy a treat at the pastry shop. Mamma would buy fancy clothes for herself in the boutiques. We were allowed to drink Cokes through a straw and eat coconut buns. She laughed loudly, she always sang in the car, and she made delicious ham sandwiches to take to the beach. I loved to place my ear against her flat stomach, which always gurgled merrily. And she smelled so good. The skin under her chin was soft and smooth, and I felt so warm when she hugged me.

Her sobbing was heartbreaking. It split me apart.

When I was little, I thought she was perfect – an ideal human being. I was never ashamed of her. And everyone thought she looked so young. In my eyes, she was the most magnificent person in the whole world.

I don't know what happened after that.

*

Whenever Mamma calls, I'm filled with sorrow, tenderness and loathing. I have to stop myself from slamming down the phone when I hear her voice. I force myself to suffer through the conversation. Limit my replies to a few words. Allow her to dump all of her complaints on me, as usual. I hold the receiver several centimetres away from my ear and try to think about something else. But my patience is wearing thin. The conversations have been getting shorter. I can't stand to listen to her voice.

Soon I won't be able to control myself any longer.

That inescapable thought keeps rumbling in the back of my mind, like an approaching thunderstorm. I dread what might happen when the storm breaks loose. When the lightning flashes in the sky and the clouds open up to send rain down upon us. Then there will be no turning back. Then all hope will be lost.

And then there will be only one option if I'm going to be free.

Knutas celebrated Walpurgis Eve with his family at the cottage in Lickershamn. They had a relaxing holiday playing cards, making a fire in the fireplace, eating good food, and taking walks along the shore. Just the four of them.

Normally they spent the Walpurgis holiday with good friends, but this year he and Lina had declined all invitations. Much to the disappointment of his elderly parents, they had even decided against the traditional 1 May dinner at their farm. And the twins weren't allowed to bring along any friends, as they usually did. Knutas and Lina had agreed that they needed to shut out everything else so the family could spend some time together.

Knutas was nervous before they left, anxious about how things would go. He was uncertain how to act in order to regain Nils's trust. If that was even possible. The stunned despair that he'd felt immediately after the big scene with his son had gradually subsided. But Nils's words had left deep wounds, and he wondered if they'd ever heal.

After the fight they had both been polite but cautious towards each other. Knutas didn't know if it would be wise to broach the subject again, or whether that might just make matters worse. He wished that Nils would take the first step towards reconciliation. When the kids were younger, he'd made sure he had a talk with them after he had yelled at them or they had argued. It was his responsibility as an adult to make things good again. He had always thought that the process of reconciliation was very important. But now he was unsure what would be best. It felt as if everything had been turned upside down. Deep in his heart, he probably thought that Nils should apologize for his cruel words. Provided he hadn't really meant what he'd said, of course. But maybe he did. Knutas felt ill at the thought.

He wondered how this breach of trust had come about. He and Lina seldom fought, he didn't have any sort of addiction problem, and he wasn't a violent man. They had a good life together; he did his job and paid the bills. There was always food on the table, and they always attended the parent-teacher meetings at school. The family took a holiday trip every year, and they spent time at their summer cottage. They seldom said no if the children wanted money for the cinema or asked if they could invite friends home. How much could realistically be expected of parents?

He thought that he was always willing to listen to his kids. He made a point of asking them about school and sports practice. But he couldn't very well have deep, therapeutic conversations with the kids every night before bed. That would be intolerable.

Apparently Nils had an entirely different view of things. Maybe even different from Petra. Knutas hadn't yet dared ask his daughter about that. All he could do at the moment was to try to be as nice a father as he could be. Without acting too pushy.

He was sure that with time things would get better.

At any rate, the Walpurgis holiday had been pleasant and calm. There were no arguments, not even any minor spats between the twins. It was as if they were both feeling a bit subdued after what had happened. They played cards in the evening, and Nils even laughed once in a while. Each time he did, Knutas felt happy for a moment, but then his uneasiness returned. He noticed every gesture and glance, and tried to interpret each one.

He was finding it hard to really relax.

On the first day back at work after the holiday, Knutas walked from police headquarters over to where Veronika Hammar lived on Tranhusgatan. The sun was out, and Visby's streets were practically deserted. At this time of year the city is at its loveliest, he thought as he passed the high cliff. From there he had a view of the sea and the horizon. In the foreground stood the magnificent cathedral amid a cluster of picturesque buildings, medieval ruins and winding lanes. He went up the cathedral steps and continued along Biskopsgränd, past the ruins of St Clemens and over to Tranhusgatan, which ran parallel to the Botanical Gardens. Veronika lived in a small, whitewashed house that looked as if it had been built in the early 1900s. There was no one in sight. The police surveillance had been discontinued on the previous day, even though Knutas had tried to convince the county police commissioner to keep it in place until the end of the week. He was given the usual answer: lack of resources.

Knutas was dreading this meeting with Veronika

Hammar, considering her outburst the last time he'd seen her. But he had still decided to go alone. If there were two officers, she might feel at a disadvantage, and he realized that with this particular woman it was essential to tread lightly. He had phoned her yesterday to say that he would be coming to see her. She had sounded friendly and amenable, as if she'd completely forgotten how their last meeting had ended.

He went up to the front door and rang the bell. No answer. He rang three more times and was just about to give up when the door opened a few inches.

'I wanted to make sure who it was first. They took away the police surveillance, those stingy bastards,' explained Veronika Hammar, looking at Knutas with a dull expression. Her hair was limp and lank. She was wearing an ugly pair of sweatpants and an old spotted cardigan that was missing its belt. This woman who was usually so elegantly attired looked as if she'd simply given up.

He greeted her politely, hoping that she wouldn't see how concerned he was about her appearance. She led the way into the house. They walked through a lovely living room with ceiling beams and floral-patterned curtains and continued out to the terrace at the back. The sun was shining on the small courtyard, and they sat down at a patio table.

'How are you doing?' he asked.

Veronika smiled wanly.

'Well, I'll live. At least I hope so.'

Knutas studied her in silence as she served the coffee from an old-fashioned ceramic pot adorned with roses. He noticed that the cup she handed him wasn't quite clean, but he took a sip anyway as he gathered his thoughts. Veronika seemed almost bewildered. The coffee was weak and barely lukewarm.

'How have things been going since you got out of hospital?'

'Fine. Thanks for asking.'

Knutas frowned. The impression he was getting from Veronika indicated that things were far from fine.

'Have you noticed any strangers around here, or anything suspicious?'

'You wouldn't believe how many strange and unsavoury people there are wandering about. I haven't wanted to leave the house since I got back from hospital.'

'So how have you been managing?'

'I ask my son, Andreas, to get groceries for me. He's the only child that I have here on Gotland.'

She pressed her lips together to keep them from quivering. Then she pulled a pack of cigarettes out of her cardigan pocket and lit one. Knutas noticed that her hand was shaking.

'Well, it was actually your children that I wanted to talk to you about. How would you describe your relationship with them?'

'I live for my children and always have. They're a real

blessing, and I'm so lucky to have them. Otherwise I probably wouldn't have lasted this long.'

Knutas shifted position uneasily.

'Why don't we start with Andreas. How do you view your relationship with him?'

'It's wonderful. He's my safety net. I can always count on him, no matter what happens. He's been a bachelor all these years since he moved away from home, but we've always had each other, and that has been a great support for me.'

'So you're saying that you've been single all these years too?'

Veronika gave him a disapproving look.

'More or less, after I got divorced. Yes, I think you could say that.'

'But weren't you having an affair with Viktor Algård?'

'My dear inspector, that had been going on for only a couple of months. We'd just met.'

Knutas stared at her pensively. When they last spoke, she had described Viktor as the love of her life and claimed that they were on the verge of getting married.

'What about your other children? Simon, for example?'

'He's the one I'm closest to. We think so much alike, Simon and I. We understand each other.'

'But he lives in Stockholm now.'

'That's just temporary. He had to get away for a while, you see. Away from that awful Polish woman he was living with. Or was she Hungarian? She treated him horribly, to tell you the truth. I could tell from the start that it wasn't going to last.'

'Why was that?'

She grimaced, her expression almost spiteful.

'Well, my dear. First of all, they were polar opposites. Simon is a gentle and open person, just like me. But that Katrina was harsh and silent and uptight. Always sullen and surly. I'm really glad he's rid of her.'

'From what I understand, he's not doing very well.'

'And no wonder. She broke his spirit over the years. She was terribly domineering, and he was always having to dance to her tune. She ruled that home with an iron hand. You could see that the minute you stepped in the door. I'm sure he'll be feeling better soon. And then he'll come back here where he belongs. I've told him that he can live with me. I have plenty of room, you know.'

'How often do you speak to each other?'

'Every day on the phone.'

'Every day?'

'Yes. Ours is a special relationship. We understand each other. We're on the same wavelength. He always knows what I mean. But it's not good for him to be all alone over there in Stockholm.'

'If you get along so well, why doesn't he move in with you now? Then he'd be closer to his own son. What's stopping him?'

'My dear sir, that's not really so surprising, is it? Simon

is suffering from depression. He needs peace and quiet for a while. But soon he'll be back on his feet, and then he'll move back over here. I'm convinced of that.'

'How long has he been gone?'

'I don't really remember. Now wait a minute, I think it's been since Christmas.'

'So over four months.'

Veronika Hammar didn't reply. Her lips were pressed so tight that they were no more than a thin line.

'What about your daughter Mikaela? How often do you see each other?'

'Ah, yes, Mikaela.' She sighed a bit and then smiled again. 'My little daughter. She's always gone her own way.'

'She lives quite a distance from here. Is it difficult to stay in contact?'

'Difficult? Why should it be difficult? Some people have children living in Australia.'

'From what I understand, you never see each other. Is that right?'

'What do you mean? Why wouldn't I be in touch with my daughter? That's the most absurd thing I've ever heard.'

She stood up abruptly and gathered up the coffee cups. Without a word she carried the dishes into the house. Knutas waited as he tried to decide how to proceed without risking another outburst. The sun was hot, and he was sweating under his jacket. He suddenly felt trapped in the small courtyard and wanted to leave. There was something very unpleasant about Veronika Hammar. She was unpredictable. It was impossible to foresee how she was going to react. Why had she denied so strongly that her daughter had broken off their relationship?

That was as far as he got with his muddled thought before Veronika appeared in the doorway, her expression tense.

'I'd like you to leave now,' she said, sounding stressed.

'But I do have a few more questions,' Knutas said. 'How are things with your eldest son, Mats?'

A cloud passed over Veronika's face. She had to gasp for air before she repeated her demand.

'Didn't you hear what I said? Get out of my house. Now,' she snarled, spraying saliva.

Knutas stared at her in astonishment. He saw a hint of insanity in her eyes. This woman is off her rocker, he thought.

He stood up and slipped past her.

'Thanks for the coffee,' he said quietly.

After his meeting with Veronika Hammar, Knutas rang Jacobsson at the police station. She told him that everything was going smoothly, and his presence wasn't immediately needed. He decided to pick up his car at headquarters and drive out to have a look at the site of the fire near Holmhällar. The techs had finished their search of the area without finding anything new, other than to reinforce the theory that the fire was the work of an arsonist. It had apparently started in the kitchen, which indicated that the perp had also been inside the cabin.

Knutas was frustrated by the fact that they didn't have the faintest lead on a possible suspect. The perpetrator's shadow kept dancing before his eyes but he couldn't distinguish any features. There was no pattern. First a man was poisoned to death, and by all indications it was the wrong victim who had died. Now they were dealing with an attempted murder by arson. This was clearly not someone who was a hardened criminal or a cunning murderer. In fact, all the circumstances pointed to someone whose actions were prompted by intense emotions, someone who had a strong personal connection to Veronika Hammar. Maybe it's one of her children, thought Knutas. Or else she has a relationship with somebody that we don't know about yet. He needed to talk to her again. And her children too. He would have preferred to meet all four of them in person, but her son Simon refused to answer any phone calls. And both Mats and Mikaela were still away.

Knutas drove south along the coast road. It was a beautiful day, offering a hint of the summer that would soon arrive. The birches were sprouting leaves, and spring flowers were just starting to come up along the road.

As he approached the exit for Holmhällar, he happened to think about Sten Bergström. Had anyone interviewed the man again? Knutas reminded himself to check with Rylander. Viktor Algård's former competitor lived only a kilometre or so from the summer-house area where the fire had occurred. Was that just a coincidence? Maybe Bergström's fight with Algård over clients was not the only thing he was hostile about. He was about the same age as Veronika Hammar, and they were practically neighbours out here in the country. When they interviewed Bergström, he and Karin had confined their questions to the conflict between the two companies owned by Algård and Bergström. Could there be something else behind their animosity?

There was one other person that he kept thinking

about: Elisabeth Algård. After the initial interview, he had essentially crossed her name off the list of potential suspects. She did have an alibi for the night of the fire, but was it possible that he had let her off too easily? He was well aware that it could be disastrous for a detective to lock himself into one line of thought at the beginning of an investigation.

The police in Stockholm had finally got hold of Veronika's son, Simon, and had gone over to talk to him. The interview had produced very little. The officers reported that he seemed physically weak and in a much too fragile psychological state to have committed a murder. That's one way of looking at it, thought Knutas sarcastically. Normally the conclusion would be just the opposite. People committed murder precisely because they were in a fragile psychological state.

Before reaching the Holmhällar bed and breakfast, he turned on to a narrow forest road. The area around the cabin was still cordoned off.

Knutas spent a long time walking through the rubble on Veronika Hammar's property. All that remained of the cabin were the soot-covered foundations. He looked in the direction of the sea. It wasn't visible from where he stood, but he could hear the roar of the surf. Knutas tried to conjure up the image of Veronika in this setting. Her contorted face appeared before him, as she'd looked during her outburst at the hospital. An emotionally unstable woman. Unpredictable and perhaps dangerous. Could she be the person behind all of this? He toyed with that thought as he made his way over to the charred remains of the cabin. A woman could easily have killed Viktor Algård. Death by poisoning required no physical strength and it was quick and effective, with no blood.

Veronika had a complicated relationship with her children, and that was putting it mildly. Her parents were dead, as was her ex-husband who was father to three of the children. When Jacobsson had looked closer into Veronika's family history, she had been unable to find out who was the father of the eldest son, Mats. Veronika had attended the party at the conference centre, and she had just started having an affair with the victim. Her art studio was located in the courtyard where Algård had his own pied-à-terre. She had definitely been at the crime scene, since her fingerprints were everywhere. She could have staged the whole episode with the cocktail. It was true that the bartender had confirmed that he'd served her a drink, but who was to say that Veronika hadn't asked someone to make the request and then doctored the drink herself?

And she might have a good motive. Maybe Viktor Algård had changed his mind and decided to stay with his wife. Jealousy was a common reason behind a murder.

An enraged woman who felt hurt, insulted, and betrayed – and on top of all that was emotionally unstable – might be capable of anything. That sort of person could be seriously dangerous.

Knutas scanned the scene of destruction. Had Veronika Hammar gone so far as to sacrifice her own cabin in order to fool the police?

Questions whirled through his mind.

Feeling discouraged, he walked back to his car.

When Knutas returned from his expedition to Holmhällar, he ate a late lunch at his desk, wolfing down two cheese sandwiches with a cup of coffee. Then he slowly spun his chair as he filled his pipe. He was trying to gather all the impressions from the day, all the thoughts he'd had about Veronika Hammar's odd personality.

The police had interviewed two of her sons. Neither of them had an alibi. What sort of motive could Andreas possibly have?

The relationship between him and his mother seemed basically chilly and sporadic, but it wasn't any worse than in many other families. He hadn't been willing to say very much during the interview.

Through an aid worker in Bolivia, Jacobsson had finally managed to get in touch with the daughter, Mikaela. She seemed to have left behind both Gotland and her mother for good. A few years back she had broken off all contact with Veronika and had never tried to resume their relationship. She said that she simply couldn't take any more of her mother's martyr act, which wreaked havoc with her own life and had done so ever since she was a child. Of the four children, she was the most candid, explaining that her mother had nearly annihilated her. Veronika lacked any sense of boundaries, and she had prevented Mikaela from living her own life. Or rather, a decent life, as the daughter expressed it.

As a teenager, Mikaela had started cutting herself, and she had also been anorexic for many years. She didn't want to risk developing any more psychological problems now that she was responsible for her own children.

Was it possible that she might have decided to take her revenge? She'd been away ever since her mother's cabin had burned to the ground. Was that merely a coincidence, or was it actually part of a carefully devised plan? Knutas still hadn't met her in person. She was expected home on the following day. Veronika's eldest son Mats was also supposed to come home from his trip abroad within the next few days.

The youngest son Simon was perhaps the most likely candidate. He had closed up like a clam when the police in Stockholm had tried to interview him, but his former live-in girlfriend, Katrina, had been more than willing to talk about him. She said that she'd left Simon several months ago because she realized that his mother occupied too big a place in their life. And he was too weak to free himself from Veronika, always giving her priority over Katrina and their son Daniel. Finally she had come to the conclusion that things were never going to change. Simon then fled to Stockholm, where he was living in a borrowed flat. And he had sunk into a deep depression.

Knutas felt a strong urge to meet Veronika Hammar's other children. He was literally itching with impatience.

He glanced at the clock. It was four fifteen.

There was still time.

I'll never forget that day. The day when everything fell apart. I had left work around four in order to pick up Daniel from the day-care centre by four thirty. It was already dark. Christmas was approaching and everyone had lit the Advent stars that hung in the windows. To the delight of the children, it had been snowing for several days. Daniel was completely worn out after playing outside all day. They had gone sledding on the little hill behind the centre and made snowmen that were lined up in the snow-covered yard.

Daniel was allowed to sit in the pushchair all the way to the Konsum supermarket. We had to buy groceries because I was planning to make Falun sausages with macaroni. When we got home, I put my son in front of the TV to watch cartoons while I cooked. Katrina came home just before dinner was ready. When I gave her a hug in the doorway, I noticed that she looked pale and tired. But who doesn't these days?

After dinner she let me relax while she cleared the table and filled the dishwasher. I watched her in silence. We never really talked much to each other. I thought that was just fine. I worked as a mechanic and she was a personal assistant. We lived a quiet life in a flat on Bogegatan. Katrina was from Hungary and had been in Sweden only six months when we met at the home of one of my co-workers. She was dark-haired and beautiful. The first thing I noticed about her was her smile. Those red lips and the dark eye make-up. Women on Gotland didn't usually wear that much make-up. She was tall and slender, and she smiled at everyone. I'd never had a long-term relationship before, and hadn't really been interested in having one. I liked doing my own thing without interference from anyone else. I enjoyed the silence in my flat and the solitude of eating my meals in front of the TV. At work, I kept to myself. I was doing fine, and nobody complained. I spent much of my free time at the gym, working out for several hours every other day. Those gleaming machines were my best friends. I exercised so hard that my body practically screamed, but I enjoyed the feeling of straining my muscles to the limit. That was how I could empty my mind of all thoughts and relax completely. Body-building was my lifeline. Maybe it was my body that Katrina fell for. I can't help thinking that was the case, even though I know it sounds bitter and most likely wasn't true at all.

After we put Daniel to bed, we had our coffee in front of the TV, as usual. When the Swedish programme that we always watched was over, Katrina got up from the sofa and turned off the TV. 'There's something I want to talk to you about,' she said. I felt a jolt of excitement. My first thought was that she was pregnant again. I was eager to have another child and kept waiting for that to happen. Maybe a little sister for Daniel. A daughter. We hadn't used any contraception after Daniel was born, and he would soon be three. I remember closing my eyes briefly, wanting to hold this moment in my heart. My eyes had filled with tears even before she came back to the sofa and sat down beside me.

She seemed to be having a hard time finding the right words. She took my hand and looked at me with a serious expression. Her face was almost translucent. I was filled with tenderness, and my gaze fell on her waist. Her raspberry-coloured T-shirt was tucked into her jeans and she wore a narrow, black belt. Very chic, as always. Nothing showed. Yet. Then she broke the silence. She spoke slowly, hesitantly. As if the words came from far away.

'This isn't going to work any more.'

I stared at her, uncomprehending. She looked away and swallowed hard. Then she cleared her throat and went on.

'I love you so much. That's not it. But we're too different. Daniel and I aren't a priority for you, and you allow your mother to take up too much space. She keeps worming her way into our life and I can't take it any longer. I always have to share you with her. The minute she calls for help, you rush right over there. Every weekend she comes here. She's poisoning our life. She never gives us any peace. Sometimes you talk to her four or five times in one day. I feel sick to my stomach every time the phone rings, because I'm afraid it's your mother. I've tried to tell you this so many times before, but you never take it seriously. You just brush my concern aside. You let her intrude on our plans, you allow her to be rude to me, and you let her totally control you. I can't take it any more. We can't even have a holiday in peace. You're a wonderful father to Daniel. That's not it. It really isn't.'

She squeezed my hand as if to underscore her words.

'It's because you either won't or can't free yourself from your mother in order to live your own life. I'm not saying that you should ignore her completely, but you need to see less of her. Not let her take up so much of your time. But you refuse to listen to me, and I don't want to do this any more. I give up. You think she's more important than I am. You think of her as the most important member of the family, not me and Daniel. I've been disappointed so many times, and it's never going to change. I've been over and over this in my mind, thinking that we should stay together for Daniel's sake, but I've decided that it's not good for him if things are so bad between you and me. Children notice that sort of thing. We can share taking care of him. It'll be fine. He can stay with you every other week. The important thing is that we remain friends even though we split up.'

The words poured out of her, as if she had planned in advance exactly what she wanted to say. Practised, as if she were giving a bloody speech. I sat there paralysed. Her words rolled over me like tanks, crushing me.

'I've been thinking about this for a long time, and now I've made up my mind. This isn't going to work any more,' she repeated. 'I'm going to stay with Sanna tonight. I've already packed a suitcase.' She nodded towards the front hall. 'We'll talk more about this tomorrow. I've taken a few days off from my job, and I'm going to take Daniel with me so you can think about things in peace and quiet.'

She squeezed my hand again, as if asking for my approval. Wanting to know that I agreed. That I wanted the same thing. My lips felt dry; they refused to move. Not a word came out of my mouth. When she closed the door I was still sitting on the sofa in the exact same position, staring dry-eyed at the blank TV screen.

And at my shattered world.

The plane landed at Bromma airport at five thirty. Jacobsson had instantly agreed to go to Stockholm with Knutas, which made him happy. Whenever it was necessary to conduct sensitive interviews, it was best to have a colleague along, especially someone he trusted. And he didn't know the officers in Stockholm very well. He'd been in contact with Mikaela Hammar's husband to warn him that they would be paying his wife a visit the following day. That was fine, even though she was expected home from her trip to South America that same day. Her plane was due to arrive at seven in the morning. Knutas and Jacobsson were going to rent a car and drive out to Vätö, which was about a hundred kilometres from Stockholm. They agreed to meet with Mikaela around noon.

The setting sun cast a crimson glow over the capital. Their taxi crept its way through the city streets. The rush-hour traffic was heavy, so they had plenty of time to look out of the window. Everywhere they saw people sitting at outdoor cafés and restaurants.

'I can't believe there are so many people. It's way too crowded,' said Knutas.

'Pretty soon it's going to look like this in Visby too.'

Jacobsson gave him a crooked smile. She seemed more relaxed than usual.

The cab dropped them off at a grand-looking building on Kornhamnstorg in Gamla Stan, the old part of the city. Surrounding the square, like beads on a necklace, were countless outdoor restaurants filled with people dressed in summer attire who were enjoying a drink as they sat in the fading sunshine after work. Right across from them was Skeppsbron where the ferryboat had just pulled away, headed for the verdant island and the zoo across the water. Near the Karl Johan sluice a few boating enthusiasts, getting a head start on the season, sat in their vessels, waiting to pass into the locks. From there their boats would be lowered to the water level of Saltsjön. They were probably going out to the archipelago for the weekend since the weather was so nice.

Knutas tapped in the code on the door of the block of flats. Then they took the lift to the fifth floor.

Knutas thought Simon Hammar looked younger than his thirty-three years, and he bore a striking resemblance to his mother. He was dressed in worn jeans and a wrinkled T-shirt.

'Come in,' he said listlessly, and he turned to lead the way.

It was a typical early-twentieth-century flat. The high ceiling embellished with plasterwork, the wainscoting which reached halfway up the walls and the hardwood floor all suited the style of the building. The rooms were lined up along one side, providing a fabulous view of both lakes, Mälaren and Saltsjön. Knutas and Jacobsson were amazed when they stepped inside the magnificent living room. They went over to the window to look at the view.

They felt as if they were truly standing in the centre of Stockholm. Jacobsson, who knew much more about the city than Knutas did, pointed out the characteristic red-brick Laurinska building with its pinnacles and turrets situated on Mariaberget, the yellow façade of Södra Theatre near Mosebacke Square, and the statue of Karl XIV Johan seated on his horse and proudly gesturing towards the city.

The furniture in the living room, which easily measured over 45 square metres, consisted solely of a sofa, coffee table and two armchairs. An old-fashioned tile stove stood in one corner. The room was so empty that any sound echoed. They sat down around the coffee table. Even though it was hot and stuffy in the flat, their host offered them nothing to drink.

Simon Hammar immediately lit a cigarette.

'Would it be possible to open a window?' asked Knutas.

'Can't do that. Too noisy.'

Knutas and Jacobsson exchanged glances. This wasn't going to be easy. Knutas decided to get right to the point.

'Do you know whether your mother has any enemies – someone who might wish to harm her?'

Simon stared at the police officers, his expression inscrutable.

'No. Why do you ask?'

'We think her life is in danger. We have reason to believe that someone is trying to kill her. Her boyfriend, Viktor Algård, was murdered, but all indications are that he wasn't the intended victim. We think the killer was after your mother. And then someone tried to kill her by burning down her cabin.'

'Viktor Algård? He and Mamma were an item?'

'Yes.'

Simon managed a lopsided grin as he shook his head.

'You didn't know that?' asked Jacobsson.

'No, she's never mentioned it.'

'So you are in contact with each other?'

'Sure, but only by phone at the moment. Although it's been a while since she called.'

'And you haven't called her?'

'No.'

'Could you describe what sort of relationship you have with your mother?'

'Why should I do that?'

'Because we think it's relevant to our investigation.'

Simon looked at Knutas with suspicion. He didn't say

anything for so long that both officers began to feel uncomfortable.

'What exactly do I have to do with all this?'

'We're not saying that you have anything to do with it. But we'd like to know how you view your mother.'

'What the hell do you mean by that?' he asked heatedly. 'How I view her?'

'Take it easy,' said Jacobsson, annoyed at Simon's stonewalling. 'We're in the process of investigating more than one serious crime, and your mother appears to be the target. So I want you to tell me now what sort of relationship you have with her. Just answer the question.'

'And how the hell do you expect me to answer that in five minutes? What do you want to know? How often we see each other or talk on the phone? What kind of criteria am I supposed to go by?'

'It hasn't escaped our attention that your sister has broken off all contact with your mother. Why did she do that?'

'Mikaela probably wanted to be able to live her own life,' he said quietly.

'What do you mean by that?'

'Mamma has a tendency to suffocate her children. What Mikaela did was the only right thing to do.'

'And why haven't you done the same thing?'

'I suppose I'm too weak. Or too strong, depending on how you look at it.'

'What do you mean?'

'I think that despite all the things she has ruined for me, I still hold on to a faint hope that everything will turn out OK in the long run. That we'll be reconciled and that one day she'll be happy. We'll have a happy ending.'

His voice faded. For a while none of them spoke. Simon lit another cigarette.

'You don't really think that you can fix things in her life so that she'll be happy, do you?' Jacobsson asked at last.

'I guess I do. I've always thought that.'

'Can I bum a smoke from you?' asked Jacobsson. 'And how about a cold beer? I'm going to open a window, whether you like it or not.'

They stayed in that flat for several hours. Surprisingly enough, Simon decided to open up and tell them about all the difficulties he'd encountered, both in his childhood and more recently. Jacobsson proved to be very sympathetic, and she was the one who was able to encourage him to talk. Knutas mostly kept to the background, listening and watching. It was 9 p.m. by the time they left.

As they took the lift down, Jacobsson looked at Knutas and said, 'I don't think it's him.'

The minute I got on the commuter train to Nynäshamn, I knew. The end was near. Mutely I gazed at the landscape rushing past outside the window. The rolling hills, horse pastures, and fields of Södertörn.

In Nynäshamn I got off, bought a newspaper and some chocolate biscuits at a kiosk, and then strolled down to the ferry terminal. It was an overcast day, and the sea looked forbidding. A strong wind was blowing at the dock, and I pulled up my jacket collar over the turtleneck of my sweater.

The weather suited my mood. I was filled with foreboding. It had to end. The boat was half empty. The tourist season hadn't really begun yet, and it was an ordinary weekday.

I sat down on a deckchair and closed my eyes. I didn't want to go to the cafeteria, even though I could have used a cup of coffee. But I had no desire to talk to anybody.

I am empty of all feeling, spent, used up and broken down like an old tractor. All those ruined expectations, all the hysterical outbursts and insane demands that I've had to fend off for as long as I can remember. I have no right to my own life. That's what I have finally understood.

She is stronger. She has won. There is only one way that I can get rid of my tormentor, my own flesh and blood, the person who long ago brought me into this wretched life. I wonder why she even decided to give birth to me. Was it in order to torture me, suck all the life out of me, obliterate me? To pass the sins of the parents down to the children in a pattern that would repeat itself, etched into the family tree for all eternity? So that the children would be afflicted, one generation after another? Trying to keep them from having a real mother and father because you never did, you fucking bitch? No one is allowed to have anything that you never had. Your children aren't allowed to have good relationships since you never did. Your children are trying to live decent lives, but you keep trying to stop them. You're like a huge, malicious demon standing in the road, imbuing your children with the same hatred that fills you. And they are repeating the irrational pattern that you created.

I refuse to play along any more. There is only one way to put an end to this. And it's finally going to happen – what I have so long yearned for. But the realization doesn't fill me with joy or anticipation. Only a deep and profound sorrow.

I keep my eyes closed all the way to Gotland.

It was a relief to get outside. Dusk had arrived, but the air was still pleasantly warm.

'Let's go get a bite to eat,' Jacobsson suggested. 'I'm starving.'

They had booked rooms at a hotel near Slussen, so they decided to walk up to the Mosebacketerrasse restaurant. It was packed, but they managed to get a table all to themselves. Soon they were enjoying lamb cutlets and a bottle of red wine.

'What makes you so sure that Simon isn't the killer?' asked Knutas as he dug into his food.

'He just seems too unstable. Do you really think he could have got hold of some poison, and then cold-bloodedly murdered Viktor while a huge crowd of people were having a party upstairs? And after that, do you think he could have gone to Holmhällar and burned down his mother's summer cabin where he'd spent his childhood summers? I think he seems far too weak to have done any of those things.'

'Well, maybe you're right.'

'Katrina, his ex-girlfriend, says the same thing. He'd

never be able to do that. Even if he might want to.'

'OK, but that's what the wives and girlfriends of criminals always say. *They never would have imagined* . . . And *he never would have hurt a fly* . . .'

'It must be terrible to have a mother like her,' said Jacobsson emphatically. 'Someone who acts like a big baby who always needs help with everything – and then is never satisfied! From what Simon told us, it sounds as if it'd be easier to fill up the Grand Canyon with water using only a teaspoon – and at least the canyon has a bottom!'

'I agree. It seems like Veronika Hammar has some kind of mental problem. That sort of behaviour doesn't sound healthy.'

'In a way, all of her children really have sufficient motive,' said Jacobsson pensively. 'The only way they can have their own lives is by breaking off all contact with her. Or by killing her.'

'There might be something to what you're saying. If Simon isn't capable of it, maybe his sister Mikaela or his brother Andreas is. Or why not Mats, who was sent to live with a foster family?'

'But he hasn't had any contact with her all these years. I'd put my money on the sheep farmer,' said Jacobsson.

'Andreas Hammar? He could certainly pull it off. And isn't there cyanide in the prussic acid that's used as rat poison? He must have plenty of that stuff on the farm. What do you think?'

'Possibly. And we're going to talk to Mikaela tomorrow. But there's one other potential perp. And that's Veronika Hammar herself.'

'Why would she want to murder the man she was in love with? Or burn down her own cabin?' asked Knutas.

'She could be more mentally disturbed than we suspect. Maybe Viktor Algård discovered the less attractive sides of her personality and wanted to leave her. As irrational and unbalanced as she seems to be, she could have taken revenge by murdering him. Then, to divert suspicion from herself, she burned down the cabin. She could have staged the whole scene with the drink to lead us off the track.' Then Jacobsson gave Knutas a doubtful look. 'But that theory seems like a long shot. Maybe we're way off the mark by deciding that it has to be someone in the immediate family. What if the killer is somebody else entirely?'

Knutas was starting to feel a bit drunk. He was worn out after all the events of the past week, and it was nice to be sitting in the midst of the Stockholm hustle and bustle, drinking wine with Karin.

'That's possible,' he said. 'But I don't think we're going to get any further tonight. I need to put aside everything from work and just relax. Would you like some more wine?'

'Sure.'

On his way to the bar, Knutas phoned Lina. He was feeling guilty about going off to Stockholm the minute they got back from their holiday in the country, and on top of that deciding to spend the night in the capital. He also felt guilty because it was so pleasant to be sitting here in the restaurant with Karin, far away from everyone and everything. Annoyed, he ordered another bottle of wine. What was wrong with him? He had no reason on earth to feel guilty. During all the years of their marriage, and they would soon celebrate their twentieth anniversary, he had never been unfaithful to Lina. His relationship with Karin was strictly professional. Only on one occasion had something like a sexual attraction occurred, and that was last summer when he had ended up at Karin's flat after a night of drinking. All they did was sit on her sofa and listen to the Weeping Willows band while they drank champagne, but suddenly there was something in the air, something new between them that had scared Knutas. It made him so uncomfortable that he had jumped to his feet, saying that he had to go home. At the door she had kissed him on the lips. Fleetingly, but it was enough to make his head spin.

When he'd elbowed his way back to the table, Karin gave him a smile. He noticed that she had touched up her lipstick.

'By the way, I forgot to tell you. I talked to Kihlgård today. He got back the results of all the tests they did. And it was nothing. He's fine.'

'That's good to hear. I was really concerned about him.'

'The problem is that he's overweight and doesn't get enough exercise. So now he needs to start working out – at the gym. Can you see Kihlgård in gym shorts?'

Knutas smiled. The image was amusing, to say the least. He pictured the stout, boisterous inspector from the National Police scampering around a room with a bunch of buff twenty-year-olds.

Jacobsson lit a cigarette.

'So what should we talk about now?' she teased him. 'Since you don't want to discuss the investigation.'

'It's not as if I'm the one who has a hard time talking.' Knutas took a sip of his wine, his eyes searching her face. 'I've noticed that something has been weighing on you all winter. Actually, ever since last summer. Won't you tell me what it is?'

Karin didn't answer immediately. She took several sips of her wine while deciding what to say.

'There are certain things that I can't share with you, Anders. No matter how good friends we are. I thought you realized that long ago.'

'Of course I respect the fact that you don't want to tell me everything. But can't you at least give me a clue? Because I can see that something is bothering you, and it's affecting your work.'

Karin's nut-brown eyes flashed.

'Are you saying that I'm not doing my job properly?'

'Come on, Karin. Of course that's not what I'm saying. You're an excellent police officer and you always do a good job. But you haven't been yourself for the past six months, and I'm talking about your mood, not your professional efforts.'

'OK, OK.'

She took another sip of wine. Knutas filled her glass. He noticed that she suddenly looked nervous.

'Some things that happened during the murder investigation last summer stirred up old memories from my own life. Memories that I would have preferred to forget.'

'What do you mean?'

Knutas could see how tense she was now, preparing to divulge what was bothering her. He could tell that it was something important. She sighed heavily. Her eyes filled with tears, and she looked so small and vulnerable that Knutas wished he could put his arms around her.

'The fact is that I've wanted to talk to you about this for a long time. I've been on the verge of telling you several times. The problem is that if I do, I'm risking my whole career with the police force, and I'll be putting you in a terribly difficult situation. I've wanted to spare you that.'

'What's this about?'

'But I really have no choice, no matter what the consequences may be. In my heart, I've wanted to tell you all along. Remember Vera Petrov? She was pregnant, right?'

'Yes?'

'When we were searching for her on the boat, I looked in all the cabins on the upper deck. And afterwards, I told everybody that I didn't find her. Well, I was lying.'

Knutas stared at Karin in astonishment.

'She and her husband were inside one of the cabins when I opened the door with my gun drawn. I recognized him at once from the boat to Gotska Sandön. And I knew that Vera was pregnant. She was in labour when I found them, and I was forced to help her give birth. The baby was literally about to pop out. I acted as the midwife, and everything went fine. She had a little girl. It was a tremendously emotional experience for me, seeing the two of them and the baby. They were so filled with joy, in spite of the hopeless situation that they were in. As if nothing else mattered at that moment.'

Knutas listened with a growing sense of alarm. Vera Petrov had executed two people in cold blood. It sounded as if his closest colleague had actually allowed a double murderer to walk free. And she'd been lying the whole time, while he had worked so hard to solve the case, bringing in Interpol, trying to track down the killer. The hunt had gone on for months without success. The double murderer and her husband had disappeared without a trace. And here sat Karin, babbling about how happy they were to have a baby. It was one thing that she had betrayed him and the rest of her colleagues. But this was such a gross dereliction of duty that she'd never be able to work as a police officer again. She was going to end up in prison, maybe for several years. In all seriousness, he wondered whether Karin had gone mad.

Not noticing how upset her boss was, she went on: 'Of course I had planned to arrest them and call for back-up as soon as the child was born. But something happened. I found myself enveloped in my own grief.'

Karin's expression changed drastically, as if she were unbearably exposed. She looked pale, in spite of a slight suntan, and her eyes were more solemn than he'd ever seen them before. As if she were truly looking at him for the very first time. No longer hiding behind anything.

'The thing is, I also had a baby once. I was only fifteen at the time, so that was twenty-five years ago.'

Knutas stared at his colleague in surprise.

'Do you mean that you're the mother of a twenty-five-year-old?'

'Yes, that's right. Although I haven't seen my child since the day she was born.' Karin's lips quivered and her eyes filled with tears.

'Come on. Let's go,' said Knutas, helping her up from the table.

He put his arm around Karin, who sobbed all the way back to the hotel. Knutas escorted her to her room, unlocking the door with the key card. He made her sit down on the bed and then put some pillows behind her back. He brought her some toilet paper so she could blow her nose and gave her a glass of water.

'Do you mind if I smoke?' she asked.

'Go ahead.'

It was a non-smoking room, but what the hell.

Karin lit a cigarette, her hands shaking. Knutas pulled over the only chair in the room and set it next to the bed. He cursed the wine for making his head spin and tried to gather his thoughts. He'd never seen Karin look so weak. The room was only dimly lit, making shadows fall across her face. Suddenly she looked like a stranger, and he wondered how well he really knew her. Maybe their close friendship was merely an illusion. He sat there in silence, waiting, with his hands clasped on his lap. His palms were sweaty, but he didn't care; he clasped them even tighter, as if his hands needed to support each other because of what he was about to hear. Karin's voice shook when she finally began to speak.

'Just after I turned fifteen, I was raped. I was out riding my horse in the woods. The horse fell and went lame, and I had to lead him back home. On the way I stopped at the riding teacher's farm to ask if I could use the phone. He was married and had children, but he was home alone when I arrived. We put my horse in the stable and then I went inside the house with him.

Instead of letting me use the phone, he raped me, right there in the living room. I remember staring up at the big family photo over the sofa when he forced his way inside me. It hurt terribly.'

Karin turned her head to look up at the ceiling, and the tears kept pouring down her pale cheeks. Her skin looked so thin, almost transparent. Knutas felt a shiver run down his back. He didn't want to see the images that appeared in his mind; they made him feel sick to his stomach.

She took a deep breath and then went on.

'When he was finished, he said that he'd make a lot of trouble for me if I ever told anyone. Then he let me use the phone. I was in shock. It seemed so unreal. I asked my father to come and get me. I was ashamed. I felt so dirty. I'm sure you've heard it all before. I got home, took care of the horse, and then showered. We had dinner and I went to bed early. All I wanted was to go to sleep. When I woke up the next morning, it was like it never happened. I tried to put the whole thing out of my mind. I thought that if I tried hard enough to pretend it was just a bad dream, then I might make it go away. That's why I didn't say anything, not to my parents or to anyone else. A few days later I ran into him at the post office. He smiled and said hello. As if nothing had happened. My legs buckled and I almost fainted. I was so scared of him that I nearly died. I almost wanted to die. I lost all interest in horseback riding, and my parents couldn't understand it. I did poorly in school and kept mostly to myself. I started skipping classes, pretending to have a stomach ache or thinking up some other excuse.'

Her voice faded, and Knutas tried to digest this horrifying story. So this was the secret that Karin had kept buried all these years, the sorrow that he'd always known was there, and yet it was incomprehensible.

He glanced at her surreptitiously as she sat there on the bed, looking like a little girl. He felt guilty, as if he were intruding just by being in the room and listening. She didn't look in his direction; her eyes were fixed on some invisible spot on the wall. Now and then sounds were audible from outside on the street, but they were of no significance. The only important thing was right here, inside the room – what Karin was saying, the words that Knutas had unknowingly been waiting to hear for so many years. She lit another cigarette.

'Then the unthinkable happened. My periods stopped, my breasts felt tender, and I started throwing up in the morning. I continued to deny the situation. I just went on as usual, ignoring the trouble I was in. Eventually the nausea subsided, but my jeans were getting too tight. After a while I couldn't hide my condition any longer. One morning when I went into the kitchen wearing my nightgown, my mother gave me a strange look. I remember opening the refrigerator and looking for something inside. She was standing next to the stove and I could feel her looking at my stomach. In a flash she was at my side, her hand on my belly. I'll never forget the tone of her voice. It was ice cold, accusatory and filled with contempt – even hatred. "Are you pregnant?" she asked. I panicked. I'd been refusing to think about it for so long. She pulled up my nightgown to look at my breasts. "They're twice the normal size. And just look at your stomach!"

'I started sobbing as she showered me with questions. Pappa appeared, standing in the doorway as if frozen to the spot. Staring at me with horror, as if I were some sort of monster. Then I told them about the rape. Exactly how it happened. All the details. As I talked, I felt more and more ashamed. I was filled with nausea, as if I'd done something wrong. When I was finished, I just sat there, crying. And neither of my parents said a word. It felt like being inside an airless bubble. No one spoke. No one tried to comfort me. Mamma just left me there in the kitchen. And then Pappa followed her out.'

Karin fell silent. Knutas gently patted her arm.

'Then what happened?' he asked cautiously. 'What happened next?'

Karin blew her nose and drank all the water in her glass.

'What happened next?' she said bitterly. 'They refused to contact the police. They didn't want to talk about it at all. Mamma took care of the practical arrangements. They decided that the child should be given up for adoption right after the birth. I agreed. I just wanted to get rid of it so I could go on with my life. Keep going to school. Keep being a teenager. I wanted everything to be the same, like it was before all this happened. I didn't think of the baby as a real child; it was just something bad that had to go away. I managed to finish the school year, although my grades were terrible. In the autumn I gave birth to my baby. On the twenty-second of September.'

The tears were pouring out again, but Karin continued her story.

'It was a girl. I was allowed to hold her for a short time after the birth. I could feel how warm she was, and how her heart beat against mine. Like a little bird. At that moment I regretted my decision. I wanted to keep her. In my mind I gave her the name Lydia. But all of a sudden they took her away from me, and I never saw her again.'

Her voice faded away. Karin sank back against the pillows, as if all strength had left her body.

'But couldn't you tell them that you'd changed your mind?'

'What say did I have in the matter? Nothing. My parents told me that it was too late, that all the papers had been signed, even though later on I found out that wasn't true. They lied to me.'

Karin closed her eyes.

'I've never told this to anyone,' she added faintly. 'You're the only person who knows.'

Knutas lit his pipe. A thick haze of smoke had settled over the small room. He was stunned, devastated by Karin's story. The outrage he had initially felt when she confessed that she'd let Vera Petrov and Stefan Norrström escape was gone, at least for the time being. Right now he shared Karin's suffering and was appalled at what she'd been forced to go through. He'd had no idea about any of this during all the years they had worked together. He looked down at her vulnerable face. She lay on the bed with her eyes closed. He felt overcome by a great sense of weariness. He leaned down and kissed her lightly on the forehead. Then he pulled the blanket over her, turned off the light, and left the room.

Knutas tossed and turned all night, lying on the narrow hotel bed, unable to sleep. The small room was stifling. Heavy curtains in a drab, rusty-brown colour hung at the window. He could hear a fan whirring somewhere. The traffic noise was clearly audible, now and then interrupted by the siren of a police car or ambulance. Occasionally some passerby would yell or laugh out on the street. He couldn't for the life of him understand how Stockholmers could stand all this racket. The city was never silent. He would go crazy if he had to live here.

Thinking about Karin kept him awake. At this moment he regretted insisting that she tell him what was bothering her. How strong could a friendship be? She had put him in an impossible situation. She had deliberately allowed a double murderer to go free; that was totally unacceptable. It was very unlikely that Vera Petrov would ever kill again, and any reasonable person would understand how a terribly tragic and heartbreaking episode in her past had motivated her actions. But that was no excuse. Karin could not remain on the police force. She had been his colleague for almost twenty years, but now she was going to have to leave. The thought was so alarming that it made him shiver. Imagine going to work every day and not seeing her there. She wouldn't be getting coffee out of the vending machine or sitting at the conference table for a meeting. He wouldn't hear her laugh or see that gap between her front teeth. Karin Jacobsson was his sounding board, both professionally and personally. He couldn't even picture what it would be like at the station without her.

In the past he had sometimes worried that she might quit. She was still single, as far as Knutas knew, which had always seemed to him incomprehensible. She was so beautiful with her dark hair and warm eyes. He used to worry that she might meet someone who would take her away from Visby. She was so intense, so lively. Sometimes he had wondered how she viewed him. What did he have to offer her? He was just an ordinary middle-aged man with pitiful personal problems, which he never hesitated to discuss with her. He wasn't a particularly inspiring friend.

When he thought about what she had been through – the rape, the birth, her parents' betrayal – he was filled with anger. Finally he got out of bed, found his pipe and sat down in the armchair next to the window. He pulled aside the curtains and opened the window. It was four in the morning, and he realized it was hopeless trying to sleep.

He lit his pipe and sat there until dawn, watching the city wake up outside the window.

The yard is filled with children playing. Their raincoats – yellow, blue, red, green and pink – form a colourful bouquet against the backdrop of the black asphalt and surrounding grey buildings. The rain has just stopped, but the air is dripping with moisture. Cold winds keep the temperature down. A low-pressure area has settled over Gotland, instantly and brutally dropping the temperature from 20 to 9 degrees Celsius. The change in the weather doesn't seem to bother the kids, who are running from one side of the playground at the day-care centre to the other. A few teachers are chatting as they keep an eye on the children. Their conversation is constantly being interrupted when someone falls down and starts crying, or another child stuffs something in his mouth, or a few of the kids start fighting. The youngest toddlers, who can barely walk, are sitting in the sandbox with buckets and shovels, happily digging in the rain-soaked sand.

It takes me a minute to spot him. He's wearing a dark blue rain jacket, waterproof trousers and a matching sou'wester hat. He's busy with a bright yellow bucket and shovel. He's sitting next to a friend, and they seem to be talking and playing well together.

I feel a pang in my heart. I'm having a hard time breathing, and I have to squat down. I'm hiding behind a warehouse, not wanting to draw attention to myself.

My boy. His dark hair is sticking out from under his rain cap, his cheeks are a glowing pink, and I catch a glimpse of his dark eyes. A contented child. What does his future hold? How will he be affected by what is about to happen? What will he think when he gets older? How many questions will he have? And how much will he suffer? That little boy sitting there, playing so happily in the sand. Innocent, carefree. He has the right to a safe and secure childhood. To deny him that would be reprehensible. And now here I am, about to shirk my responsibility.

But there's no other way out of this straitjacket, none at all. Mamma will continue to plague me for the rest of my life. I will never be free. Other people die – from cancer or in a car crash. She will presumably go on poisoning the lives of everyone close to her until she's a hundred years old. By then I'll be almost eighty.

I once had a dream that I was leafing through the newspaper until I came to the obituary page. There I saw her name. And the only thing I felt was relief.

I stand up and look at my son one last time before I turn on my heel.

And with heavy steps, I walk away.

When Knutas came downstairs to the hotel breakfast room, he found Karin sitting next to the window with a cup of coffee and the morning paper in front of her. She had dark smudges under her eyes and she was frowning. As usual, she wore jeans and a T-shirt. Around one wrist was a leather strap with a green stone. On her feet, which stuck out from under the table, she wore purple trainers. She was deeply immersed in the article she was reading and didn't notice when he paused in the doorway to study her.

Knutas was overcome with tenderness for the slight figure sitting near the window. He felt a prickling in his hands and legs, as if tiny needles were sticking into his skin. For a second everything went black, and he had to hold on to the doorpost. He hadn't slept a wink and his body ached with fatigue. When he left his hotel room, he had made up his mind. There was nothing else to do. He had to ask Karin to resign. To leave the police force. He took a step forward, then another. The distance to her table was about 10 metres. Moving like a sleepwalker, he continued forward, his eyes fixed on her face. Suddenly she felt his approach and looked up. Their eyes met.

No, he thought. I can't make a decision right now. I need more time to think things through.

'Good morning,' he said.

'Good morning.'

'Listen, I'd rather not discuss what we talked about last night. I need time to think.'

'OK. But when we get home, I plan to hand in my resignation. Just so you know. I don't want to cause you any problems, Anders.'

Her words made him feel panic-stricken. Once before she had almost quit her job, and he didn't want to go through that again.

'Let's not do anything hasty. You're not responsible for my bloody welfare. Whatever I decide, it'll be my decision. Please give me some time to think it over,' he pleaded. He could hear for himself how insistent he sounded. 'You've had to carry too much on your own. Try to let it all go for the time being.'

She gave him a wan smile.

They got the rental car from the Katarina garage, just a stone's throw from the hotel. They did their best to ignore what they were both thinking about and tried to focus on the task ahead of them. Their personal problems would have to wait until later.

Knutas found it surprisingly easy to make his way

through the city. At first he kept to the shoreline, driving along Skeppsbron and Strandvägen, past the TV and radio building on Oxenstiernsgatan. Then he turned on to Valhallavägen, one of Stockholm's most fashionable streets, which was designed like a French boulevard, very wide with a double row of trees down the middle. It came to an end at Roslagtull, and from there they continued straight ahead along Norrtäljevägen. Presumably he could have taken a more direct route through the city, but at least he had found the right road. And the view was spectacular, with the water glittering in between all of Stockholm's islands and the magnificent buildings of the royal palace, the National Museum, the Dramaten theatre, and the Nordic Museum on Djurgården, which resembled a renaissance palace with its turrets and towers.

As the investigation had progressed, Knutas had grown more curious about Mikaela Hammar. She had created a whole new life for herself away from Gotland. She had married a mainlander and moved to Stockholm's archipelago. There she started a riding school, which she and her husband ran together. At the same time, she worked for a humanitarian aid organization.

It was quite a drive. Knutas checked his watch as they passed Norrtälje, with at least 10 kilometres still ahead of them. It was just past eleven. Their plane home left at three thirty. They had plenty of time.

When they drove across the bridge to the island of Vätö, he was reminded how different the archipelago was from Gotland. An entirely different kind of landscape. No long sand dunes here. Instead, he saw cliffs, boulders and skerries. Vätö was one of the bigger islands in Stockholm's archipelago, with about a thousand permanent residents, shops, a post office, library and school. Many people who lived on the island commuted to Stockholm or Norrtälje. Mikaela Hammar and her family lived in Harg, at the centre of the island.

They came to a big old gate at a curve in the road and turned into a horse pasture. The car bumped along on the narrow tractor track, and then the farm appeared beyond a hill. It stood there in lonely majesty, atop a plateau with hills on one side and an expansive view of the countryside on the other.

Several Fjord horses came trotting towards Knutas and Jacobsson as they climbed out of the car.

Knutas, who was rather frightened of horses, hurried towards the gate. The farm consisted of a main building, painted Falun red, and two smaller buildings forming wings on either side of it. Further away on the property was a barn with a paddock in front. A riding track was visible beyond the barn. The front door of the house opened and a plump suntanned woman in her mid-thirties came out on to the porch holding a tray with a coffee pot and cups. She smiled and welcomed them warmly.

'I was thinking we could sit outside. It's such a beautiful day.'

She led the way to some patio furniture at the side of the house with a view of the hills. Cowslips and lilies of the valley were already in bloom. It was almost like summer.

'Thank you for your willingness to meet with us right after returning from such a long trip,' Knutas began.

'It's no problem. I understand that this is important.' A trace of sorrow was evident in her voice.

'You know what's been going on. By all accounts, your mother was first the target of a murder attempt by poisoning, and then barely escaped an arsonist's fire. We're still not entirely sure whether the murder at the conference centre was actually aimed at her, but that's what she claims. And we've had her story at least partially confirmed by witnesses. What's your reaction to all of this?'

'If somebody is trying to kill my mother, I'm not really surprised, to be quite honest.'

'Why's that?'

'There's a reason why I've broken off all contact with her. My mother has a talent for obliterating everyone close to her.'

'In what way?'

Mikaela Hammar sighed. Knutas noted that she was not at all like her mother. She was tall and quite stocky, with long, wavy light brown hair and blue eyes. There was actually nothing about her that reminded him of Veronika Hammar.

'I grew up with a mother who was so self-absorbed that she never really saw me or my siblings. I'll stick with describing my own experience. As a child I was made to feel invisible and I was never treated with respect. Each day brought new offences, any problems were simply shoved under the rug, and my mother always acted the martyr. Our lives were filled with dishonesty. It was like living on a stage set. I went through long periods of depression, which got worse when I was a teenager. Things got so bad that I started cutting myself and developed eating problems. I would binge on food and then throw up afterwards. That went on for five years, and she never noticed a thing.'

'How old were you at the time?' asked Jacobsson.

'It started when I was fifteen and lasted until I moved away from home. That's when I met my husband, thank God. He was my salvation. Without him, I wouldn't be alive today.'

She spoke in a matter-of-fact tone, without a shred of self-pity.

'What caused these problems?'

'I think that I'd been suffering for a long time because no one really paid any attention to me. There were probably two reasons why I started cutting myself. Partly from anxiety and partly because deep inside I wanted someone to see me, notice me. Discover what was going on. But nobody did.'

'What happened when you met your husband?'

'I met him in the summer. He came to Gotland on holiday, like so many other people. Of course my mother criticized everything about him. The way he looked, the fact that in her eyes at least he didn't have a very good job, and that he lived in Stockholm. She complained about everything. But for once I refused to listen to her. And I thank God for that. For the first time in my life I felt truly loved, and it was wonderful. Here was someone who liked me just as I was, without reservation and without making any demands. He listened to me, let me speak my mind, let me have my own opinions. Because of him, I grew as a person and I started believing in love. I saw that love actually existed and could last. I will always be eternally grateful to him for that. He healed me.'

Mikaela Hammar spoke with such genuine feeling and warmth that both Knutas and Jacobsson were moved by her words.

'You and your mother haven't been in touch for a while. How long has it been?'

'It's been ten years since we talked to each other.'

'What exactly happened?'

'I finally had enough. The children and I went to visit Mamma at the summer cabin. We were only going to stay a few days. That was as much as I could stand. My kids were young then. Linus was four, and Doris was two. One afternoon I needed to go grocery shopping, so I asked my mother to look after the children while I was gone. It wasn't going to take more than two hours. She said that would be fine. Mamma never babysat for us, but I didn't think anything could happen in such a short time. Besides, it's so much easier to shop for groceries without having little kids tagging along. Linus was playing with his plastic cars on the lawn, and Doris was asleep in her pram when I left. When I came back, both of them were howling. Doris had blood on her cheek, and the neighbours were standing around, shouting. A huge commotion. It turned out that Linus had gone to the privy, which is a short distance from the cabin, and Mamma was supposed to wipe his bottom when he was done, but she forgot about him. So he sat there and cried for over an hour while she was inside the cabin, talking to someone on the phone. In the meantime, Doris had toddled over to the neighbours' place and their dog bit her. That was the last straw. After putting up with my mother's selfish behaviour for so many years, I finally told her off. Then I packed up all our belongings, grabbed my kids, and left.'

'And afterwards? Did she try to get in touch with you?'

'According to my siblings, she thought that I had treated her terribly. In her words: That's not how anyone should treat their mother. I refused to phone her. After a month or two she started sending me letters. Long furious tirades in which she described all the things she had done for me and how grateful I ought to be. I read the first couple and then tossed the others out. I didn't even bother to open them. She had always been on my back, and it was so liberating to break off all ties with her. It's the smartest thing I ever did. The best present I ever gave to myself and to my husband and children. Even though I know how awful that must sound.'

Mikaela Hammar spoke in a firm voice, but her hand was shaking as she lifted her coffee cup. For a moment no one said a word. Knutas could easily picture the scene in his mind. He sipped his coffee.

'Considering how long it has been since you communicated with each other, I can understand that it might be hard for you to say anything about possible threats to your mother's life. If that's what we're actually dealing with, that is.'

'In reality, I think any of us could be pushed so far that we might want to kill her. That's how hard she has stomped on us, abused us and exploited us. Plus she has always kept certain things secret. Has either of my brothers told you anything about Mats?'

She hadn't set foot outside the house since coming home from hospital a week ago. She got up every morning, ate breakfast, read the paper, and listened to the local radio station. Then she waited for lunch, which usually consisted of soup or a salad. Around two in the afternoon she had coffee, and she ate dinner in front of the TV, watching the news. The hours in between meals dragged along. She couldn't concentrate on anything. Had no interest in doing any cleaning or painting or pottering about in her little garden, which was what she usually did at this time of year. She felt frozen. As if waiting for something, but she had no idea what it might be. The days passed, and she longed for the cabin that no longer existed. The realization that it was gone had hit her suddenly, making her sob for hours. She lay on her bed like a child, shaking all over. She felt overwhelmed by fear, but no one came to her rescue. Viktor was dead, and none of her children answered the phone when she rang. She was utterly alone.

The fact that she couldn't get hold of Simon was something she'd grown accustomed to over the past few months. But what about Andreas? He had changed lately. His tone of voice was harsher, less amenable. And he wasn't as easy to reach as he had been before. Maybe because he'd met someone. There were clear signs in his house. She'd found an eyeliner pencil in the bathroom, a hair clip on the hall table. All of a sudden he had plain yoghurt in his refrigerator. And he never picked up the phone when she called.

This morning she was feeling even more anxious than usual. She got up and went through her usual morning routine, but she was filled with nervous energy. She wandered through the rooms of her small house, then went out in the courtyard and tried to read the paper. But she couldn't sit still. She washed her hair, but that kept the anguish at bay for only a brief time. She tried to do a crossword puzzle but her thoughts kept drifting in different directions. She couldn't focus. Nothing held her attention for long. When she decided to have her afternoon coffee, she was dismayed to discover that there were only a few grounds left in the bottom of the tin. And there wasn't another one in the cupboard. Andreas still wasn't answering his phone. She was going to have to go out. She gave a start when she saw her own reflection in the mirror. She needed to do something about her appearance.

She spent almost an hour fixing herself up. She chose an elegant white trouser suit that was probably a bit excessive for a walk to the ICA supermarket, but what the hell. She carefully put on her make-up and then spent time blow-drying her hair, which was getting too long. And the roots were showing. She needed to get her hair coloured and cut.

When she studied her transformation in the mirror before leaving the house, she was definitely satisfied. She looked almost like her old self.

The pressure in her chest returned the minute she stepped out on to the street. She cast a surreptitious glance in both directions. Not a soul in sight. No police car either. The surveillance had been stopped. The police chief had explained that they just didn't have the resources to continue it. No resources. The thought was appalling. Viktor had been murdered, and she herself had almost been killed by an arsonist. Was the threat really over? On the other hand, she couldn't very well spend the rest of her life locked inside her house. The situation was both incomprehensible and frightening. She simply couldn't imagine who would want to harm her; she had never hurt a fly. She'd spent her whole life helping others and standing up for her fellow human beings, without giving a thought to herself. She had devoted herself to her children, colleagues, neighbours, friends and acquaintances – and received nothing but ingratitude in return. That was the bitter lesson she'd learned. But who on earth would want to kill her? She could think of only one person, and that was Viktor's widow, Elisabeth Algård. Who else could it possibly be? Elisabeth had gone completely berserk when he told her that he wanted a divorce. Later he'd also said that his wife was crazy with jealousy.

Veronika couldn't understand why the police hadn't arrested her. She hoped they were at least keeping an eye on her and it was just a matter of time. Maybe Elisabeth was being escorted over to the station at this very moment. The idea gave her renewed strength as she walked along the deserted street. So far there were still very few people in Visby, but soon the hordes of tourists would invade the town. She wouldn't be able to retreat to the cabin this summer, but eventually it would be rebuilt. For now she would have to make do with staying at Andreas's farm for the summer holiday. At least it was out in the country, even though it was rather far from the sea.

What if she stopped for coffee at Rosengården before she did her shopping? It was her favourite café, and she hadn't been there in weeks. Besides, she was desperate for a cup of coffee, and they had the best espresso. She came to the entrance and, without further hesitation, went inside.

The usual waitress smiled at her, saying how nice it was to see her. 'How are you?'

'Fine, thanks,' replied Veronika. She ordered her coffee and a piece of carrot cake. A few customers had taken seats on the outdoor patio. A couple of tables were occupied, but she avoided looking at the people sitting there.

She chose her favourite table at the very back, close to the garden. It stood next to a small lilac bower, which was already starting to bloom. From there she had a good view of the Botanical Gardens and all the flowers. This was an oasis and one of the few places in town where she could relax, even when she was alone.

A few minutes later the waitress came back carrying a tray, clinking and clattering. Veronika thanked her and then took a sip of the strong coffee, feeling her energy level revive. Everything was going to be fine. She refused to give up. The birds were chirping, having a calming effect on her. The carrot cake she'd ordered was big and moist. As she raised the fork to her mouth, a man entered the restaurant. She thought he looked familiar.

But she just couldn't place him.

The café was on the outskirts of Visby, with a view of the Botanical Gardens. The sun was shining and it was a warm day. Emma wanted to go someplace where she could sit in peace and think. And it had to be outdoors so she could smoke. Over the past few years she had sometimes smoked a lot, sometimes not at all. She had stopped when she was pregnant with Sara and Filip and while she was breastfeeding. But afterwards she had started smoking again. The same thing had happened with Elin. As soon as she stopped breastfeeding, Emma had resumed smoking even though she had actually weaned herself of the habit. Lots of her friends and acquaintances thought it was odd for her to be so addicted to nicotine. She worked out several times a week, taught young children and loved to take walks in the woods. In fact, she was considered a real outdoors person. Emma couldn't explain why she smoked. Right now she needed to think, and that meant being able to light up a cigarette.

She walked through the gate in the ring wall to the garden café and looked around. A dozen or so tables had been placed outside among the blossoming apple trees and lilacs. Here anyone wanting both shade and solitude could find a place. Three tables were occupied. At one of them sat an elderly man working on the crossword puzzle in the newspaper, with a cup of coffee and a piece of marzipan cake in front of him. At another table sat two teenage girls drinking lattes from oversize cups. They had their heads together, deep in conversation. At the third table sat a young man with a salad and a book. Emma couldn't see the title. He was the only one who looked up as she went over to the counter to place her order. She asked for a double macchiato and her favourite dessert: Italian almond biscotti dipped in chocolate. She chose a table at the far end of the garden where she could sit in peace without being disturbed. The sun was so warm that she took off her jacket and draped it over the back of the chair next to her. Then she sipped her coffee and lit a cigarette.

She didn't think it would do any harm, this early in the pregnancy. And besides, she wasn't positive that she wanted to go through with it. She wasn't going to tell Johan yet. Another child. What would that mean? When she saw the results on the pregnancy test she'd done at home this morning, she was seized with panic. To make things worse, her ex-husband Olle had rung the doorbell thirty seconds later. It was his turn to take care of the children. She had tossed the test in the waste-paper basket, covered it with some toilet paper, and then splashed some water on her face before going to the door. She had managed to pull herself together enough to send Sara and Filip off with the usual hugs and kisses, reminding them to phone her to say good-night before they went to bed. But the test results had shocked her. She had to get out of the house and have time alone to think about the unexpected situation she now found herself in. Her friend Viveka was willing, as usual, to take care of Elin for a few hours. Emma hadn't even dared tell Viveka about her condition. Not yet.

As she drove to town, her head was a whirl of contradictory thoughts. The idea of yet another pregnancy, yet another child, made her feel sick. The next instant she was ashamed of herself. Shouldn't this kind of news make her happy? She was thirty-eight years old, married, with a good job and a wonderful husband who loved her. They had all the prerequisites for welcoming another child into their lives, and she assumed that Johan would be overjoyed.

Feeling dejected, she had parked the car near Stora Torget, bought a pack of cigarettes and the evening paper at ICA, and then walked over to the Botanical Gardens.

Now she was sitting here in the shade under the apple trees with the newspaper open in front of her so it would look as if she was reading. Silently she cursed herself. How could she have been so careless? Birth-control pills made her feel sick, and using an IUD didn't work for her, so they had used condoms, but a few times they'd forgotten and had unprotected sex. Which was irresponsible, of course, since she got pregnant so easily. She had been foolish enough to think that it wouldn't happen this time because she was getting older. She was almost forty.

She ran her hand over her stomach. A new life had taken root inside. What should she do? She was on the verge of tears, and that made her feel even more ashamed. She was a grown woman, after all.

The teenage girls had apparently finished their conversation, because they got up and left. The man reading the book followed close behind. The elderly man doing the crossword puzzle was still there, deeply engrossed in trying to find the right word, which he entered with a trembling hand. Then he took a sip of his coffee. Emma was grateful that the café was so empty. There weren't many places she could go for some peace and quiet. As a teacher, she knew so many people, and wherever she went, she ran into parents and students.

An elegant woman came into the restaurant and paused for a moment to take a look around. She was in her sixties, petite and slender, wearing a white trouser suit. Her blond hair was cut in a pageboy style, and her lips were painted bright red. There was something glamorous about her, and Emma guessed that she must be a celebrity whose name she ought to know.

The woman sat down at an out-of-the-way table, half

hidden by a lilac bower at the far end of the garden. Emma lost interest and absently leafed through the newspaper.

After a while someone joined the woman at her table. A man who looked about the same age as Emma came in and strode over to the woman sitting in the bower. He was tall and well built, wearing jeans and a shirt. Blond with a beard and dark sunglasses. He seemed very tense and somehow unpleasant. Emma forgot about her own problems for the moment as she surreptitiously studied the man and woman while she pretended to read the newspaper. Something had stirred her curiosity. She had the feeling they weren't there to drink coffee and share a friendly conversation. There was something strained about them. In spite of the obvious age difference, she thought they might be lovers who had quarrelled.

The old man with the crossword puzzle finished his coffee, slowly got to his feet and left the café. Now Emma and the odd couple were the only customers. She could see the man only from the side, and his body practically hid the woman from view. He was leaning forward, speaking in a low voice. It was clear that they were talking about something important. She couldn't make out any words, but she could hear the urgency in the man's voice. Maybe the woman wanted to end the relationship, and he was trying to convince her to stay? Or was he the one who wanted to call it quits, and he was offering a lengthy explanation? Wanting her to understand his decision? The woman said very little. Emma lost interest and went back to brooding over her own thoughts. Suddenly the woman stood up. She went over to the waitress and apparently asked for a key to the toilet, which the girl handed to her. The man remained sitting at the table, barely visible behind the lilac bushes. He must have changed position because now Emma could no longer see him clearly. Her mobile was ringing. It was Johan.

'Hi, sweetheart. Where are you?' he asked.

'I'm in town, running some errands.'

'Oh. Because I called the house and nobody answered.'

'Uh-huh.'

'How's Elin?'

'She was tired, so Viveka is babysitting her. I thought it was best for her to stay at home in peace and quiet. So I left her with Viveka.'

'Really?' Johan sounded surprised. 'Is anything wrong?'

'No, not at all. I just needed to take care of a few things. It's nice to have a little time to myself.'

'I know what you mean. It was a rough night, but it won't last much longer, sweetheart. And she'll never have whooping cough again. At least that's a relief.'

'Yes.'

Emma thought about the child inside of her, and all

sorts of images raced through her mind. Another birth, more breastfeeding, getting the child used to the day-care centre, dirty nappies and more illnesses. Just the thought of all that made her panic.

Suddenly she heard a clattering sound from the table where the man and woman sat. Or had been sitting. At first she couldn't see either of them. Then she heard a whimper and caught sight of an arm flailing about, chopping at the air. The younger man had left the table. Their eyes met as he passed Emma.

The older woman was also on her feet. But there was something odd about her. She looked as if she felt sick.

'Johan, I have to go. I'll call you later.'

Mikaela Hammar poured herself more water and drank half of it.

'None of us had a clue that we had a half-brother until Mats contacted us. Mamma had never said a word about him. Then one day the phone rang, and it was a man named Mats Andersson. He said that he was my half-brother, and he wanted to see me, so we agreed to meet at a café in Norrtälje. Of course I didn't know whether he was telling the truth. Yet I had no reason to doubt what he said.'

'How long ago was this?' asked Knutas.

'Almost exactly two years ago. In May, to be precise. I remember that we sat outside to drink our coffee because it was a warm day.' Her face lit up in a smile. 'And it was an incredible meeting. I knew as soon as I saw him that he was telling the truth. He looks so much like Mamma and my brother Simon that it's ridiculous. The same eyes and mouth. The same narrow face and high cheekbones, dark eyebrows and naturally red lips.' She ran her hand over her own face to show what she meant. 'Unfortunately, I wasn't blessed with the same colouring. He also showed me his birth certificate.'

'Who was his father?' asked Jacobsson.

'It didn't say. Mats doesn't know who his father is, and Mamma refuses to tell him.'

'So he's been in contact with her?'

Mikaela sighed bitterly.

'He's tried to meet her several times, but she doesn't want anything to do with him. She pretends that he doesn't exist. The first time she refused to see him, he was only thirteen. Can you imagine anyone doing such a thing? Giving away her child and then refusing to see him?'

Knutas cast a quick glance at Jacobsson. He put his hand on her arm.

'Are you feeling all right? Should we take a break?'

'No, it's OK.'

Mikaela gave them a surprised look but didn't comment.

'So how did this all start?' asked Knutas.

'Mamma got pregnant the first time when she was only fifteen. Long before she met Pappa. It was a brief fling with a guy who just disappeared afterwards. And then she had Mats in 1966. She didn't want to keep the baby, but she didn't give him up for adoption. She placed him with a foster family. Mats has had really bad luck and ended up with several different foster families, staying with each of them for only a few years before being forced to move. Because of that, he has never dared get really attached to anyone. His life has been very lonely and rootless. He was forced to keep moving during his whole childhood. And she never cared about him.'

'Why didn't she give him up for adoption?' asked Jacobsson tonelessly.

'That's a good question. Maybe her parents advised her not to. I have no idea. But it certainly would have been better for Mats. Then he would have had a real family, someone he could call Mamma and Pappa.'

'But then he got in touch with you. Did he also contact your brothers?'

'Yes, all three of us thought it was great. It was like getting an unexpected gift. And Mats is an easy person to like. He's so warm and sensitive. We talk on the phone several times a month if not more. Before midsummer we had a party here, and Simon's family came too. It was wonderful. Mamma didn't know about it. She was travelling abroad.'

'Do all three of you have a good relationship with Mats?'

'Yes, I think so. Especially Simon. They're so alike, and they took to each other right away. They have the most contact. Mats actually lives very close to Simon, in Söder. I think that's a good thing right now, since Simon is having such a hard time.'

Knutas gave Mikaela a long look.

Emma jumped up from her chair and ran over to the other table. The older woman was blue in the face. She was gripping her throat with both hands, gasping for air. Her eyes were filled with terror, and her body was shuddering with convulsions. All of a sudden she collapsed and fell to the ground.

'Help!' Emma screamed at the top of her lungs. 'Help! Come here! This woman needs help!'

'What's wrong?' The young waitress appeared, staring at Emma in bewilderment.

'Call an ambulance! Now!'

The waitress nodded in alarm and ran off.

Emma had vague memories of a first-aid course that all teachers were required to take, but that was aeons ago. The woman didn't look as if she were breathing, so Emma decided to try CPR. She tilted the woman's head back and leaned over her. She pinched her nose with one hand and opened her mouth with the other. When she pressed her lips over the woman's she instantly recoiled at the terrible smell. She couldn't identify what it was.

Then Emma steeled herself and began blowing into the woman's mouth.

The call came in at 3.27 p.m., and within ten minutes the first police officers were on the scene. By then the medics had already declared the older woman to be dead. The younger woman who had administered CPR had collapsed and was rushed off to the hospital in an ambulance. A large number of officers descended upon the café, including a unit with dogs. The perpetrator had only just left the scene of the crime, so he might still be in the vicinity. Jacobsson and Knutas had gone to Stockholm, and neither of them answered their mobiles, presumably because they were on the plane returning to Visby.

Wittberg and Sohlman arrived a few minutes later. Wittberg brought the police car to a screeching halt in front of the café, and then they both jumped out and ran into the garden. A pale and upset waitress who looked to be no more than twenty was sitting on a chair with a blanket around her shoulders, smoking a cigarette.

'It's just awful. She comes here so often. She's one of our regular customers,' she said, her voice shaking.

'The woman who died – what's her name?' asked

Wittberg, while Sohlman hurried past him to have a look at the victim.

'Veronika Hammar. She comes here a lot. At least several times a week, sometimes every day, although not lately.'

Wittberg swore. Veronika Hammar.

He sank down on to a chair next to the young girl, pulling a notebook and pen out of his pocket.

'Tell me what happened.'

'She came in and ordered a double espresso and a piece of carrot cake. Then she sat down at her usual table.'

The girl pointed to the spot at the end of the garden which was now cordoned off with police tape.

'That table set for four. Over there near the arbour. She liked sitting there by herself. After a while a man came in and ordered coffee and a bottle of Ramlösa mineral water. When I came out later to clear away some of the dishes I noticed that he was sitting at her table. A few minutes later she asked me for the key to the toilet.'

'Did you recognize the man?' asked Wittberg.

'No, I've never seen him before.'

'What did he look like?'

'Tall, stocky but not fat. Muscular. And older. Around forty.'

'Did he have a moustache or a beard? Was he wearing glasses?'

'Actually all of the above. And he had really thick hair, kind of tousled-looking.'

'What colour?'

'Blond.'

'What was he wearing?'

'I don't really remember. Something blue, I think. A jacket and jeans. Nothing special.'

'Did he say anything? I mean, did you hear him talking?'

'No, he didn't say anything except to place his order.'

'Then what happened?'

'Well, I don't really know. She went to the ladies' and brought back the key. Then she went back to her table. It wasn't busy so I went out to the kitchen to help the cook who makes the *smörgåsbord,* and then I got a phone call. Just a few minutes later I heard someone screaming. When I came out, the man was gone, and Veronika was lying on the ground.'

She closed her eyes and shook her head, as if trying to shake off the memory.

'Oh, it was horrible. A woman who was here by herself shouted at me to call an ambulance. So that's what I did. I didn't dare look, but I know that Veronika died almost instantly, even though the other woman was trying to revive her with that mouth-to-mouth method. She kept blowing and blowing, and then she fell over too. The next second the ambulance arrived.'

'And you don't know who that woman was? The one trying to help?'

'No, I've never seen her before.'

'What's your name?'

'Linn.'

'Can you stick around for a while? Is that OK?'

'Sure. That's fine.'

Wittberg went over to Sohlman, who had squatted down next to the dead woman. The crime tech looked up at his colleague.

'The same shit as before. Without a doubt. You can smell it.'

'Bloody hell.'

Someone tapped Wittberg on the shoulder. It was the young waitress.

'The woman who was hurt and was taken to the hospital? This is her bag.'

She handed Wittberg a handbag, which he opened eagerly. When he took out the wallet with the woman's ID, he gave a start.

Emma Winarve. Johan Berg's wife. Emma, who had almost been killed in a drama that had played out on Fårö a few years back.

And now her life was in danger again.

Knutas's mobile started ringing the minute he turned it on after they landed in Visby. He and Jacobsson were on their way to baggage reclaim.

It was Wittberg, reporting on the dramatic events of the past hour. Veronika Hammar had been murdered just as they were boarding the plane in Stockholm. Knutas had to sit down. He felt as if the air had been knocked out of him, but he also felt a growing anger. He had tried in vain to persuade the county police commissioner to continue surveillance for Veronika Hammar, at least till the end of the week. Now it was too late.

He and Jacobsson took a taxi to police headquarters. A crowd of journalists had gathered outside, but Knutas had no comment. He hurried past, promising them a press conference before the night was over. He realized that would be unavoidable.

The café and surrounding area had been blocked off and the tech guys had gone over everything with a fine-toothed comb. The police had interviewed the neighbours, as well as several witnesses who had seen a man walking away down the street just after the murder was committed.

The investigative team met in the conference room as soon as Knutas and Jacobsson arrived at the station.

Wittberg began by describing the course of events.

'Linn Blomgren, the young waitress at the café, gave us a very clear account of what happened. Just after three o'clock, Veronika Hammar came in alone. She's a regular customer at the café, although she hadn't been there for a while. She seemed tense and exchanged only a few words with the waitress. She ordered coffee and a piece of cake and then sat down at a table at the back of the café's garden. The table is almost hidden by a lilac bower. A few minutes later the man turned up, bought coffee and a bottle of Ramlösa, and paid in cash. Then he sat down at Veronika Hammar's table.

'At that time there were six people in the café – four customers, Linn Blomgren, and a cook who's in charge of the *smörgåsbord* in the kitchen. The customers were Veronika Hammar and the unidentified man, an elderly man sitting at a table doing a crossword puzzle, and Emma Winarve. The man with the crossword puzzle left the café first. Which means that Emma was the only witness to the crime. When the murder was committed, the cook was busy in the kitchen and Linn had received a phone call and was still talking when the unidentified man passed by her and disappeared. The next instant she heard someone screaming in the café garden. It was Emma, who had discovered that the woman sitting at the other table had collapsed. Linn called an ambulance.'

'What a brazen bastard that man is,' said Smittenberg. 'To think he had the guts to do something like that.'

'Ice cold,' Sohlman agreed. 'Why does he choose such public places for his murders? Is he the kind of perp who gets off on the risk of being caught?'

'Very possibly,' said Knutas. 'Both of these murders certainly point in that direction. He seems to crave attention. But we'll come back to that later. First I want to have all the facts on the table. What can you tell us, Erik?'

Sohlman told his colleagues about what had been found at the crime scene.

'The perp succeeded in what was apparently his goal right from the start. Judging from what we know so far, Veronika Hammar died from cyanide poisoning, just like Viktor Algård. The poison was put in a glass of Ramlösa that stood on the table. She died in a matter of minutes. Emma Winarve, who administered CPR, ingested enough of the cyanide gas to make her lose consciousness. She's in intensive care, in a serious condition. Veronika Hammar's body has been taken to the morgue, and I'm hoping to have a medical examiner here by this evening. We've been having trouble locating one. The man came into the café just a few minutes after Veronika Hammar. They apparently knew each other. Maybe they had agreed to meet there, or else he was following her. Unfortunately, we had called off the police surveillance. And in this instance, Veronika didn't have much use for the security alarm we had installed at her home,' he added sarcastically.

'There was no real evidence other than the glass and its contents,' Sohlman went on. 'No fingerprints on the Ramlösa bottle or on his coffee cup. According to the waitress, the man was wearing thin leather gloves, typical driving gloves with little air holes, the kind people used to wear in the sixties, if you'll recall. The perp sat there for about ten minutes, tops, before he vanished without leaving behind so much as a strand of hair.'

'Did the waitress talk to him?' asked Jacobsson.

'No, he didn't say a word after paying for his coffee. We do have a good description of the perp, although it sounds as if he was wearing a disguise, so I'm not sure how much the statements from the witnesses can really tell us,' he said with a sigh. 'But there's one thing we do know, at any rate. The killer is a man. The question is: Who is he?'

'Just a minute,' said Knutas.

He got up and pulled down the white screen at the front of the room. Jacobsson, who sat closest to the switch, turned off the lights. Knutas used his computer to project an image on the screen. He'd had only a few minutes to tell Wittberg about his theory. No one else knew the identity of the killer they were looking for. The silence in the room was palpable.

A face appeared on the screen. It was a passport photo of a man in his forties. He was blond with dark eyes and an open, pleasant-looking face. It was obvious that he bore a striking resemblance to Veronika Hammar. The man was clean-shaven, and his hair was cut short. He looked like rather a decent person as he mustered a vague smile for the camera. Hardly the image of a double murderer. Knutas clicked to bring up another photo of the same man.

This one had been culled from the police records, taken fifteen years earlier. An unshaven young man with a crew cut and a wild look in his eyes, staring with hostility at the camera. Two very different portraits of the same man.

'This is the eldest brother, Mats. According to his boss, he's been in Mallorca for the past two weeks. But that's not true. The charter company says that Mats never showed up at the airport to check in for his flight. Instead, he's been shuttling back and forth between Stockholm and Gotland. I think this is the man we're after.'

The news caused a ripple to pass through the room.

'So it's the half-brother. The one who grew up with foster families,' said Smittenberg with a sigh.

Everyone was staring at the photo on the screen.

Knutas told them what Mikaela Hammar had said about Mats Andersson and then added more details.

'He's forty-one years old and lives in Södermalm. Veronika gave birth to him at Visby Hospital in 1966. She was only fifteen at the time. Nobody knows who the father is. The birth records list the father as "unknown". Mats is a bachelor with no children. He works at a silver-plating company in the industrial district of Länne in Haninge.'

'A silver-plating company? What the hell is that?' asked Wittberg.

'They apply the finished surface to metal. And according to the CEO, there's a specific substance that's needed for the manufacturing process. Potassium cyanide.'

Knutas paused for effect as his colleagues digested this piece of information.

'The man has quite a troubled past. He grew up with a whole series of foster families, and has been convicted of assault on numerous occasions. He has also been arrested for receiving stolen goods and for petty theft. But he's had a clean record for the past ten years. Seems he's been behaving himself.'

Sohlman looked at his watch.

'It's seven fifteen. The murder was committed around three thirty. So where is Mats now?'

'He hasn't left Visby, at least not using his own name,' said Knutas. 'The boat for Nynäshamn left Visby at four forty-five, and he could have easily made it on board.

It arrives in Nynäs at eight o'clock, and we've asked to have all the passengers remain on board until the police search the whole ship. It's going to cause a big ruckus, but that can't be helped.'

Memories of the previous year's hunt for a murderer flickered through Knutas's mind. On that occasion the police had also been forced to delay a Gotland ferry-boat, but their search had proved fruitless, even though the killer was actually on board. Knutas cast a surreptitious glance at Karin. A searing pain passed through his body as he remembered what a dilemma he was in. Was he really going to keep her secret?

Then he went on. 'Our colleagues in Stockholm have been to his flat, but he wasn't there. They're also going to see if he might be visiting his brother Simon, since Mats has the most contact with him. And they live just a stone's throw from each other, on either side of Slussen.

'The question is: Where has he been staying when he comes to Gotland?' said Knutas. 'I've asked all the hotels, B and Bs, hostels, cabin rental agencies and campground owners to look through their records. Unfortunately, it's going to take time before we hear back from all of them.'

'He has a brother here on Gotland,' said Jacobsson. 'Who's to say he's not staying with Andreas?'

Johan's mobile rang as he and Pia were on their way to the café where Veronika Hammar was murdered. As soon as Johan took the call, Pia could tell that something was seriously wrong.

The doctor told him that Emma was in intensive care. She had been found at the very café they were on their way to visit. But she was just running some errands, Johan thought in bewilderment.

At that moment they had entered the roundabout at Norrgatt; Pia was driving towards the northern gate in the ring wall.

'Go to the hospital!' he shouted, still holding the mobile to his ear. 'We have to go to the hospital!'

Pia quickly turned the steering wheel the other way, casting a startled look at her colleague.

'What's going on?'

'Emma's in intensive care. She was at the café when Veronika Hammar was killed, and she tried to save her. Now she's in a serious condition herself.' He pounded his fist on the side of the passenger door. 'Shit, shit, shit.'

Pia brought the car to such an abrupt stop at the hospital entrance that the tyres shrieked against the asphalt. As Johan jumped out of the car, she yelled after him: 'It'll be OK. She'll be fine!'

She could hear how hollow her words sounded.

When the meeting of the investigative team was over, Knutas sat down at his desk and punched in the phone number for Simon Hammar in Stockholm. No one answered. The phone rang and rang, echoing in his ear. He sighed and went out to the corridor to get himself a cup of coffee from the vending machine. The whole station was buzzing with activity, and a nationwide alert had been issued for Mats Andersson. Knutas speculated what his motive could be. Was he so eager to kill his mother because she'd abandoned him when he was a newborn? If so, why had he decided to do it now, at the age of forty-one?

Thoughts of Karin and her baby flitted through his mind. It was impossible to ignore the similarities. At the same time, there were distinct differences. Mats had tried several times to contact his biological mother, to no avail. Karin had never heard from her daughter. And Mats had not been put up for adoption. Instead, he'd been sent to live with various foster families. And what role did his new-found half-brothers and -sister play in the drama? Again he tried to phone Simon at his temporary address in Gamla Stan. He was just about to give up when someone picked up. But the voice wasn't Simon's.

'Hello?'

'This is Detective Superintendent Anders Knutas. I'm looking for Simon Hammar.'

'Anders Knutas? What in God's name is going on?'

There was no mistaking that deep, morose voice. Knutas had worked on several cases with Inspector Kurt Fogestam of the Stockholm police.

'Kurt? I might ask you the same question. Why are you answering this phone? It's urgent that I speak with Simon Hammar.'

'Well, he's here all right,' said Fogestam glumly. 'But I'm afraid you're too late. Simon Hammar is dead.'

Knutas's jaw dropped.

'We just got the call. He fell out of a fifth-floor window. Landed on Kornhamnstorg here in Gamla Stan. The square that faces Slussen, you know? We've got a huge problem on our hands at the moment. Traffic is at a standstill, and a big crowd has gathered in the square. We haven't even removed the body yet. It looks like murder. There are signs of a struggle in the flat. I can call you back later. But why are you looking for Simon Hammar?'

'His mother was murdered here on Gotland just a few hours ago. She was poisoned with cyanide, just like Viktor Algård at the conference centre.'

'You've got to be fucking kidding me.'

A paralysing sense of inadequacy settled over Knutas as he put down the receiver after talking to Kurt Fogestam in Stockholm. The police seemed to be always one step behind. By all indications, Mats Andersson had first murdered his mother and then his brother. Had Simon known that he was the killer and threatened to expose him? Was that why he'd been silenced? It sounded as if Simon's death had come suddenly, the result of anger. Knutas reasoned that if a murder were premeditated, this would not be the preferred modus operandi. Mats Andersson seemed to crave an audience, yet not to the extent that he wanted to get caught. Surely it would be almost impossible to toss a man out of a fifth-floor window in the middle of Stockholm without being seen. And Simon must have put up a lot of resistance; he was both tall and muscular. Unless he was first drugged or poisoned, of course. But why throw him out of the window? Couldn't Mats have killed him with cyanide, just as he'd killed his other two victims?

Another puzzling element was the fact that the murderer had been able to leave the building and vanish without getting caught.

Knutas didn't think for a minute that the perpetrator would have purposely chosen to make things so difficult for himself. No, the decision to kill Simon must have been made in great haste.

Was it even possible for the same person to have committed the two murders within only a few hours of each other? He did a quick calculation in his head. The flight between Stockholm and Visby took only thirty minutes. A taxi ride from Bromma airport in Stockholm to Gamla Stan took about the same amount of time.

Knutas wondered again what the motive could have been for killing Simon. Was Mats in the process of murdering all of his half-siblings? Or had he already done so? Andreas Hammar lived alone out in the country, and his body might easily go undiscovered for days. Suddenly Knutas was filled with dread.

He jumped up, grabbed his service weapon, and then knocked on Jacobsson's door.

'Get in touch with Stockholm!' he shouted to Rylander as they rushed out of the station. 'Make sure the sister on Vätö has police protection. ASAP!'

Silent and grim-faced, Knutas sat in the passenger seat as Jacobsson stomped on the accelerator, racing south. Mikaela had told them that Simon and Mats were in the habit of having lengthy, heart-to-heart talks. Simon had told his sister how much these conversations meant to him, and what a support Mats had been. Was this what had prompted the murders? Andreas Hammar wasn't answering his phone and Knutas's anxiety grew. Mats couldn't possibly have reached the sheep farm after killing Simon, but he could have gone out there earlier.

Jacobsson sped towards Hablingbo, screeching around the curves. The siren was on and the other cars on the road obediently got out of their way. Knutas's mobile rang again. It was Inspector Fogestam.

'Anders, I have to tell you that we've decided this wasn't a homicide after all. We assumed it was because several chairs had been toppled. But now we've found more than one suicide note. And several reliable witnesses have independently confirmed that they saw Simon Hammar jump from the window.'

'Really? What do the notes say?'

'There are four of them. They were on the mantelpiece, addressed to different people.'

'Who?'

'One for Veronika, one for Katrina, one for Daniel, and one for Mats.'

'Could you fax them over to us as soon as possible? Have you read them?'

'Yes. I've had a quick look at them. Simon writes that he's sorry for doing what he's about to do, but he sees no other option. The letter to his mother is quite nasty. He seems to be blaming her for the fact that he can't bear to live any longer. Apparently her demands were so great that he couldn't take it any more.'

'And now she's dead too. She died at just about the same time, damn it.'

'Yes. It's terrible. I've got to go. But I wanted you to know what we found out.'

It was dark by the time Jacobsson parked in front of the farm in Hablingbo. The yard was deserted. No barking dogs. Not a soul in sight. The red pick-up that Andreas had driven the last time they visited him was gone. Knutas glanced at his watch. It was ten fifteen.

Cautiously they approached the house. No one seemed to be at home, and no lights were on. Knutas crept up on to the porch and tried the door. It wasn't locked. With their guns drawn, they slowly made their way from room to room, but they soon realized that the house was empty.

The gravel crunched under their feet as they walked around the side of the main building. As they searched the property, more police vehicles turned up.

The officers gathered in the yard and then split up to continue the search. Knutas and Jacobsson got back in the car to drive over to the lambing shed and the pasture where they had previously interviewed Andreas while he was weighing the sheep. Maybe that was where they would find him, together with Mats. Knutas fervently hoped that they wouldn't arrive too late.

They turned on to the road, which was cloaked in darkness, and headed for Havdhem. There were no streetlights and very few buildings. Occasionally they caught a glimpse of lights shining from a distant farm. They drove in silence, as if they were both expecting the worst.

'Do you remember where to turn?' asked Knutas.

'Yes. It's right up ahead.'

Jacobsson turned on to the narrow gravel road, but they hadn't gone more than a few hundred yards before a flock of sheep blocked their way. Karin was forced to stop the car.

'What the hell is this?' she said with a sigh.

More and more sheep came crowding on to the road. All of them were bleating loudly. The sound grew to a deafening cacophony. With their open mouths and blank stares, they looked ghostly in the glow from the car headlamps. Jacobsson honked and tried to inch the car forward, but the sheep refused to budge. They surrounded the vehicle, pressing against it, as if the vehicle were their only refuge.

'What do we do now?'

'It can't be that far to the lambing shed,' said Knutas. 'Let's get out and walk.'

Johan sat in the waiting room outside the intensive care ward at Visby Hospital. He hadn't yet been allowed to see Emma. A nurse had offered him something to drink, but he found himself barely able to speak. His body felt anaesthetized; his mind was empty. He just sat there, utterly still and staring at the floor. He didn't want to move until they came out and told him that Emma was going to be OK.

Suddenly the door to the waiting room opened. Johan didn't even lift his head to see who came in.

Somebody sat down on the chair next to him.

'How's she doing?'

He recognized the voice, but hadn't expected to see him here. It was Emma's ex-husband Olle.

'I don't know,' he replied. 'I don't know anything.'

The clock on the wall was ticking monotonously. The minutes plodded along. Both men, who were the fathers of Emma's children, sat next to each other in silence and waited, not knowing what to expect.

Olle drummed his fingers on his leg. Johan stared at his veined hands. The ring finger which, for so many years, had worn a wedding ring given to him by Emma. Those hands that had held Emma, changed the nappies of their two children, cooked meals and built the house in Roma. In the past such thoughts had always made Johan feel angry or jealous. But this time he felt a strange sense of solidarity. Emma was important to both of them. He would never be able to erase the years that Olle and Emma had shared. And why should he? The faces of Sara and Filip flitted through his mind. This was their father sitting next to him, burying his anxious face in his hands. Johan closed his eyes.

Neither of them spoke.

Bodies everywhere. White, woolly, bulky, warm. And all those eyes. Hundreds of eyes staring at him. He saw nothing in their expressions. And yet there was something reassuring about them. They were clustered together in one corner of the pasture, closest to the building.

He had jumped on the motorcycle and driven into town. He had left the café and the dark angel in the throes of death. That had always been his secret name for her: the dark angel. When he was a boy, he saw her as a bright and beautiful angel who would one day come to rescue him. But she wasn't the person he thought she was. She was a malicious, evil destroyer. He had done the right thing.

The relief he felt made him dizzy and nearly forced him off the road. He steeled himself. He had to get away, and quickly. He was on his way home. For him, home meant the three people who were the only ones who cared about him. Genuinely cared. They had opened their arms to him, taken him in, welcomed him warmly. His three siblings. It was a new feeling, and it had profoundly changed how he viewed the world. Suddenly he had a real reason for living.

Right now he longed to tell Simon what he'd done, but first he was going to talk to Andreas, since he lived so near. He couldn't help himself. He would burst if he didn't share the news with someone.

For the first time in his life, he felt that he had a purpose.

He passed the harbour terminal with the big white ships, which later in the evening would take him away from here. But before he left, he wanted to see his siblings one more time. It might be a while before he had another opportunity to visit them.

His heart warmed at the thought of them. Andreas was the strong, confident brother he could always turn to. With Mikaela he felt an intense connection. She had spoken to him with great candour, telling him about her eating disorder and how she had started to cut herself as a teenager. And about the problems that she'd had in relating to other people, never daring to trust anyone. Things had finally turned out well for her. She had found a husband who loved her with all his heart.

But he felt the closest to Simon. From the very beginning he had shared a special connection with his youngest brother. They belonged together. They'd had so many long conversations. At first Simon mostly listened, as if understanding perfectly what he was trying to say. Simon took everything he said to heart, encouraging and supporting him. Listening to all the shit he'd been carrying around for years. Suddenly he no longer had to bear the burden alone. He could share it with someone else, and the sense of relief he felt was enormous. He had found his family.

Then Simon had broken up with Katrina, and the roles were reversed. He'd been surprised to hear about everything Simon had endured as a child. Utterly alone, without support from anyone at all. He was struck by how isolated and vulnerable his three siblings had been, even though they had a mother, had their own family. The grief stripped him of all strength. Then he was seized by anger. He was the one who needed to make things right. Above all, he needed to save Simon, who was sinking deeper and deeper into a terrible depression.

Their regular conversations had made him desperate. In an attempt to get Simon out of the borrowed flat into which he'd practically barricaded himself, he had forced his brother to come over to his place. Just to talk, and at least once a week. As the picture of their mother gradually emerged, hatred began growing inside of him, getting stronger and stronger each day. Along with a desire for revenge.

He had watched as his new-found little brother fell apart, bit by bit. Simon was the only one who hadn't yet managed to break free. And the more time that passed, the more details he heard, the more convinced he became. There was only one way to set Simon free and give him a chance to live his own life. He was certainly entitled to that much.

There were obvious similarities between them. Both harboured something deep in their hearts that kept them at a deadlock, preventing them from living fully. He himself was forty-one years old and had never managed to sustain a long-term relationship.

He felt an urgent need to save Simon from going under.

At the same time, his brother started hinting that he no longer wanted to live. That had made the whole matter even more pressing.

He took a deep breath, and then slowly exhaled through his nose.

Things were going to be different now. With their warm and loving reception, his three siblings had made him believe that he was actually a worthwhile person, in spite of everything. That there might even be someone for him to love.

His real life was finally about to begin. He had saved his brother and made peace with himself. He listened for police sirens but heard none. There wasn't a single police car on the road. But he wasn't afraid any more.

When he reached the farm, he parked the motorcycle and hurried towards the house. He rang the bell. No one answered, and the door was locked. The dogs weren't out in the yard, and he couldn't hear any barking from inside the house. Andreas's car was not in the driveway. That meant there was only one place he could be.

He jumped back on the motorcycle and drove off, spraying gravel in his wake.

Knutas and Jacobsson made their way forward in the dark. The sheep had followed them for a short distance but gradually fell behind after realizing that they weren't going to get any food, no matter how much noise they made. Someone must have let the animals out, either deliberately or by mistake.

The two officers hurried across fields and meadows. Because it was so dark, they couldn't move as quickly as they would have liked. The ground was uneven, covered with stones and stumps, and Knutas had already tripped several times.

Jacobsson's heart was pounding hard. All the recent events flitted through her mind as they jogged along. Three faces kept appearing: Andreas, Mikaela and Simon. Each of them marked by sorrow and loneliness. And then there was Mats, the man with two faces. The boy who had been handed over to strangers, just like her own daughter, whom she had known for only a few minutes. But those minutes had affected the rest of her life and everything she did. She raced along as fast as she could. She was determined to save him. She had to save Mats before he did something crazy again. If only they could get there in time.

Then they saw the lights of the lambing shed. Thank God. It wasn't far now. It was a wooden building, nearly a hundred metres long, with a corrugated metal roof. It was divided into stalls where the ewes could have their lambs in peace and quiet. The lambing season was over, so the ewes and their offspring had been sent out to graze.

Several sheep in an outdoor pen began bleating as they approached. Both the red pick-up and a motorcycle were parked outside the building. The door was ajar, but it was dark inside. Knutas crept over to the door and stuck his arm inside, attempting to turn on the light switch. Nothing happened. The light was broken. The door creaked as they stepped inside. The faint light that seeped in through the dust-covered windows allowed them to fumble their way forward. The only sound was an occasional mournful bleating from the sheep outside.

Slowly they moved past the rows of stalls. Suddenly Knutas gave a shout.

'I see something! Come over here!'

Among the bales of hay inside one of the stalls they saw the figure of a man lying on his back on the ground.

'Damn it to hell!' exclaimed Jacobsson. 'We're too late.'

To her embarrassment she felt tears well up in her eyes. Stop it, you idiot, she thought to herself. You don't even know these people.

Knutas cautiously opened the stall door and stepped inside. He gasped when he looked at the man's face.

It wasn't Andreas.

Johan had no idea how much time had passed when the door finally opened. He saw a man wearing a white coat and glasses, his expression sombre. Johan's vision blurred, as if he were looking through a fog. As he watched the doctor coming down the long corridor towards them, all sorts of memories flashed through his mind. Fragments of his life with Emma.

Her hand frantically clutching his when she gave birth to Elin; her smile when she said 'I do' in the church; her fevered expression when they made love. A minor quarrel at the breakfast table a few days ago; Emma wearing a white bathrobe with a towel wrapped around her head after taking a shower and then making coffee in the kitchen.

The doctor had reached them now. He stood very close. Johan didn't dare look up.

'It's over now. The worst of it, anyway. She's out of danger, and she's going to be fine. The baby too.'

'The baby?' whispered Johan.

Knutas stood motionless, trying to gather his thoughts. He recognized Mats from the photographs. Now here he lay, looking up at the ceiling, his eyes unseeing, his body limp. But he was breathing.

'Mats, my name is Anders Knutas and I'm a police officer. You're under arrest for the murder of Viktor Algård and Veronika Hammar. Do you hear what I'm saying?'

He crouched down and shook Mats by the shoulder. No reaction. The man seemed almost catatonic.

The next moment two people appeared in the doorway, carrying torches. They stopped abruptly, surprised to see the police officers. Knutas looked in confusion from one person to the other. He couldn't make sense of what he saw: there stood the sheep farmer Andreas Hammar and the TV camerawoman Pia Lilja, hand in hand. To make matters worse, Jacobsson had fallen to the ground and was staring glassy-eyed into space. As if she were the victim of a blackout.

*

Then the man on the floor suddenly turned his head to look at Knutas. His expression displayed such pain that Knutas almost shrank back. Slowly Mats lifted one arm, holding something in his hand. For a fraction of a second a danger warning flashed through Knutas's brain. Was it a weapon? The next second he was relieved to see that it was a mobile phone. Mats's voice shook as he whispered his question: 'Is this true?'

Puzzled, Knutas tried to make out the words on the tiny, illuminated display. The message was brief but devastating.

'Simon is dead. Call me. Mikaela'.

Knutas was standing next to the window in his office, looking out at the car park, which was wet with rain. He filled his pipe as he thought about the dramatic events of the past few days.

From the very beginning this particular case had affected him more strongly than others. Maybe because it had made him think about his own role as a parent. Just before the murders occurred, Alexander Almlöv had been assaulted at the Solo Club. His own son Nils had witnessed the vicious attack but hadn't dared tell his father, the police officer.

Over the past weeks Knutas had spent almost as much time wrestling with that issue as he had trying to discover the identity of the killer.

The fate of Mats Andersson was a tragic one, from start to finish. He had hoped to save his new-found and beloved brother from succumbing to despair by killing their mother. But before that happened, Simon had taken his own life. Knutas could understand how shocked Mats must have been to receive word of his brother's death. Everything he had done was in vain.

The plan he had spent months putting together was to no avail.

Mats had ended up recounting the whole story about his desperate attempt to free his younger brother from their mother. Ultimately it seemed to him that there was only one option. He had to kill Veronika – destroy her before she destroyed the family that he had found at last. Simon, in turn, had tried all his life to save her, to make her happy and content with her life. But that had proved to be an impossible task. Both Mats and Simon had seen themselves as angels sent to the rescue. And it had all ended in disaster.

Nobody can save anybody else, thought Knutas bitterly. Everyone has to save his own life.

It was strange that things had gone so well for Veronika Hammar's children, in spite of the difficult circumstances they had endured while growing up with their excessively demanding mother. At least Andreas and Mikaela had succeeded in creating a satisfactory life for themselves, and they seemed reasonably happy.

They also had shown an ability to love. Was that something they'd learned from somebody else, or was it an innate part of being human?

His thoughts were interrupted by Jacobsson knocking on the door.

'Come in.'

She sat down on his visitors' sofa. Knutas sensed that

she had something important to say, so he sat down across from her.

'How are you doing?'

'Fine, thanks.'

She smiled. Her dark eyes had regained their familiar alert expression. He was happy to see it.

'I've decided to try to find my daughter. Lydia.'

Knutas didn't reply. Instead, he got up and went over to sit next to her, giving her a hug. She relaxed into his arms, not moving as he stroked her hair.

He had been pondering what to do about everything that Karin had told him in Stockholm. He had agonized over the decision he needed to make. He had no idea what to do, and there was no one he could consult.

Karin had deliberately allowed a double murderer to escape. Maybe she was unbalanced. Maybe he would come to regret the decision he was about to make.

Yet, at that moment, he knew that he could never tell anyone her secret.

Never.

EPILOGUE

The light in the flat is a heavy grey, just like in the city far below. Slussen's never-ending circle with its constant stream of cars. They stubbornly continue to come from every direction, like arteries to a pumping heart. Then they disperse into the stinking body that is Stockholm.

It's time. I feel closer to myself than I ever have before. In the past I always lived through other people and for other people, wanting to please them. Trying to live up to something. And I always failed.

I've merely been playing a role from the very beginning.

I feel immensely tired. I no longer need to keep going. Or keep fighting. Or suffering. Soon it will be over. I gaze out at the city. I'm a stranger in the midst of everything going on around me. I no longer want any part of it.

I had a dream that I was allowed to live my own life, just like everyone else. Work, travel, live. Give and receive love. Spend time with people, accumulate experiences, build relationships and mature. I imagined a future with a family, security and love.

That's no longer a possibility. It's not meant to be. I had a son, whom I love. I hope that he will experience all those things. That he will take charge of his own life.

My time on this earth is over. Sun, wind, snow, rain – never again will I witness the changes in weather. Or hear the howling of the storm over the sea. Or see the dawn.

Soon there will be nothing but night.

I'm looking forward to the embrace of darkness. I imagine death as sinking into the enveloping comfort of a woman's arms. Maybe it's true that we return to where we started. Inside our mother's body, inside her womb, inside the soft, rocking, silent darkness, unaware of what is to come.

Maybe that's what happens.

*

I pick up the photograph of Katrina and Daniel and kiss it tenderly. I will hold these two, whom I love, in my hand when I die.

Then I won't be alone.

ACKNOWLEDGEMENTS

This story is entirely fictional. Any similarities between the characters in the novel and actual individuals are coincidental. Occasionally I have taken artistic liberties to change things for the benefit of the book. This includes Swedish TV's coverage of Gotland, which in the book has been moved to Stockholm. I have the utmost respect for SVT's regional news programme *Östnytt*, which covers Gotland with a permanent team stationed in Visby.

The settings used in the books are usually described as they actually exist in reality, although there are a few exceptions.

Any errors that may have slipped into the story are mine alone.

First and foremost, I would like to thank my husband, journalist Cenneth Niklasson, who is always ready to be my sounding board and offer me the greatest support.

Special thanks to:

Magnus Frank, detective superintendent with the Visby police
Johan Gardelius, crime technician, Visby police
Ulf Åsgård, psychiatrist
Martin Csatlos of the Forensic Medicine Laboratory in Solna
Lena Allerstam, journalist, Swedish TV
Mian Lodalen, author and journalist
Anita Forsberg, sheep farmer, Havdhem
Nina Pettersson, conference coordinator, Wisby Strand
Sara Hullegård, marketing director, Wisby Strand

My thanks to everyone who has helped me with my books at Albert Bonniers Förlag, especially my publisher Jonas Axelsson and my editor Ulrika Åkerlund – your support is invaluable.

Special thanks to my agents Bengt Nordin and Anna Rytterholm at Nordin Agency.

And of course thanks to my children, Rebecka and Sebastian, my biggest supporters!

Mari Jungstedt
Stockholm, April 2008

COMING SOON

The next riveting thriller
from the bestselling Swedish author

MARI JUNGSTEDT

THE DOUBLE SILENCE

A man is pushed from a cliff; a woman is missing after a bike ride; an elderly man is washed ashore.

The friends are closer than most – too close, some might say. Every year they leave their cosy suburban neighbourhood to go on holiday together to a remote Swedish island. But this year, their holiday won't go as expected.

There're always *some* secrets we keep, even from our friends . . .